GRIM BEGINNINGS

• THE ASHEN PLANE - BOOK 1 •
A LITRPG SERIES

MAXWELL FARMER

This novel is dedicated to my wife Rachel who has supported and challenged me throughout this dream of mine. I would not be the man I am today without you. I love you.

PROLOGUE
2037

FOR THE PAST TWENTY YEARS, digital realism and the immersive qualities of video games have grown tremendously. VR, or Virtual Reality, headsets expanded from players having to move the physical body to interact with a less-than-real world to truly connecting with the mind. Players can actually lie down in their beds and be completely transported. One can experience all the sensations of the physical world without any of the dangers. Players who are particularly good at the new gaming style can quickly rise up in stardom like any athlete.

John mopped the front entrance of the middle school while listening to the *Video Game Informant* podcast over his headphones. The twenty-five-year-old, slightly balding janitor didn't care about much in life, but video games were his one true joy. Not that he was any good at them. The best he'd ever done was win a couple of local tournaments, which had amounted to a grand total of $70 and a new wireless mouse. It was not something he could rely on as a sole source of income.

There was this new game though, called *Kingdoms & Valor*. It was a VRMMORPG (or Virtual-Reality Massively Multiplayer Online Role-Playing Game) in a fantasy-based world. And it required the newest virtual reality headset, with which players could experience almost everything! All five senses would be engaged, so people could feel like they were living a brand-new life in a magical world where mysteries waited to be discovered! It was a gamer's dream! John had been saving up to buy the headset and game since he'd learned about it eight months ago.

Truly, all he ever bought were movies, books, and games. He was a particular fan of the classics and a variety of older series. Most were classified as "nerdy," like *Starfighter Foxy 64*, but they were what interested him. It was not like he had much else to spend it on. He had no family, and the only friends he had were online. He didn't care about anything else. Nothing really motivated him. John did not believe he had any purpose at all, actually.

John's musings were interrupted by laughter loud enough to be heard over his headphones. He looked down the hallway and saw two teen boys scoffing and laughing at a girl as the trio walked in his direction. There were always a few stragglers after the initial end-of-day wave of students leaving school. The two boys had short hair. One was skinny, and the other…not so much. The girl had long, straight black hair and carried a bedazzled pink backpack. She was unhealthily thin, and her skin had an abnormal yellow tinge. John knew immediately who she was. She was Becky. He did not know her personally, just that she was very sick. There had been posters throughout the school advertising a fundraiser for her treatment. She did not acknowledge the teasing boys as she focused straight ahead, looking out the glass door and watching for her mom's car to pull up. Her stern look and increasingly red cheeks betrayed the anger she was holding in.

"Ha ha! Look at the sick girl's car!" the nasally-sounding chubby boy said while pointing at a very rusted vehicle struggling across the parking lot toward the front doors.

"Stop it!" she yelled at them, tears swelling in her eyes. "We can't afford a new car because my medicine is so expensive!"

The portly bully continued undeterred. "Aww, the sick girl is crying. Maybe if your parents had adopted a normal kid instead of you, they would have a nice car and wouldn't have to deal with such a sick crybaby!"

John dropped his mop and sprinted toward them. "Hey, you punks get out of here!" he said, waving his arms to shoo them on toward the school entryway.

The two boys ran out the doors, laughing the whole way.

John turned back to the girl. "Are you okay?" he asked.

She sniffed and wiped her eyes, then looked up and nodded.

"Good. Now, I might get in trouble for saying this, but those boys were acting like straight douche-canoes."

Becky laughed, and her red face returned to its usual yellow tinge.

John smiled as he walked with her toward the doors.

Before anything else was said, a car horn honked twice from outside. Becky's mom's car had made it to the front of the school.

"Thank you, sir," the thin girl said before running out to the car.

John's mood turned bittersweet as he watched the girl wrestle the car door open and climb in.

I wish I could help her.

3

The hooded figure leaned over the enchanted well. His skeletal hands grasped the edges firmly as curiosity overtook him. Knowing his time was limited, he was desperate to find his champion. Searching through the alternate universe of possibilities in the well, the figure considered desirable attributes. The person must be a warrior, a competent leader, loyal, and like himself, familiar with death. In a world without magic, though, it had not been easy. The figure did find an avenue, fortunately, through the humans' technology. It had shown them a way to interact with the basics of magical power. He searched frantically against the clock to locate the person. He wanted—no, he needed—the best. Then he found him. His champion!

"Yes!" the hooded figure said in his haunted tone of voice. "Hahahaha! Yes!" he cackled maniacally, lifting his arms in the air and clinching his fists in celebration.

The only other noise accompanying his laughter was the sound of his chains dragging on stone and clanging against each other, echoing inside his dark prison. Though he knew the end was near, he had found a way to have his vengeance. He would be free.

4

CHAPTER 1

MAY 18, 2038

(7 MONTHS LATER)

"ALRIGHT, EVERYONE. IT'S BEEN AN intense evening of competition, but all good things must come to an end!" the announcer proclaimed. "Now, let's get on with our final event!"

The crowd roared.

John still couldn't believe he was at the final stage of the *Kingdoms & Valor* World Championship. The fantasy-based game had been played at a professional level since its release and already had become the highest-grossing game ever! Though John had never been good enough at VR games to get paid, this one was different. A twenty-five-year-old janitor, he'd become one of the top players in the world in only two months! He'd spent his days cleaning up vomit at his local middle school and his nights cleaning up his enemies in a fantasy world with spells and spears. Then it had only taken another couple of months to find a professional team and sponsors. The Straight As focused on Death Magic and Undead effects, an unorthodox style as Life Magic was long assumed to be the top magic discipline, and it had taken them very far.

The team's charitable nature, being part of something bigger than themselves, also really hit a chord with John. They had been donating half of all profits to St. Baldrick's Foundation for kids with cancer, and the nonprofit organization had directly helped a child named Becky with her treatments. With their help and contributions, she had made a full recovery. She had even become the team's number one fan. He'd never really had friends or a worthwhile purpose before. Now he had a job he loved and was helping children in need. He had found his calling. Once this tournament was over, he planned to continue trying to make a difference with his life by being a full-time professional gamer.

"Now, to bring out our first contenders. First, we have the Straight As with their captain, Ace!" the announcer said.

Hearing his avatar name called, John snapped out of his daze and looked toward the curtain separating them from the stadium.

He and his team walked out from the stadium entrance and headed toward the right side of the raised stage with the table where their six computerized headsets waited. John couldn't hear anything over the thousands of fans cheering all around him. State-of-the-art gaming chairs were neatly lined up in front of each player's station. The team sat down, put on their headsets, and adjusted their settings. The headsets were made from a gel-like substance that surrounded the players' eyes and engaged their nervous systems.

John heard the familiar hum of his equipment as he lost sensation with his real body and aligned with his avatar, Ace.

An advantage of putting on their headsets first was that they could not hear the cheering for the home crowd favorite team, In 4 Life. John had met them once before. They were rather overconfident and had an obnoxious team captain who was ridiculously muscle-bound both in real life and in the game. He was the gold-standard definition of a sore loser and was well known for getting in fights with both teammates and opponents alike post-match. Once the Straight As saw their opponents' avatars fully load, the countdown started.

John's avatar looked at his team as they nodded. He smiled, excitement causing his heart to beat rapidly in his chest, and said, "Let's do this."

The audience counted down with the timer, "Three, two, one, fight!"

CHAPTER 2
SORE LOSER

"DIE, PUNK!" A MINOTAUR MEMBER of the opposing team yelled as it activated a Barbarian-class talent called Berserker's Fury.

"Watch out!" John yelled to his teammates, but he was too late.

The minotaur swung his greatsword clean through one of the Straight As who happened to be the team's healer, then swung repeatedly at John's last teammate, Abraham. The barbarian managed to get one good hit in, causing severe damage before a Death Magic Shield of Translucent Bones was cast by the player.

"Crap!" John muttered, frustrated.

"What do we do now!?" asked Abraham, whose now-wounded avatar was a skeletal mage.

They were outnumbered. Both of them were injured and did not have much in the way of healing magic. The opposing team was in a much better situation, with their minotaur captain serving as the team tank, taking and giving most of the damage, while the two Life Magic mages could only cast buffs and heals, maintaining a protective shield continuously.

John knew time was limited. He could see cracks starting to form on Abraham's shield. They needed to eliminate the number advantage of the opposing team. He could try summoning a death creature. Unfortunately, one of the opposing team's two mages, being masters in life magic, would kill it off quickly.

"Give it up!" the minotaur said while repeatedly swinging his sword. The brute wasn't running out of Stamina because he was constantly being replenished by one of his mage teammates.

Where can I catch them off guard? Where can I summon a creature that they kill immediately? Well, their shield covers them completely, except for the ground, of course. John's introspection struck an idea. "Rimi," he said to invoke his spell. If he couldn't summon a creature out in the open, he could conjure a ground-dwelling Ghul to burrow over and catch them off guard, he hoped.

Hearing John's incantation, the opposing team's two mages went on high alert and stopped casting buffs on their tank. The pair looked all around them for a portal somewhere. Suddenly, a gray hand with open sores and sharp claws appeared from underground and grabbed one of the mage's legs. In an instant, the player was pulled down and completely engulfed under the ground before anyone could respond. Only a brief, muffled yell had been heard.

It worked! John thought.

As the other mage looked down and the tank looked back to see what had happened to their teammate, John and Abraham capitalized on the distraction. John ran toward the minotaur while conjuring a Death Magic handaxe in his left palm. Abraham buffed him with increased death damage, increased weapon damage, and a poison weapon spell. By the time the minotaur turned back, John was right on him. With a primal yell, he took his translucent magical handaxe and sliced right through the neck of the player's avatar.

Kingdoms & Valor was just a game, but it had very realistic special effects. John felt arterial blood spray on his face as it erupted from the decapitated body of the minotaur before the hairy brute dropped to his knees and collapsed on the ground. Though the players couldn't hear it because of their full immersion, the audience erupted at the dramatic turn of events. The last opposing player was so flustered by the situation that he completely forgot about the Ghul under his feet and quickly suffered the same fate as the other mage.

"We did it!" John yelled out. He and Abraham high-fived and gave each other congrats with their avatars. A loud clap echoed as John's flesh touched the bony hand of his teammate.

"Let's go celebrate, man!" Abraham replied.

"Good call. Let's go," John said.

The skeletal mage disappeared.

John took a moment to savor his time as Ace and being in the game that meant so much to him. Then he logged out, took off his headset, and, as he opened his eyes, was struck suddenly with a sharp pain in his chest. He blinked once and looked down, finding a knife sticking out of his chest. He looked up at the muscular minotaur player standing in front of him, his hand still holding on to the weapon and a smug look plastered across his face.

Screams of terror erupted from the crowd.

"How do you like that, you cheating bitch?! No one beats us and gets away with it!" The musclebound player pulled his knife out of John's chest with a wet thunk.

John sat there stunned. Warm blood ran down his body.

Everyone around them stood wide-eyed, completely thrown off by this real act of extreme violence.

The attacker raised his hand to go for the killing blow.

John's mind raced. *My life is over? Just like that? There is still so much I want to do!* With a strange mix of melancholy and fear, he thought, *If only I could get a second chance!*

The knife came down, and John's world went black.

CHAPTER 3
CHARACTER CREATION

JOHN FLINCHED, THINKING THE DAGGER was still coming. When nothing happened, he opened his eyes and found himself in pure darkness. He could feel his body but couldn't see anything. Before he could think straight, purple words that looked like a bad text message appeared across his field of vision.

DO U S33K POW3R?

He answered hesitantly, "Um, yes?"
The words disappeared and a new question showed up.

DO U WANT S3COND CHANC3 @ LIFE?

"Uhhh," he stammered, thoroughly confused now. *Wasn't I just stabbed? Was that all a dream? Is this a dream?* Not sure what was going to happen, he responded honestly, "Yes!"

R U W1LL1NG 2 PAY THE PR1CE?

John didn't know what this meant, but he had gone this far. "Yes."

White words appeared right in front of John's vision.

> Welcome Traveler!
> You have been summoned to the Ashen Plane,
> a land of danger and adventure. Please choose your race.

A search bar with a downward arrow button appeared.

What is going on!? John thought. The concept of not being able to see his virtual body still bothering him, he decided to go along. He tried to touch the arrow button to show the race options but was not able to. "What? Mmph!"

Being stuck at the loading screen was not a fun idea to John. When he was a child, he remembered playing his grandfather's *Pokemon Red* game on an old-school video game system, the Gameboy Advance, and being stuck inside the first house for an hour. How was he supposed to know that you had to walk on top of the rug to the wall? Not wanting a repeat event, he took a deep breath and thought more about how to interact with the screen. After half a minute, an idea hit him.

"I wonder," he said. He had seen a video interview of some of the creators of *Kingdoms & Valor* and remembered them talking about transitioning from a virtual touch screen to interacting with virtual screens with your thoughts. John looked at the screen, thought that he wanted to click the arrow button, and... "Yes!" he exclaimed.

The downward arrow disappeared, and a list of races showed up before him.

The mental command worked! Even though this strange

prize was unexpected, the new development was definitely interesting.

There were many classic options, such as elves, dwarves, orcs, and humans. There were also some unique options, such as spriggans, lycanthropes, and celestials. John scrolled down and mentally clicked on the human option. Even though he was an undead elf last time, he wanted to try out being a normal human male for this alpha test.

A race description appeared before him.

Race: Human

Gender: Male

Humans are by far one of the youngest and most diverse races in the Ashen Plane. They live short lives but have an unquenchable drive to achieve. It may in fact be owing to their short lifespans that they have such determination to attain much success. They work hard to make their lives count.

Humans start off with base stats but can represent a variety of different stat point investments. They do not gain any boost in stat points in every level but do gain +5 stat points, +1 Skill Level, and +10 (Health, Manna, or Stamina).

Then a list of statistics scrolled through the black as John read along at a quick clip.

Strength: 10—Determines effectiveness of physical weapons whether held or thrown. Each point allotted increases overall strength by 5 kg. This statistic also affects physical tasks, like carrying, hand-to-hand combat, etc.

Agility: 10—Determines overall speed, whether moving or changing equipment. This stat is helpful with focusing and taking aim as well. Determines overall grace and fluidity when moving. Affects stealth, overall balance, and ability to dodge.

Vitality: 10—Determines health and bodily fortitude and helps with resistance to pain, poison, and other bodily assaults. Improves regeneration of endurance and health at a rate of .1/second for health and .2/second for endurance. Also increases health by 5 for each point invested.

Intelligence: 10—Determines total manna, helps with logic and reasoning, and increases manna by 5 per point invested.

Mind: 10—Determines manna regeneration rate and can represent awareness, insight, and intuition. Increases manna regeneration rate by .05/second for each point invested.

Endurance: 10—Determines total Stamina. Each point invested increases Stamina by 5 points, directly affecting how well the body exerts itself (running, swimming, and other bodily movements).

Charisma: 10—Determines overall likability. Increases in this stat will allow greater and more beneficial interactions with others

Your new human character will begin
with the following stats:

Health: 100

Manna: 100

Stamina: 100

Experience Points: 0 (points to next level: 0/100)

Feats: 2 Randomly Assigned

Skills: 2 Randomly Assigned

Resistances: None

Languages: Common

Do you wish to continue on as a Human?

Yes or No

John mentally clicked yes.

Bright light blinded him, and he was rapidly pulled upward as if something had grabbed him.

CHAPTER 4

ZORDELL

JOHN FELT A LARGE, BONY hand throw him up in the air, as if someone had launched him out of his family's pool, while his eyes tried to adjust to the sudden brightness.

"Ow!" he yelled upon landing on his side on a rocky floor. *What is this?* he thought.

With all of the other VRMMORPGs, character creation had been much more in depth. He was used to taking an hour just to customize his characters before playing. This was definitely different. Just the pain of falling to the ground felt more real than anything he'd ever felt before in the VR systems. He stood and looked all around himself, letting his eyes adjust. It looked like he was underground or in a cave, but he couldn't tell. There were torches with purple flames evenly spaced along the walls on both his left and right, then a large stone wall in front of him that went up at least a hundred feet. He couldn't tell for sure, though, because he couldn't see the ceiling, which was well beyond the reach of the torches. The scene showed no signs of pixilation. Seeing nothing else of note, John looked back in the direction he had been thrown from.

There were a few stairs carved in the rock that went upward to what looked like an altar around three feet tall. The being standing behind the altar made John's blood run cold. There was a twelve-foot-tall figure covered in what looked to be a large, ragged black cloak that didn't cover the body completely. It looked like a raincoat that wasn't zipped up to John. The majority of the creature's body was completely shrouded in darkness under the cloak, and two large skeletal hands and legs stuck out. There were chains connecting shackles on its appendages to the rock wall behind it, and a purple orb floated in the center, where its chest should have been.

"Hello. Hahahaha!" the figure chuckled in a coarse and haunted voice that was almost a whisper.

Whoa! This is a creepy beginning to a new game. Is it a horror genre? What is going on?! "Contact moderators," John said, looking up and hoping someone was monitoring him on some screen.

Nothing.

"Contact Team Straight As."

Again, nothing.

"Arrrgh!" John grunted in frustration. "Logout."

Nothing but the sound of the ghostly figure's chains clanging against each other.

"Emergency logout!"

When still nothing happened, John became concerned. He had heard of VR systems making it difficult for people to log out before, but it was so rare these days with the increased safety regulations. The longest forced log-in he knew of was a week. So, when the game wouldn't even acknowledge his presence, let alone log him out, his heart started racing. What if there was a glitch in this game? What if he'd had a mental break, and the game was trying to deal with his ill mind? Had he actually been stabbed? Did he actually die? He had battled with anxiety for a good part of his life, but he'd never had an issue in-game before. His mind swirled in confusion and anxiety.

Taking a deep breath, John said, "Okay, if I'm in a game, I just need to find a message board in a town. When I do that, I can hopefully write a message to the moderators to get me the fuck out of this glitchy program." With a set mental game plan for how he was going to get back, John looked back down.

"Are you finished?!" the cloaked figure said, its haunting voice raised in anger. As it said those words, the ground shook, the sconces on the wall grew bigger and brighter, the purple part of the chest orb grew brighter, and it conjured a ball of purple energy in each hand.

John bent down, bracing himself and keeping his balance. *What is going on?* he wondered.

"I assure you that I did not bring you here just so you could ignore me, boy!" The being noticeably calmed, and the chamber went back to its original state.

John stood back up straight and looked at the hooded figure. "Um, okay. My name is J—Ace. Why did you bring me here, um…?" John realized he hadn't caught the being's name yet.

"Hmph," the large figure smirked, then dispelled his magic. "That is not your name. My name is Zordell. This is not a game, boy! You are John. This is not your world. You are in the Ashen Plane."

A chill went down the John's spine. *How does this game know my actual identity?* "Wait, what? What do you mean this is not a game?"

The figure chuckled in its haunted tone, then four red eyes glowed from inside the hood and locked onto John. He was immediately stuck, frozen and staring into the red, pupil-less eyes of the creature in front of him.

John felt as if his privacy was being invaded. Like all of his secrets were being revealed to this statue and he couldn't stop it. Eventually, it felt as if the creature knew everything about him on the deepest level, and the tension that had frozen John stopped. In control of his movements again, John fell to the ground, breathing heavily. *What was that?!*

"What did you do to me?" John asked apprehensively.

"Just learning about you, John. Now I know everything I need," Zordell said, making John feel uncomfortable. "This is not one of your VR games. This is real. You've realized you cannot use any of the verbal commands you normally would. Don't you think there's a reason?" The creature paused to let John reflect for a moment. "In case you still have any doubts," Zordell said, interrupting John's musings. The hooded figure flew down to John and tackled him to the ground, then drew a wicked-looking curved black dagger with a bone handle from beneath his cloak.

John's recent trauma flashed in the forefront of his mind. "Wait, wait, wait, wait, wait!" he pleaded.

The being paused only for a moment, then stabbed John in the left shoulder, through his trapezius muscle. The blade went through with such force that it pinned him to the ground.

John screamed in pain. *This feels just like before!*

"Quiet!" Zordell yelled as he glared down at John.

John gritted his teeth and stared right at the hooded creature above him.

Zordell took his now free dagger hand and used it to pull back his hood.

It was fair to say that John was thoroughly thrown off by

what he saw. He was confused and almost wanted to laugh despite being stabbed. The being revealed the skeletal head of a unicorn with two red eyes on each side and a small horn jutting out from the front its head. The strong smell of decay permeated John's nostrils.

The large being slightly twisted his dagger and asked, "Is this pain familiar?"

John tightened his lips and nodded his head.

"Do you believe me now?" Zordell asked.

John did his best to keep his composure and nodded his head in agreement with his lips still pursed from the pain. He could also feel blood pooling under him from the wound. *This is real. This is real! Crap, this is real! How?! What is he?! A monster unicorn?*

"Now, you may be wondering what a being such as myself would want with such a weak and little creature like you? Well, it turns out that we both need something, and we can help each other," he said with a creepy smile.

"What…what do you want?" John asked.

Zordell took his free hand and rattled the chains binding his other arm. "As you can see, I am trapped here. I need you to collect some things for me, and you need a second chance at life," the skeletal figure said smugly as he reached down and pulled the dagger from John's body.

John grunted from the sharp pain.

The skeletal being pulled a red potion from inside his cloak and offered it to John. "Now, drink this."

John hesitated at first, but then felt blood dripping from his shoulder wound and decided it was best not to argue in his current state. He uncorked the vial and drank the potion. It had a mild bitterness and while he was drinking it, he felt his wound heal and close. *Healing potion?!* In his games there were increased sensory receptors, but he'd never actually tasted a potion or felt this…good. *This is definitely real,* he thought.

"Good," Zordell stated. "Now, follow me."

John got up and did as the large creature said. He was led to the top of the stairs, to the small stone altar sticking up from the ground, and they stood on opposite sides of it.

Zordell said, "As I told you before, you are no longer on Earth. This world is known as the Ashen Plane. It is the former battlefield where the gods fought for millennia. Their magic shaped the very landscape itself. I am an Arch Necroid, a being of pure death. I have brought you here because you died. Seeing as you no longer had any concerns in your plane of existence, you were available and in possession of the skills to help me."

"I still don't understand. I'm a janitor. I don't have any skills. Wait. Did you say I died!?"

The Arch Necroid laughed. "You did, boy! The pain of the dagger was to remind you of that pain, to show you that you actually were stabbed and actually did die. Do you believe that now, or do you need another reminder?" After a brief pause with no reply from John, Zordell continued. "As for the skills, you actually do have them. You see, to ensure a fair fight, the gods came up with rules and settings to which those in this world must abide. At first, it only applied to the gods and us higher beings, but we learned that they affected you lesser beings as well, after you came into existence."

John had squinted his eyes while listening to the monstrous being in front of him, then they widened in comprehension at its last statement. *It's like a game! It's like* Kingdoms & Valor *back home!* "Your rules, am I correct in assuming they're something I'm familiar with?"

22

Zordell nodded his head, confirming John's assumption.

John looked away, trying to wrap his mind around all his racing thoughts. His musings were interrupted when Zordell continued his explanation.

"So, that is why I've summoned you here, John. I want you to be my champion," the Arch Necroid said resolutely.

"Um, not that I'm ungrateful, but I was wondering, why me? Why not someone who's more familiar with your world? And how am I supposed to free you?" John said.

"Fair questions. In truth, my prison prohibits me from interacting with the outside world." Anger seemed to appear in Zordell's face as his voice rose. "But I will not be defeated by those audacious pieces of filth! I found a loophole in the magic that's imprisoned me! Normally I cannot contact any other being in my isolation, but I learned that only applied to those from this plane. Seeing as you are not from here, you can inherit my power and provide justice for these offenses!" he said with zealous intensity. "You see, I've been watching you, John, and after analyzing, I know everything about you. The way you led your team, your familiarity with death magic, and your unique approaches to situations make you an excellent candidate. After centuries of imprisonment, I've managed to slowly accumulate enough manna to summon only one being, and that is you!"

"And if I say no?" There were so many details John did not know about the situation. He was still wrapping his head around the fact that he'd died.

Quicker than John could process, the Arch Necroid pinned John against the stone wall with the dagger, this time through his abdomen.

John coughed blood a second later, his body responding to

23

the instant sharp trauma. A notification appeared in his vision stating that he had received a bleeding status and was losing three points of health per second. He mentally removed the notification and looked at Zordell, who was bending down to look at him square in the eyes.

"I do not have time for this!" Zordell asserted. "I assure you that if you die here, you will very much not come back! I used a century's worth of magic to reincarnate you, and I will not have you waste it!"

Every slight movement John made caused him pain from the dagger, so he made sure not to expand his lungs too much. Panic raced through his mind. *He just stabbed me again! This fucker!*

"Now, let's reevaluate the situation, shall we?" Zordell said. "You are a janitor with no real friends or family and barely any education, who has wasted almost every opportunity given to him in life. You were too scared to take a chance and pursue any worthwhile goals and have only ever made an impact by playing a mere game that soon will no longer exist owing to bankruptcy. All you have ever done is watch life from the sidelines! Before you could do anything else, you died. I not only brought you back but am offering you the ability to use magic and giving you an opportunity to shape the world to your will. You said you wanted a second chance at life. You said you were willing to pay the price. If you now choose to reject my offer, you will die of blood loss within the minute. All you have to do is destroy the wards keeping me here. I do not care what else you do with your new life in this world! Do. We. Have. A. Deal?!"

The sconces once again grew bigger flames to match the in-

24

fluence of the being, and another notification appeared before John.

> Quest Unlocked
>
> A Deal with Death
>
> Zordell the Arch Necroid has offered you his power. If you accept, you must promise to destroy the wards keeping him imprisoned. Be warned! In accepting the branches of magic the Arch Necroid has, you may have those abilities for all eternity, and they will have instant effects on your relationships to beings of the plane. You may be welcomed with open arms or you may be a target.
>
> Rewards:
>
> Death Magic
>
> Soul Magic
>
> Progenitor of the Arch Necroid Title
>
> Novice in Soul Magic Title
>
> Novice Death Magic Title
>
> Unknown
>
> Do you accept?
>
> Yes or No

Uncertain what all the information meant and too distracted to focus completely, John was getting light-headed. He could feel arterial blood pulsating out of him, dripping down his body.

Fuck, he's right! Shit! What do I do?! Well, I'm dying...umm, but he needs me! Maybe I can get something out of this! "Okay, I'll do it, but I get the dagger and...uh, uh, some starting equipment!" John said, fighting the urge to slur his speech.

25

The skeletal deity first let out a grunt as if in frustration, but then chuckled.

An update to the notification screen appeared to John, adding Zordell's dagger and starting equipment as rewards. Then John quickly clicked yes with his mind. He thought he somehow saw a smile from Zordell's mouth.

A couple of moments later, Zordell shoved another potion down John's throat.

From the immediate elation he felt, John knew it was another healing potion. But that feeling was cut short as Zordell pulled the dagger out of his body, bringing renewed sensations of pain. He landed knees to the stone floor and vomited. Blood continued to pour out of his body, though the Arch Necroid did not allow him to die. John ended up drinking three high-quality potions after the dagger had been removed before he could stand.

John moaned as he stood, a strand of drool hanging out of the side of his mouth.

"Quickly," Zordell said in a rushed tone.

John looked at the death creature as it reached inside its own chest and forcefully ripped something from inside it with an audible crack. *That's one tough dude!*

Zordell only let out a slight grunt, then produced a purple crystal shard and held it out to John. "Time is short. Touch the fragment now!"

John did as commanded. Upon touching the shard, he felt a shocking sensation as his life was forever changed.

CHAPTER 5
CHANGING

ONCE JOHN PUT HIS HAND on the crystal, it started dissolving. The bits didn't fall to the ground though—they were sucked into John's hand. To his surprise, it started breaking down faster and faster. Locked into place with his arm extended, it was like his hand was a vacuum cleaner that couldn't turn off. His entire body was tense as if he were flexing every muscle he had, and his skin was turning white as snow. More and more he felt like he was being overloaded, like a balloon with too much water. Trembling in his stuck state, he could only hope he would not explode from the overflow of energy.

He began screaming from the pain. His hair started to turn black and grow longer, until it was shoulder-length and he'd grown a long beard to match. Still yelling, he could feel his body growing too. Strength was emerging from inside him. Then the crystal was no more. The pain stopped, and he was released from his frozen state. He stopped yelling and leaned over, breathing heavily.

Then the pain returned. John jerked upright, looked to the ceiling of the cave with his arms held out, and began screaming again. His skin and muscles tightened down his body like he was being shrink-wrapped. The skin around his eyes, mouth, shoulders, arms, and legs constricted. His teeth started showing from the regressing of his lips, but then his skin and musculature quickly grew back to its previous state. Despite the pain, John stopped yelling and looked at his arms. Once the muscles returned, they shrank down again at the same hastened speed.

"Arrrgh!" he grunted, falling to his knees, utterly confused about what was happening. Back and forth, his skin and muscles were shrinking and growing back at a faster and faster rate. The pain was intense! He then heard a voice from within his own mind.

The voice said, *"With this magic and this quest, let justice be done. Let life and death become one."* And his vision went to black once more.

In his subconscious state, John saw a single orb floating in blackness. The orb appeared to be clear and filled completely with two different color liquids seeming to fight against each other, one clear like water and the other light purple. Somehow he knew he was looking at his own soul. Out of the blackness behind the orb, Zordell's four glowing red eyes appeared twelve feet up in the air, looking straight down at John.

The Arch Necroid placed his skeletal hand on the orb and said, "Repeat the ritual words I said."

John looked up to the skeletal creature, back to the orb, up at him, then back at the orb again. He cautiously walked to the orb filled with volatile liquids, placed his hand on it, and nervously said, "With this magic and this quest, let justice be done. Let life and death become one!"

With that, the two liquids stopped fighting each other and the clear and purple liquids became one. Once the two had combined, John looked at Zordell's eyes, and his mind was bombarded with images. He could see the Ashen Plane, primal and chaotic. There were giants and beings of great power fighting, literally changing the landscape around them. John recognized these were memories. Not just any memories, but Zordell's memories. He then saw numerous monstrous and horrifying creatures, like some undead army, surrounding Zordell.

Before John could see anything else, the Arch Necroid's voice rang loudly, saying, "Enough!"

John jerked awake, gasping for air as if he had been underwater, but he was in the same dark chamber where he'd first met Zordell. He'd passed out and was now lying on his stomach. "Uggh," he grunted as he pushed himself off the ground. Standing, he looked at his hands, now longer and bonier than before. Both of them and his arms were completely white. In fact, he noticed his entire body was ghostly white. While his hands and feet were bony, John noticed his musculature remained intact. In fact, he was more toned than before. "Nice!" he exclaimed, looking down at his new six-pack abdomen.

"Ahhh!" Zordell sighed in relief, then, with much more calm in his voice, said, "Thank you, John."

John felt a stinging sensation on his right pec and looked at it. A tattoo of a black skeletal head with red eyes, reminiscent of the Jurassic Park symbol, had appeared. Having always wanted a tattoo, he said, "Hmph, cool!"

Zordell produced a small mirror and showed John his reflection.

"Whoa!" he exclaimed, not expecting what he saw. His hair had grown long enough that he felt like a Viking. His eyes had sunken in some too. The irises flashed red with black sclera for a moment before going back to blue with white around them. *That was freaky.* While John wasn't unsightly—in fact, he looked tall, dark, and handsome—he definitely didn't appear normal. At the realization that he was only wearing a loincloth, John looked back at Zordell and asked, "About the starting equipment, will there be any clothes and armor in there?"

Zordell chuckled, slid the mirror into his robes, and walked toward the altar. Then the large creature beckoned John over with his skeletal hand.

John had already been stabbed twice by the being over the course of a few minutes, so he came over only after a moment's pause.

"Now, there are certain rules regarding Progenitors. I can communicate with you occasionally when our connection is strong. I should be able to contact you despite my imprisonment since we have bound ourselves. I can also give you physical gifts only twice a year, such as armor or skill books." Zordell let out a frustrated grunt. "That's why your negotiating for extra items will count against my limit for you. Now." The Arch Necroid raised his left hand and three floating orbs with what appeared to be equipment and armor appeared. "As you are only at level one, you can only handle so much weight and only items with mostly minor difficulties. You also negotiated for starting equipment, so I have given you three options to best pursue your path to serve me. Go, examine them."

John excitedly touched the orb on his left and a notification screen appeared.

> You have found Starting Equipment of
> Necroid's Servant (Light) containing:
> Black Clothing Set (Shirt, Pants, Shoes X 1)

> Black Leather Armor Set (Body,
>
> Helmet, Bracers, Boots X 1)
>
> Oakwood Hunting Bow
>
> Iron Arrow (X 20)
>
> Iron Dagger (X 2)
>
> 20 Gold
>
> 1 Ring of Swift Death
>
> Do you wish to equip?
>
> Yes or No

Pretty average. John tapped at the middle of the rightmost orbs to examine them as well.

> You have found Starting Equipment of
>
> Necroid's Servant (Medium) containing:
>
> Black Clothing Set (Shirt, Pants, Shoes X 1)
>
> Chitin Armor Set (Body, Helmet, Bracers, Boots X 1)
>
> Long Bow
>
> Iron Arrow (X 20)
>
> Iron Sickle
>
> Chitin Buckler
>
> 20 Gold
>
> 1 Ring of Death's Blessing
>
> Do you wish to equip?
>
> Yes or No

> You have found Starting Equipment of
> Necroid's Servant (Heavy) containing:
> Black Clothing Set (Shirt, Pants, Shoes X 1)
> Iron Armor Set (+50 Armor) (Body, Helmet,
> Bracers, Greaves, Boots X 1)
> Iron Javelin (X 5)
> Iron Greatsword
> 20 Gold
> 1 Ring of Death's Protection
> Do you wish to equip?
> Yes or No

"So we have light, medium, and heavy armor," John mused aloud. "The weapons accommodate the armor as well. I'm assuming this world is very deadly?"

With a confident air, Zordell replied, "Without a doubt."

John reasoned that if it's a super dangerous world he knew very little about, it would be best to have armor that would provide the most protection. He assumed the large being wouldn't give him something that would be too cumbersome to carry. "I'll take the heavy armor set."

"Wise choice," Zordell answered. The large creature snapped his fingers and the two other orbs disappeared.

"How come the items are so…?"

"Underwhelming?" Zordell said. "It is because you negotiated for starting equipment. Because we agreed to those terms and considering your current abilities, I can only give you such minimal gifts!" The large creature took a breath and said in a notably calmer voice, "Fear not, though. I have not made it this far by being held down by such petty rules. Know this, my Progenitor, there will always be systems in place. You just have to find a way to use them for your advantage."

John didn't understand exactly what the creature meant but nodded in response. He then thought to click Yes to accept the heavy armor set, and to his surprise, the equipment magically appeared on him. It also felt pretty decent for starting armor, comfort-wise. After admiring his armor for a bit, John looked up and thanked the creature.

Zordell stuck out his arm and revealed a more in-depth look at one of his shackles, particularly the unique symbol engraved on it. It was an open hand with seven fingers. "Your mission is to go out into the world, find the seven magic stone seals with this symbol on them, and destroy them."

Before the Arch Necroid could elaborate more, the entire cavern shook and dust fell to the ground.

Zordell looked up. "Someone is coming! Quick, stay there!"

"What?" John responded.

Zordell slapped the stone floor with the palm of his bony hand. A large, complicated rune appeared on the ground at the top step to the altar. "This is an example of twisting the rules for our benefit. You actually are about to be sent out of my prison, to the outside world. These seals keep me here, but they do not stop you as they are not attached to you, my champion. Normally, this process takes one minute, but I have just activated a rune that slows time so that one minute will last one hour for you." With that, Zordell moved down a step.

The platform John was on began slowly rising up into the darkness above as the rune and the entire circumference of the floating stone podium glowed purple.

33

"Wait, wait, wait, wait!" John pleaded. "I have so many questions still!"

Zordell looked up at his Progenitor and stuck his pointer finger up, indicating he wanted John to stop speaking. Once John halted his plea, Zordell turned his finger down slightly to point directly at his champion. "I know not exactly where the seals are, but you will be drawn to them. Take the extra time I've given you to familiarize yourself with how everything works. I'm sending you to someone who could be of use to us." Zordell's look turned serious. "I chose you for a reason. Do not fail me or we both will die. By the way, you are no longer John. You are no longer Ace. You are Grim, Progenitor of the one and only Arch Necroid Zordell."

John could tell from the lack of fear or anger in the large being's voice and the expression on his withered face that he had placed all his hopes in John. He guessed Zordell had given him, a mere human, as good of a start as he could.

A tunnel engulfed John, and he could see his new mentor no more.

Before he could process anything else, a notification appeared.

Congratulations! You have been given a new designation!

Arch Necroid Zordell has personally given you a new name—Grim. What this means for you, only time will tell. Know this, though, only the very blessed or very notable have ever been named by one of the higher beings of the Ashen Plane. Take your new name with honor as this likely means there is a great destiny in store for you.

Well, that's ominous. A lot of responsibility to so quickly throw on a guy. I guess I don't have any other choice at the moment. Looks like I'm Grim now, he thought nonchalantly. *Wait, what? What just happened!? I was stabbed to death!?* The predicament and realism of his situation was hitting him like a freight train once he'd had a moment to fully process it. His eyes dilated, his palms became cold and sweaty, and his arms became heavy as he started breathing heavily. It was a full-on panic attack. Flashes of the traumatic experience of being brutally killed went through his mind. After about thirty seconds, he looked at his hands and flexed his fingers and tensed his muscles. *I am alive. I am different now. I am no longer John. I am more. I am Grim.*

Grim then took a deep breath to help himself get a grip on his new situation. Once he had calmed and his heart rate had decreased, he took in his surroundings. The platform moved slowly upward in a tunnel that looked to be made of rock. The tunnel was lit by a bright white light floating about ten feet above his head and the purple light coming from the rune and edge of the platform. He then analyzed the icons framing his view. Three bars of different colors at the top of his vision enlarged when he focused on them. The red bar showed his HP or health points. The blue bar showed his total manna, and the green bar was his stamina. He then saw a flashing exclamation mark in a red box icon in the left side. Fortunately, this was familiar from his gaming experience. Once he focused on that, he realized most of his notifications had been auto-minimizing the large amount of new information he was receiving. Once he saw the many prompts he needed to go through, Grim was grateful Zordell had given him an hour.

Quest Complete

A Deal with Death

You have accepted Zordell's offer to become his Progenitor. Not only that, but you were able to keep a cool head while being stabbed and pinned to the wall and negotiating for better terms instead of completely cowering in the face of death. You are truly a resilient character! Take note, in making this pact, you have promised to find and destroy the seals keeping Zordell imprisoned. Be warned, you have been tied to the branches of magic (Death & Soul) that Zordell uses for all eternity, and this will have an instant effect on your relationships with beings of the plane. You may be welcomed with open arms or you may be a target.

Reward:

Death Magic

Soul Magic

Progenitor of the Arch Necroid – Title

Novice in Soul Magic – Title

Novice in Death Magic – Title

Living Dead – Status

+2 Vitality

+2 Charisma

Daria's Dagger

Starting Equipment of Death's Servant (Heavy)

A New Quest

Title Earned: Progenitor of the Arch Necroid

You are the new Progenitor of the Arch Necroid! You can create three Greater Vassals as long as the creatures have at least a 50% Affinity for Death Magic. You also gain 50% Resistance to Death Magic. Finally, your cost and stat requirements for Death Magic spells are reduced by 50%.

Title Earned: Death Mage (Novice)

You have decided to follow the path of a death mage. You can now cast Death Magic and gain a 5% resistance (overridden by Death Progenitor status). The path of a death mage is often looked upon negatively, but remember, death is just as natural as life.

Title Earned: Soul Mage (Novice)

You have decided to follow the path of a soul mage. You can now cast Soul Magic and gain a 5% resistance. The path of a soul mage is difficult but can open paths to enhance and even supersede other branches of magic.

Status Effect Gained: Living-Dead

In bonding your living soul with a being of death, you are now a creature of the living-dead. You only need to ingest 50% of the sustenance you previously required, but it has to come from a living creature (blood, meat, etc.) in order to actually provide you sustenance. The fresher the source, the more energy it will provide. It can even help heal your wounds. You are less susceptible to the cold but have an increased susceptibility to fire.

Note: Side-effects of hunger will be more severe, leading to decreases in focus, control, willpower, and your stats. You can be driven to harm even those you love if not addressed properly. You have been warned.

Skill Gained! Analyze LVL 1

You have a discerning eye. If you physically touch a creature outside of Mythic and God-Tier, you can learn information about them. As you level up this skill, it will improve so that you can learn even more and perform the skill from a distance.

Skill Gained! Commerce LVL 1

You have made a deal to improve your previous dire situation. Increase this skill to allow better bargains for yourself in the future.

-1% cost for purchases

+1% for overall better deals

Quest Unlocked! Death Comes for Us All

You have made a pact with Zordell to break the seals keeping him imprisoned. This is a mandatory quest and cannot be refused.

Requirements:

Destroy the 7 seals keeping Zordell imprisoned

Reward:

Increase in reputation with Zordell

Unknown

Well, the note about my status effect was uncomfortable, Grim reflected. Although he required 50% less food and drink, he had become a straight carnivore and could go zombie on some poor soul if he wasn't careful. Fortunately, it did seem that he could tolerate things other than meat and blood; they just wouldn't benefit him in the form of sustenance. He was still a little hesitant to try eating anything else. Overall though, he had been given some amazing power. He knew two branches of magic and also had solid resistances in both. He could also cast Death Magic at 50% less the requirements of any other mage. Back home, people would have literally paid millions of dollars to attain these skills, and he had been given them as a level 1 noob.

One thing he didn't understand was why some words, like Mythic and Master, were bolded. He focused on the bolded words, and more in-depth explanations appeared.

Mythic – There are different age classifications in the Ashen Plane. They typically represent difficulty going from New (0-1 year), Young (1 year-200 years), Aged (201-500 years), Old (501-1,000 years), Ancient (1,001-5,000 years), Mythic (5,000+ years), and God-Tier (Unknown).

Titles – Titles are given to beings when they become more skilled in whatever they do. They go from Novice (0-9), Initiate (10-20), Versed (21-29), Associate (30-49), Practiced (50-69), Adept (70-84), Expert (85-98), and Master (99 & above).

Note: There are statuses above Master, such as God-Tier, that supersede all others.

Resistance – Resistances show over ability to withstand damage of a certain type, whether physical or magic-based in nature.

Affinity – Affinity determines the percentage of likelihood that you will perform a skill or have an ability. Some creatures are born with the innate ability to do magic and other skills. Others have to be trained extensively to awaken their ability. The length of time needed is also determined by Affinity. At every title from Associate on up, a mage can awaken Magical Affinity in one being for every title as long as their Affinity is 50% or higher. Creatures in the Ashen Plane can learn only one branch of magic outside of Soul Magic.

Grim was thrilled to learn that he not only had magical power awakened, he had a good number of spells too.

You have learned Death Ward. Cast a ward of Death Magic on a creature to have its HP drop to 1 instead of 0 one time in a 24-hour period, keeping you from dying. You will also stabilize from any debuffs you would have suffered. As you level up, benefits and improvements will come.	Cost: 5 manna Duration: 24 hours Cast Time: 1 second Range: Touch Cooldown: 1 minute

You have learned Death Orb. Cast a ball of concentrated Death Magic at your enemies that will do +5 base Death damage. As you level up, benefits and improvements will come.	Cost: 5 manna Duration: Detonates on impact Cast Time: 1 second Range: Up to 30 feet Cooldown: 1 second

You have learned Commune with the Dead. Temporarily revive base consciousness of the soul of the recently deceased (within 1 hour). At your current level of this spell, you can ask three questions. As you level up, benefits and improvements will come.	Cost: 10 manna Duration: 3 minutes Cast Time: 4 seconds Range: 1 foot Cooldown: 1 hour

You have learned Decay. Cause accelerated rot and decay to anything you touch. It will spread out 5 feet from the area you touch. As you level up, benefits and improvements will come.	Cost: 5 manna Duration: Permanent Cast Time: 1 second Range: Touch Cooldown: 3 seconds

You have learned Summon Undead. Summon the soul of a weak creature to inhabit and take over the body of a dead creature. Significant decreases to Intelligence, Mind, and Charisma occur in the reanimated corpse, but it will follow your commands and feel no pain. As you level up, benefits and improvements will come.	Cost: 25 manna Duration: 1 hour Cast Time: 1 second Range: 5 feet Cooldown: 30 seconds

You have learned Fusion. Take the souls of two willing beings and unite them to create a new soul and a brand new creature with the power of two souls.	Cost: 5,000 manna Duration: Permanent Cast Time: 1 minute Range: 10 feet Cooldown: 1 day

You have learned Soul Orb. Cast a ball of concentrated Soul Magic at your enemies. Does no physical damage but drains stamina from your target. As you level up, benefits and improvements will come.	Cost: 10 manna Duration: Detonate on impact Cast Time: 1 second Range: Up to 30 feet Cooldown: 1 second

"Awesome!" Grim exclaimed. He noticed the 50% decreased cost for his death magic spells, which he was pumped about, and also figured out that he had combined with Zordell. It was the fusion spell. With a cost of 5,000 manna, the spell was crazy taxing! But it just reinforced the point that the Arch Necroid was not to be trifled with. It also showed that the Arch Necroid had waited a long time to accumulate the manna cost for the spell. The creature hadn't been kidding about the effort it had taken to summon him.

Grim took out the dagger Zordell had given him and practiced attack maneuvers. It swung smoothly, but there was a distinct weight to it. The blade definitely had some stopping power. He turned the blade over and examined it. It was around a foot long with a bone handle and a dark red gem at the middle of the cross guard. The blade was black and curved, and there were many small, complicated runes covering the blade completely on both sides. The dagger was truly a masterpiece. Whoever made it must have had some extreme precision to carve all those runes.

Grim focused intently on the blade, and its information appeared.

> You have found Daria's Dagger
> Damage: +5-8
> Durability: 1,000/1,000
> Weight: 0.7 kg
> Rarity: Legendary
> Quality: Masterwork
> Properties: +5 death damage, Unknown

"Wwhhhaatttt?!?!" Grim said.

In his game, Legendary items were *le cream de le crop*, so he was stunned to have scored one under the current circumstances. Only a few people in the entire world usually found one! He definitely became a bigger fan of the dagger, and then also wondered who Daria was and wished he could see all the qualities of the weapon. He re-sheathed the dagger, then examined his enchanted ring and greatsword.

> You have found Ring of Death's Protection
> Durability: 12/12
> Weight: 0.1 kg
> Rarity: Rare
> Quality: Fine
>
> Properties: Contains a LVL 1 Death Ward enchantment. Once a day, if your HP should drop to 0, it will drop to 1 instead and you will stabilize.

43

> You have found Iron Greatsword
> Damage: +20-25
> Durability: 25/25
> Rarity: Common
> Quality: Average
> Weight: 3 kg

Not bad! Grim thought. Having a ring that had a Death Ward spell as well as the ability to cast it could really save him in a pinch. Essentially, he could save himself from death twice! The greatsword was pretty basic but could still pack a punch if need be.

Satisfied with the examination of his equipment, he decided to make the best use of his time before being thrown into the world by practicing his newfound magical abilities. A moment of panic struck. Zordell hadn't taught him how to use magic!

"How do I…?" he said aloud even as his mind began trying to work it out.

In his game, using magic was generally based on mental commands. Grim had already experienced that even though this world had similarities, it was quite real and quite different. Looking at his right hand and feeling somewhat frustrated, he thought about how to conjure Death Magic.

Nothing happened.

After taking a deep breath, he focused on the spell he wanted to cast, Death Ward. He felt a pulse of magical power surge from inside him as something seemed to activate. He somehow innately understood the intricacies of basic magic. *I must have gained the knowledge from Zordell somehow,* Grim thought. He focused inwardly, seeing his soul as a light-purple orb with eight tubes extending out from around the circumference and one going upward from the top. Of the nine tubes, seven were dull gray. One of the orbs on the circumference was dark purple, while the one going up from the top was translucent and glowing. Grim understood that they represented Death and Soul Magic respectively. Wanting to cast a Death Ward on himself, he focused on the dark purple orb first to draw death magic from it, then on the orb that represented his soul, and sure enough, it worked. His hand glowed purple. He looked at his hand and smiled in satisfaction. He then touched his chest and cast the Death Ward on himself. Purple magic coursed over his body, then disappeared. Grim saw his manna bar slightly decrease.

"Cool!" It seemed he was finally getting a better understanding of his new power.

A log entry appeared in the side of his vision.

> Grim has cast the Death Ward on himself.

While log entries could provide important information, in Grim's experience, they usually obstructed your view more than helped anything, unless it was about a quest. He wondered how to prevent more unnecessary information from appearing. The world must have understood his thoughts because a new notification appeared.

> Would you like to auto-minimize your log to only show information related to your quests and their progress?
>
> (Note: You can always open your log manually to see all entries.)
>
> Yes or No

"That's simple enough, and also kinda creepy," he said as he selected yes.

Grim concentrated on conjuring a Death Orb spell next. Sure enough, a ball of purple magic appeared in his hand. Though it looked somewhat like purple fire, it did not burn or damage his hand, and he could throw it like a baseball. He threw it at one of the walls of the tunnel he was ascending. He didn't have enough time to examine it thoroughly, but he did notice that it left a mark on the wall before the platform went above the impact area.

With those things out of the way, Grim only needed to do two more things before he felt fully prepared to take on his new world. The first was to check his updated status because so much had happened to him in such a short amount of time. The second was to find some way to copy the rune Zordell had activated on the platform he was standing on. If he could find a way to make versions of this time-slowing enchantment, it could be a major game changer.

Grim first focused on the icons in his vision. There was one that looked like a tiny version of his face up by the status bars at the upper part of his sight. When he focused on it, his status screen appeared.

Grim (LVL 1)
Race: Human (Living-Dead)
Strength: 10
Agility: 10
Vitality: 12
Intelligence:10
Mind: 10
Endurance:10

Charisma:12

Health: 110

Manna: 100

Stamina: 100

Feats: Ogre Skin, Shrewd, Sapper

Skills:

Culinary LVL 1

Great Weapon Wielding LVL 1

Analyze LVL 1

Commerce LVL 1

Death Magic LVL 1

Death Ward

Death Orb

Commune with Dead

Decay

Summon Undead

Soul Magic LVL 1

Fusion

Soul Orb

Resistances: Death Magic 99%, Cold 25%, Slashing Damage 25%, Soul Magic 5%, Fire 25%

Languages: Common

Titles: Progenitor of the Arch Necroid, Soul Mage (Novice)

Not bad, he thought. He had started out just as a pretty basic character with no known advantages but could tell he was well on his way to becoming a powerhouse. He checked the Feats and Skills that were bolded to further understand them.

Feats are inherent to oneself. Creatures are typically born with them, and they are not acquired often, if at all. Your three new Feats are:

Ogre Skin

"Your skin is unnaturally thick, like that of an ogre."

+25% resistance to slashing damage

+10% wound healing rate (stacks with the regenerative abilities of your living dead status)

Shrewd

"Others may call you scheming. You prefer cunning."

+10% Perception

+5% chance of making a better deal when negotiating

Sapper

"No longer do you have to eat your vegetables!"

Allows you to ingest the body of any creature, living or dead, to heal your wounds.

Note: The fresher the source, the more healing provided.

The first two were random but could still prove useful. Ogre skin was especially appealing. He wondered if Shrewd had come into play when he'd negotiated with Zordell. Having the forethought to negotiate a legendary weapon while bleeding to death would be considered shrewd, he figured.

Skills are abilities you can acquire in your lifetime through effort and experience. Your 2 new skills are:

Culinary LVL 1

You are familiar enough with ingredients to cook simple but sustaining dishes. At LVL 1, your meals are not very amazing but get the job done.

+1% positive benefits to your dishes

+1% to taste

Great Weapon Wielding LVL 1

"People may say you're compensating for something with a big weapon. They stop, though, when you hold that weapon to their throat."

+1% damage with 2-handed weapon

+1% to speed for using 2-handed weapon

The Culinary skill didn't impress Grim. He had been more of a ramen noodles, microwave meals, and take-out kind of guy. He knew the next two could prove extremely useful, though. His new equipment abilities definitely favored a Tank build. His Great Weapon Wielding was a solid skill to have even though it was admittedly very minor at the moment. After going through his entire status page, Grim only had one more task left.

He didn't have any pens or paper to make a sketch of the magic rune symbol and, after a minute of pondering, decided he would carve it on a piece of his armor. He took out his new dagger and decided to engrave the rune as best he could on the bottom of his right boot. At one point he sneezed, which caused a mark to happen that wasn't supposed to be there. Realizing that he couldn't fix the mistake, he started over on the bottom of his other boot. Unfortunately for Grim, once he had finished his copy as best he could, no prompt appeared.

He clicked his tongue in frustration but thought, *Oh, well. Guess I can't have the power of an ancient powerful being and learn advanced magic symbols all in one day.*

Satisfied with the progress he'd made, Grim re-equipped both boots and sheathed his dagger. Before he could do anything else, the light above him flashed. It was so bright he had to turn his head away and close his eyes, and then the feeling of intense light was no more.

CHAPTER 6
NEW WORLD

GRIM SLOWLY OPENED HIS EYES. There was light but not as much as he had just experienced. As his vision adjusted, he felt a slight chill from the breeze against his pale white skin. The cold tickled his nostrils and lips. He saw his breath escape into the air as he exhaled. Once his eyes were accustomed to the new source of light, Grim could see he was on the edge of a cliff that gave an overview of an expansive snow-capped mountain range.

When he turned around, he saw an altar five feet in front of him that was exactly like the floating altar he'd seen in Zordell's prison. And there was a panic-stricken figure sitting on the other side, leaning against the structure. The creature had short, thick brown hair and green skin and a severe underbite with large protruding canines. As Grim approached, he could tell the creature was a shirtless orc, ribs protruding, in ragged pants made out of animal skins and furs. It also had a deformed right arm and foot that were a darker shade of green and smaller than their counterparts on the other side of its body. The orc was sitting with its back against the altar, focused forward. Grim followed the creature's gaze until he found what it was looking at—a lion stalking toward it, only ten feet away. It was a thin lion, around four feet tall with a short stubbly mane and light brown fur bespeckled with random spots of blood and dirt.

The feline looked as emaciated as the orc did. It let out a low growl and revealed its front teeth to the crippled orc.

Instantly, Grim conjured Death Ward in his right palm and equipped his other hand with Daria's dagger. He yelled, "Watch out!" and stepped between the orc and the lion.

Grim placed the Ward on the bleeding orc by touching his shoulder as he took a step forward. A surge of purple-colored magic washed over the green humanoid, preventing certain death from occurring once in a twenty-four-hour period.

The orc appeared startled as the unfamiliar power of the Ward surrounded him. He looked up at Grim, shocked and thankful that the pale-skinned, armor-clad Progenitor had appeared just in time to intercept the big cat before it reached him.

The large feline lunged at Grim. Too slow, not practiced enough, or both, Grim tried to take a backhand slice at the creature, but the lion seized his left forearm instead. Pain coursed through him as he was dragged to the ground by the lion. He lost hold of his dagger during the creature's downward pull, but pure adrenaline was his saving grace as he used his free hand to punch the lion on the left side of its face, at the eye.

The creature yelped in pain as it let go of Grim and scampered backward.

Grim quickly grabbed the dagger with his uninjured right arm and conjured Death Orb with his left. Fortunately, the iron armor he was equipped with had sufficiently protected him from most of the damage, preventing the lion's teeth from piercing his skin. Grim quickly threw the magic orb at the lion only a couple of feet away, then watched as Death Magic spread necrosis over the cat's face and neck.

The lion took a few steps back in a daze from the surprise attack.

Grim did not let the moment go to waste. He lunged at the feline with Daria's Dagger and pierced it through the temple.

The beast let out a final whine before its body dropped limply to the ground.

At the lion's departure from the mortal realm, Grim felt the dagger give out a slight pulse like that of a heartbeat. After he pulled it out of the creature, he examined the blade. Outside of being covered in blood and brain matter, he found nothing abnormal about it. He cleaned and sheathed his dagger, then shoved snow under his wrist guard where the animal had tried to bite him to ease his bruising.

Notifications appeared as he stood up from his kill.

> Skill gained! Heavy Armor LVL 1
> +1% Damage Protection
> -1% Movement Penalty

> Skill gained! Short Blades LVL 1
> "It's not the size, it's how you use it."
> +1% Damage
> +1% Attack Speed

> Congratulations! Death Magic has reached LVL 2!
> +2% Damage
> -0.2% Manna Cost

You have killed Starving Juvenile Dire Lion LVL 2! +60 EXP

After mentally closing the notifications, Grim turned back to the orc. The creature was standing, so Grim could see now that he was at least six-and-a-half-feet tall and used a wooden cane. His eyes were wide and jaw gaping open.

"Who…who are you?" the male orc said in a high-pitched voice that sounded very innocent. If Grim had closed his eyes, he would have NEVER guessed that voice belonged to an orc!

"I am Grim," he replied. "Who are you, and why was that lion attacking you?"

"I am Lukav, and the lion thought I was easy prey." He rubbed the back of his neck uncomfortably and chuckled with a hint of melancholy. "Grim, I owe you my life. My people would normally pledge our service in return for this debt, but I doubt you would want one such as me."

Grim furrowed his brow, then looked at the orc's body. His eyes widened in realization. "Why do you say that?"

Lukav showed Grim his deformed hand, looking down at it with a sad expression.

Grim sighed. He was reminded of the sick children his team had sponsored back on Earth.

"Well, Lukav, I have met others who the world around them thought were useless too. Believe it or not, despite their difficulties, they did not lose faith in themselves." Grim's mind flashed to Becky, who'd had an extremely poor prognosis when his team first started sponsoring her treatments. She had told him, "The one who says they can and the one who says they can't are both right." That spunky girl had made a full recovery and become an inspiration to him to this day. Grim put a comforting hand on the orc's shoulder. "I watched them achieve miracles when no one thought they could do anything. You are not useless, Lukav. In fact, you can be of some use to me right now."

The orc's eyes turned hopeful. He took a knee, leaning on his cane, and said with sincere certainty as he bowed to Grim, "I, Lukav of the Blood-Shield Clan, pledge my fealty in service to you, Grim, who saw my value and saved my life. In life and in death, for now and always."

A notification appeared to Grim.

> Lukav the orc has pledged his service to you!
>
> As a Progenitor, you may accept this offer or reject it.
>
> Note: If you do accept this offer, you have the option to fill one of your Greater Vassal positions. Current Greater Vassal positions filled: 0/3
>
> Do you accept?
>
> Yes or No

This was a lot for Grim to take in. He had been in this new world for less than two hours and been stabbed three times, become a living-dead person, learned magic, fought a lion, and now this?! This world, even though similar to his game, had so many foreign concepts that he was unsure of. He was unable to minimize the translucent screen without making a selection, but Grim decided to speak to Lukav before choosing.

"Before we get to that, Lukav, I would like us to get to know each other a little better." Grim took off his iron helmet with a small, curved white horn on each side like that of Zordell's. It had covered the upper part of his face and had enough of a feel to make Grim want to yell Vus-Ro-Da and be called the

55

Dragonborn. He felt the cool breeze more on his face now that it was all exposed.

The orc stared up, wide-eyed, at Grim.

"I am not interested in forcing you to do anything you don't want to, nor do I approve of slavery, if that's what being my follower means. If it's okay with you, I will reject your offer until we have a greater understanding of one another. Does that sound agreeable?"

Lukav's expression changed to that of disappointment at the Progenitor's denial, but he grudgingly nodded his head in agreement and stood. The orc showed himself to actually be a good half foot taller than the man.

Grim didn't show it, but he was relieved Lukav had agreed. He definitely didn't know enough about the orc to have the green-skinned humanoid pledging his eternal servitude to him. He selected no, and the notification disappeared.

"Thank you, Lukav. If you don't mind my saying, you look hungry and probably cold. Why don't you tell me about yourself, the Ashen Plane, and what brought you here over a meal by a fire? I'm new to this world and would like to learn more about it."

Lukav's stomach growled at the idea of food. He looked down at his thin form sheepishly and said, "That is agreeable."

Grim chuckled. "Come on. I hope you like lion for dinner."

The two made camp at the edge of the stone altar. Grim took charge of dissecting the beast's carcass. He was grateful that he'd gone hunting a few times in his previous life so that he knew what he was doing. He first decided to use his new enchanted dagger for the job, but when he saw that the death magic infused into the blade accelerated necrosis of whatever it cut into, Grim decided his greatsword would do a better job.

Even though Lukav had the obvious physical impairment with his right arm and foot, he still managed to collect wood and start a fire, albeit not very quickly. Once they had the lion meat cooking, the two sat by the fire under a long, awkward silence before any conversation was initiated.

Grim spoke first, his gaze moving slowly across the horizon as he surveyed their surroundings. "So, uh…tell me about yourself, Lukav. How did you end up here…wherever we are?"

The orc looked at Grim with a genuinely confused expression and said, "I am an orc of the Blood-Shield Clan. We are small clan, but strong, and were famous for our enchantments." His look turned sad and frustrated, and his voice filled with disdain. "I have been cursed with these deformities. I was born weak. Not only can I barely fight, I can barely do anything! I have tried to find my path, my way to benefit the clan, but it has eluded me. My right side has prevented me from being a strong fighter, and magic in any orc is rare. Those who did possess magic were unable to awaken anything inside me. I was left to clean. I maintained weapons, armor, laundry, and the latrines."

That struck Grim, and he turned to look the orc in the eyes. *This guy is a janitor. He's just like me!*

"I thought my assigned path was never my destiny. I wished to be more than one who could only clean. My mother believed in me too. She was the head blacksmith of the clan and before she died, she told me to never give up. There were some others who cared about and trusted me. I wanted to become strong to protect them. So, I snuck out of the village to discover my path. I have been here for days, and I was running low on supplies when that lion attacked me. I had given up hope, then you showed."

Lukav sighed in relief before continuing. "Before you came, I thought I was done for. Not only did you save me from the lion, you reminded me I have purpose! Those in the clan who found me worthless were wrong! I have found my path! It is to serve you, Grim," the orc said with fervent joy and watery eyes.

Grim was taken aback by what Lukav had said, that they were so...similar. *If I really am going to make the most of my second chance at life—live a life of meaning and purpose—I want driven guys like him around me!* With a touch of awe in his voice, he said, "Wow! That's amazing! My story is not as moving as yours, but there are some similarities. I once cleaned the latrines for my people too. Few ever saw worth in me, and I rarely did in myself. Then my patron, Zordell, found value in me. Though the way he went about it was, ehh, different, but yeah, he showed me my worth, and hey, he gave me my powers! I will say though, the dude is kind of a jerk. So if you can avoid ever meeting him in person, you probably should. Just forewarning you, man," Grim said as he handed a section of charred lion meat to the orc.

"I see," Lukav replied before savagely tearing into the hunk of meat.

The two ate voraciously until the meat was gone. Grim was definitely glad to have the orc on his side after seeing him eat with abandon. Finished, they stood, kicked snow into the fire, and locked eyes.

Grim said, "I think we now better understand each other, Lukav. I have a skill that would allow me to know you even more if I touch you. Would allow me to use it?"

Lukav nodded his head in approval.

Grim touched the orc's left arm and triggered Analyze.

An info screen appeared.

Lukav (LVL 3)

Race: Orc

Health: 75

Manna: 25

Stamina: 35

This orc was born with severe deformities in both his right arm and foot. Though his body has provided difficulties, it has not stopped his mind or his will.

He removed the screen from his view and looked back to Lukav.

"Well?" Lukav asked.

Grim smiled. Though the orc's stats were not impressive, the statement had given Grim hope. "I think this is the start of a beautiful friendship!"

The orc smiled, then placed his fist over his chest and bowed his head to Grim. Then he took a knee, bowed, and with certainty said, "I, Lukav of the Blood-Shield Clan, pledge my fealty in service to you, Grim, who saw my value and saved me. In life and in death, for now and always."

A notification appeared to Grim.

Lukav the orc has pledged his service to you!

As a Progenitor, you may accept this offer or reject it.

Note: If you do accept this offer, you have the option to fill one of your Greater Vassal positions. Current Greater Vassal positions filled: 0/3

Do you accept?

Yes or No

"I accept your pledge," Grim said.

The notification disappeared.

Grim glowed purple, then a thread-sized stream of purple magic reached out from his chest and touched Lukav. Once it made contact with the orc, he glowed purple as well. After a moment, the glows and the thread of magic disappeared.

A new notification filled Grim's vision.

Quest Unlocked! Devotion I

Congratulations! You have gained your first vassal. Gain 49 more to amuse your patron and receive a Boon. Current vassal status (1/50)

Would you like to make this follower a Greater Vassal?

Yes or No

Note: Your follower must undergo an awakening of Death Magic in order to become a Greater Vassal.

Grim focused on the words Greater Vassal, and an explanation appeared.

Greater Vassals are empowered with their master's specific branch of magic to become more effective at whatever task their master desires them to do. What exactly happens to a Greater Vassal of a Progenitor is unique to that individual. A ritual recitation of the words "Become More" will incite a transformation in the selected vassal. However, the master may affect the transformation with any words that preempt this phrase, so choose your words wisely before invoking the change.

Grim thought it seemed like a pretty safe bet. He selected

yes, and another notification appeared telling him to say the ritual words. Thinking about what he should say before the words, he quickly found the solution!

He looked down to Lukav and said, "My strong right hand, become more."

CHAPTER 7

LUKAV

OF ITS OWN VOLITION, GRIM'S right arm shot straight forward with the palm up toward Lukav. It pressed against the orc's thin upper chest where the clavicles met the sternum. Grim could feel Death Magic inside of him extending out through his arm and into Lukav, searching for purchase. He could tell instinctively that the Death Magic was determining the orc's Affinity. He felt as if he were somehow trying to light a magical candle inside the orc's soul. After around thirty seconds, Grim thought Lukav didn't have the required 50% Affinity to awaken Death Magic, but then he felt it. A spark!

Death Magic surged through Grim's arm and into the orc. Then the Progenitor's arm dropped back to his side and his companion's eyes glowed completely purple as his body began to change. His teeth grew longer and sharper as his facial features filled out and enlarged. Grim watched the orc's weak frame grow notable muscles and his right arm grow more quickly, as if trying to catch up with the transformation of his other arm. His formerly deformed appendages turned white like Grim's skin. Spikes protruded from that shoulder as well as a notable bony elbow spike. His fingers elongated and black claws emerged from each of their tips. A similar process occurred on his right foot as well. White streaks that looked like roots traveled throughout the orc's body, seeming to increase the strength of him. At the beginning of the process, Lukav had groaned. Then he'd started to laugh. The orc was in ecstasy at his transformation. While Grim was happy for his follower, he had to admit Lukav's metamorphosis was a little creepy.

Once the transformation was complete, the orc looked at his new master with a confident smile. Lukav had definitely become stronger! Outside of the drastic changes to his right appendages, he had gained distinct muscles over his whole body. He had also grown a few inches taller, putting him almost a whole foot taller than Grim. White bulging streaks traveled from his right arm to his chest and from the right leg up to his right ribs. Gone was the frail orc who had difficulty moving around. This was a monster! He had turned into a Tolkien version of Hellboy. He was still disproportionate, but in his favor. His right arm and foot were about one and a half to two times bigger than their counterparts.

Grim smiled as he realized he had an orc version of *Hellboy* as his ally. *Not a bad way to start out!* "May I analyze you again?" he asked.

"Certainly, Master!" Lukav replied in a chipper manner while bending down. His light and innocent voice hadn't changed at all, unlike his body.

Grim then analyzed him again. *Da fuck?!* The orc had gained a level and received a crazy boost to his stats. In fact, almost every stat had doubled and there were more statistics showing now. He had also gained enchanted claws that did

Death Magic damage in addition to becoming a mage! *I don't want to hold his hand!*

"How come I can see more information about you?" Grim asked.

"I am not sure, Master. It might be because I am your servant now."

The orc had a point. They had essentially bonded in that process, and Lukav was the equivalent of his padawan. As he looked at it again, he saw the similarities to his own profile.

"Can you see mine? And please, just call me Grim."

The orc's eyes lost focus for a moment as he stared straight ahead. "I can, Grim! All I had to do was will your information to be seen! You are blessed indeed!" The amazed orc continued examining the Progenitor's information.

"Hm, good to know," Grim replied. "So, have you ever heard of Zordell or a Progenitor before?"

There was a pause, then Lukav gazed down at Grim and replied, "I have never heard of the name Zordell before, but I have heard of Progenitors. Up until now, I thought they were myths."

"What do you mean?" Grim asked.

"I do not know much, but this is what I was told. There is a legend of eight ancient creatures in the Ashen Plane called Arch Beings. It is said they are the greatest in their individual branches of magic, and they keep the balance of power throughout the world. Which of the nine branches was not represented, I do not know. They supposedly had champions who did their will. Those champions were called the first, the Progenitors," Lukav answered.

"Anything else?" Grim asked.

"Outside of them being powerful, no," Lukav answered. "So…what has Zordell sent you to do?"

"Well, essentially, he wants me to free him. He was chained up, seemed desperate. When talking with him, I made him upset. Then he stabbed me with this dagger," Grim said, pointing to his enchanted weapon sheathed on his belt, "and basically forced me to make a deal. If I became his Progenitor, I would not bleed to death, and he would get someone to free him."

Lukav's eyes widened, and he stared slack-jawed at Grim. "Wow, that is dangerous!"

"Yeah, he was rather sadistic." Grim thought uncomfortably about his new patron for a moment, then continued. "Anyway, after I became his Progenitor, his mood improved. He told me there are seals placed to hold him in the world. He doesn't know where, but he said I would be drawn to them. I'm supposed to destroy them, then I will get rewarded. It's safe to assume, though, that the ones responsible for sealing him in will try to stop me."

"Do you have to free him?" Lukav asked. "It seems that you are safe now."

"Well, I did accept a quest from him. I'm honestly not sure what would happen if I deny it, but seeing how ridiculously strong he was, I doubt it's a good idea. Plus, even though he's kind of a dick, he actually didn't seem like a bad guy…just really desperate, you know? If I were in his situation, I might be the same way."

The orc nodded in understanding. "You have saved my life and given me power. My life is pledged to you. I will help you with this quest. So, how do you plan to do it?"

"Uh, well, I'm a foreigner in a brand new land. I need

knowledge about where I am, and I need to get stronger," Grim answered.

"If I may," Lukav replied. "Why not see my people? They should have information about the Ashen Plane and some maps to help guide us."

Grim thought for a moment, then agreed. "Lead on, my man. But first, let's get you a shirt."

They took turns using the greatsword to remove the lion's pelt. It was awkward, but after a bit, they had removed an uneven section of skin. Lukav then dried it over the fire to remove any traces of blood and gore. Realizing that making a decent shirt would be impossible, Grim cut a hole in the middle of the pelt and had Lukav put his head through it. It definitely wasn't stylish, but it served as a makeshift poncho that would keep the orc warm.

After making Lukav a "shirt," they began the journey to the orc's clan. Grim was informed that it was still morning, so they could make good progress before making camp for the night. After they left the cliffside altar, the mountainous terrain soon became a thick forest of pines, interspersed with rocks. A slight fog hovered near the ground around them as they trudged through the snow. Grim took in his new surroundings, enjoying his new world, while they walked quietly for some time. There was no distinct trail once they hit the forest, but Lukav said they were going the right way. They spent their day traversing the coniferous forest while practicing their Death Magic. There was a light layer of snow that covered the ground, which helped to guide them by revealing Lukav's footsteps from his previous journey. Grim did see impressions in the snow of multiple woodland creatures. They were able to use their Death Orb spell on some animals and actually killed a few. Grim and

Lukav started a friendly competition of who could accumulate more kills by the end of the day. In hindsight, Grim could admit that it was childish and wasteful as the magic ruined the viability of the animals' pelts and meats, but he was having too much fun with his newfound powers. Being a competitive person, Grim took Zordell's advice and decided to use the rules of this game, or lack thereof, to his advantage.

After Lukav had taken a 3-1 lead to Grim, the Progenitor decided to use a new spell. They had only found a fox and three rabbits so far, and Grim had been in charge of collecting their bodies. He knelt down to the most recent rabbit victim and once again called on that familiar feeling of channeling death magic through his body, from his soul. He could somehow visualize the purple-hued magic coursing through him. Focusing on the spell he wanted to channel, he released the summon undead spell and forcefully said, "Necro Compeli!"

Once the words were said, a wispy purple beam of light shot out of his hand, went through the mouth of the dead animal, and landed on the ground next to the corpse.

"Huh?" he said in confusion. *What was that?*

A gaseous ball of purple light came out of the ground where the beam had landed and then floated into the mouth of the dead rabbit. The animal's eyes and mouth shone the same purple hue of light, but more dully, and then the dead animal rose back to life.

"Whoa!" Grim breathed in awe. He hadn't known how the spell would go, but he definitely thought it was cool.

Apparently, instead of reviving the dead animal, he'd brought a spirit to inhabit the body of the dead creature. The reanimated beast pulled itself back up on its feet, unfazed by the large black patch of necrosis still on its side, and looked directly at Grim.

Grim petted the undead creature and used Analyze.

Snow Rabbit (LVL 1)

Race: Animal (Undead)

Strength: 1

Agility: 6

Vitality: 5

Intelligence:1

Mind: 1

Endurance: 7

Charisma: 1

Health: 10

Manna: 0

Stamina: N/A

This is a creature whose body has been inhabited by a weak spirit. Most spirits are grateful to have a new body and host and are typically very obedient to the ones who gave them a new life. Undead creatures often lose most of their Intelligence and Mind but no longer feel pain and do not tire as easily compared to when they were alive. This spirit will inhabit this form for one hour.

Grim cautiously whispered, "Take two steps to the left."

The rabbit sidestepped to its left two times.

After seeing its obedience, Grim sighed in relief. *Time for step two!* he thought.

For almost an hour, he had his undead pet lure out or chase a number of forest creatures straight to him and away from

Lukav. Pretty soon he had a respectable 7-3 lead on the orc, who had grown frustrated at the human's comeback. Unfortunately, Grim was reckless, and the magic he was using caused such severe necrosis of the carcasses that there was nothing left to salvage—no meat, no pelts, no loot. He didn't care, though. His competitive drive was leading him on.

When Lukav protested about the rabbit, Grim shrugged and said, "Zordell told me there will always be systems in place, and we just need to find ways to use them for our benefit. Work harder, not smarter, bro."

Satisfied with his logic, Grim continued forward. He was about to call his rabbit to him when he heard a high-pitched squeal behind him. He turned back to see Lukav with the undead creature impaled through the orc's new enchanted claws. The rabbit, out of health, dissolved into black sludge that ran down the greater vassal's hand and arm.

"You said use the rules to my benefit. Well, there's no rule that said I can't destroy your pet," Lukav said with an uncomfortable smile. The orc's innocent nature was obviously conflicting with his "bending the rules."

Grim smiled confidently, though. His inner competitive nature was on full display. The real game had begun!

The two companions traveled the rest of the day while having some intense competition of wit and hunting skill. After Grim was accidentally scratched by Lukav's claws, though, he thought it would be best to set some actual ground rules. They decided to use only Death Orbs since they both could cast the spell and could not interfere with each other's casting. They also had to take turns so one of them didn't take off chasing an animal, leaving the other lost. Grim already had a good opinion of the orc but grew to like him even more upon learning he was

69

a good trash talker as well after Grim pestered him repeatedly. Grim could tell Lukav was a kind person, so he would have to be the one to initiate the joking. Their good-natured competition went on into midafternoon, when Lukav stuck his arm out, stopping Grim in his tracks.

The orc stuck his finger to his mouth and whispered, "Shh." He then pointed in front of them in an upward direction.

About ninety feet in front of them was a small hill, and on top of it stood a deer. It was a large doe about five feet tall with dark brown fur.

Lukav looked at Grim and activated Death Orb in his right hand.

Grim shook his head no, then pulled out one of his javelins. It was an inch thick and a foot and a half long, made of light mahogany-colored wood, and had a sharp iron tip. "Let's use these so we can eat the deer. We need to get within about ten yards," he whispered.

Lukav nodded in affirmation and let the magic orb in his hand fizzle out.

Grim handed two of the weapons to Lukav. The pair crouched and began slowly creeping closer to the top of the hill. Lukav accidentally stepped on a fallen branch, causing a loud crack that echoed through the forest. The doe looked up as the pair froze in place. After about thirty seconds, the deer turned away from them, took a few steps, and resumed ruffling through the snow to find some grass just out of their sight.

The pair, after a sigh of relief, continued sneaking toward the hill. Once they'd made it near the top of the hill, they started a cautious crawl upward so as to not disturb the animal. They slowly peered over the crest. The deer was still eating grass and only ten feet away from them, unaware of their presence.

70

They lowered their heads under the hillcrest and looked at each other.

"Okay, whoever kills this, wins," Grim decided.

Lukav nodded agreement.

The two prepared to hurl their javelins at the animal.

Grim whispered, "Three, two, one, now!"

CHAPTER 8
GNOLL

GRIM AND LUKAV APPROACHED THE fallen cervid, finding a large spear impaled in its chest and a pool of blood forming under its body. A figure approached the downed beast from the other side of the hill, about fifty yards away. Grim squinted to see what the creature was when Lukav grabbed him by the chest plate and pulled him back down the hill. Frustrated, Grim was about to say something to the orc when Lukav shushed him, wide-eyed and with a noticable layer of sweat on his forehead.

The orc whispered, "Gnoll."

"Wait, there are gnolls here?" Grim whispered. There had been gnolls in his previous games, and they were bad news!

"Yes! They are savages!" Lukav replied, panic growing more apparent in his voice. "They are a barbaric people! My clan has been warring with a tribe of them since before I was born. I have only ever seen a dead one once at the village, but my mother told me about them. They are driven to do only a few things: kill, eat, and breed. Even the very young ones can kill you if you are not careful."

"Well, what should we do?!" Grim asked.

"It depends. Males run in packs with a matriarch serving as their protector. Some males have been seen alone or with a group of other males, though. I have been told they're looking for anything that walks to mate with. The monsters will eat, rape, and kill anything that has a pulse. Sometimes in that order," Lukav said with a look of true fear on his face, his innocent nature assaulted by the reality of his situation.

Grim frowned. "Crap!" After considering their new set of circumstances for a moment, he whispered, "I'm going to see how many there are. We may have to fight, so get ready."

Lukav sucked his teeth but nodded agreement to the plan.

Grim started crawling back up to the hill, hoping the creature hadn't seen them. He cautiously peeked over the brush line of the hill, being more careful than the last time. He saw an up close view of the horrific creature for the first time. The gnoll had one foot on the corpse of the deer for leverage is it pulled the spear out of the creature's body. Grim assumed it was a he because it wore only a loincloth. It was humanoid, about six feet tall, with gray skin and a hyena's head, and it smelled like rotten flesh mixed with cat urine. There were blisters and scars on its face. After it pulled its crude spear out and set it on the ground, it buried its head into the dead creature and ate with abandon. Grim scanned the surroundings for any sign of other gnolls, finding none.

He crouched back down next to Lukav and whispered, "Okay, I only saw one. If they are as dangerous as you say, we could either take him out or go around. Do you know another way?"

Before the orc could answer, something slimy fell on his arm. The Greater Vassal and Progenitor looked up, finding the gnoll glaring down at them from about ten feet above them. It

73

was leaning over the edge and drooling with desire at its new meal. It lifted up its rudimentary wooden spear and let out a blood-curdling battle cry.

"Attack!" Grim yelled in panic.

Both he and Lukav threw their javelins at the being in a panicked reaction. Grim missed, but Lukav managed to hit the gnoll in the left shoulder, throwing it off balance and causing it to back up. The weapon did not do much damage, given their short distance from the gnoll. The duo ran up the hill, choosing to try to overwhelm their attacker. Grim grabbed his greatsword while Lukav decided to use magic with his left hand and his enhanced claws on his right. The gnoll had just pulled out the javelin from its shoulder when they crested the hill. Lukav took a wide swing with his claws, but the gnoll used its spear like a club and hit the orc in the head, knocking him down before he could connect. Grim used the distraction to swing his sword into the creature's upper right arm, but the gnoll blocked it with the spear. They stood there with their weapons against each other, eyes locked. The gnoll barked at him in a harsh language that he couldn't understand. Grim stomped on its foot and used Analyze as they made contact.

Gnoll (LVL 3)

Health: 175/200

Manna: 0

Stamina: 105/150

Gnolls are feral humanoids that attribute their origins to demonic rituals. They have an insatiable bloodlust. They often take advantage of their prey before killing it.

Lukav was right! Before Grim could figure out what to do with the information, the creature reared back and swung its weapon at the Progenitor's chest, knocking him on his back a few feet away. It jumped on top of Grim but was forced to retreat just as quickly to avoid a backhand slice from Grim. It hopped backward, then screamed in pain as black claws pierced through its right side, followed by dark necrotic energy spreading outward from the new wound.

Grim got to his feet, thankful Lukav had gotten back in the fight when he did.

The gnoll attempted to reach back at its impaler, but Lukav managed to slam a Death Orb into its back with his free hand. The blow knocked the monster to its knees. It looked up in time to see Grim swing his sword down with a war cry, and its eyes were frozen in the realization of its imminent death after its skull was cut in two. Grim felt a rush of power, and then notifications appeared.

> You have defeated a LVL 3 Gnoll!
> +136 EXP

> Level Up!
> You have acquired enough EXP to reach LVL 2!

> Congratulations! Great Weapon
> Wielding has reached LVL 2!
> +2% Damage
> +2% to Attack Speed

75

> Congratulations! Heavy Armor has reached LVL 2!
>
> +2% Damage Protection
>
> -2% Movement Penalty

> Skill gained! Stealth LVL 1
>
> You are able to sneak about unnoticed by others.
>
> +1% Stealth Speed
>
> -1% Chance of Being Detected

> Skill gained! Tracking LVL 1
>
> You are able to discern and follow the tracks of others. Many have lost their lives from the pursuit of a master tracker.
>
> +1% Tracking Speed
>
> +1% Chance of Finding Tracks

> 5 Stat Points, +1 Level Point, and +10 Health, Manna, or Stamina are available to distribute for your race: Human
>
> Do you wish to distribute them now?
>
> Yes or No

"Yes!" Grim said with a celebratory fist pump in the air. "I just leveled up! I feel...*great!*"

Then he selected no to distributing his Stat Points. He was new to this world and the allocation of stat points, from his experience, could mean life or death. And that was literally the case for him now.

Both Progenitor and Greater Vassal stood catching their breath for a moment.

Grim asked, "Are these creatures common around here?"

"I leveled up too, and no," Lukav huffed, still trying to regain his Stamina. "Seems like it was alone. I have never heard of them being this close to our village. We have to let them know!"

"Okay. How far away are we from your village?" Grim asked.

"About half a day's journey, but the forest is even more dangerous at night. We should make camp," Lukav replied.

Grim nodded agreement and took off his helmet, then the two went to work. They first dragged the gnoll's smelly body a good distance away so they would not attract predators, and they looted his body only to find a random animal tooth and a few small, salty seeds that Lukav called hanzos. They were apparently uncommon and made a tasty snack. Lukav convinced Grim they had to cut off what was left of the monster's head as proof or his clan wouldn't believe them. Grim agreed as long as the orc didn't expect him to carry it. They built a fire and dressed out some of the deer meat for their evening meal. Before they actually started cooking, Grim had a moment of inspiration. He took the seeds they had found on the gnoll's body and pressed them into the meat. He held the venison over the fire on a skewer. After their meal had been thoroughly cooked, a notification appeared.

> Recipe Discovered!
>
> Hanzo Venison
>
> You have discovered that if you season venison with salty hanzos, you can make a tasty dish!
>
> Ingredients: Hanzo seeds (varying amounts), raw venison (varying amounts)
>
> +6% to taste
>
> +2% to positive mood

77

Grim wondered if it was his Culinary skill that had given him the idea. He thought if he could find better recipes with better bonuses, he could find substitutes for potions. The small increase in taste showed on Lukav's surprised face, then the orc tore into the meat with a large smile.

"Good?" Grim asked.

Lukav nodded without stopping his attack on the meal.

Enjoying his meal, Grim thought it'd be a good time to get more information. "So, Lukav, where are we exactly? I know we're in the Ashen Plane, but where specifically?"

The orc looked up at Grim with his cheeks distended from the food he was chewing, a bit thrown off by his question. After swallowing, he answered, "We are at the Spine of Zulnixia. It is a mountain range located on the northern side of the continent of Frassisi."

"Okay." Grim wiped his mouth with the back of his hand. "Do a lot of people live here? Are there any humans?"

"Oh, no!" Lukav answered with a chuckle. "This is a very difficult area to live in! First, the winters here are very harsh. Second, many dangerous creatures live throughout this region. You saw how tough that gnoll was, and that was a grunt. The dangers also make trade difficult here, though human traveling merchants do occasionally pass through."

"Earlier you said your clan was in a war with a gnoll tribe. Are you sure the one we killed was part of them?" Grim asked between bites.

Lukav shrugged. "Maybe, but from what I've been taught, any gnoll is bad news."

"Well, will your village allow you to come back since you left?" Grim asked.

Almost choking on his food, Lukav coughed and beat his

chest to relieve the discomfort. Then he gave Grim a concerned look and said, "Uhhh, there are some things you need to know. My clan is a noble and honorable clan, holding the aspects of truth and freedom above all others. Unfortunately, we are losing our war with the gnolls. Though we are stronger and better trained, they have higher numbers and are extremely violent by nature. Many of us have died. We have not been even allowed to undergo our pilgrimage trials for concern that our clan's location would be compromised."

"What is a pilgrimage trial?" Grim asked.

"At eighteen every villager must leave our people to gain perspective and bring back a useful item or skill that will benefit the clan. They call that rite of passage a pilgrimage. So, I snuck out, deciding to perform my pilgrimage. You see, I thought we could use the help. We have been practicing and getting stronger, increasing our numbers and skill, here in the mountains. While this has been helpful, my clan has not welcomed outsiders recently for fear of a spy. Soooo…"

"So they'll attack me unless I'm with you, and they may attack you too for leaving?" Grim asked, his voice rising as the reality of the situation struck home.

"Hopefully not." Lukav chuckled uncomfortably.

Just as Grim was about to scorn his new companion for the poor timing of that information, he felt something sharp pressed against his back.

A deep voice said swiftly, "You move, you talk, you die."

A feminine figure appeared from behind a nearby tree, gripping a large spear. She swiftly hit Lukav in the side of the head with the blunt end of her weapon. The orc fell to the ground, and she pinned him down with her knee on his back and twisted his enchanted arm into an uncomfortable position while holding her spear against his neck.

She turned her head to Grim and demanded, "Who are you? Why are you here?"

She had a deep but feminine voice that was sharp and commanding, and now that she had stopped moving, Grim was able to examine her. She had green skin and a large amount of long, dark brown dreadlocks and wore a mixture of leather armor and animal furs. There was a choker necklace of what looked to be animal teeth wrapped tightly around her neck. She had brown eyes, and even though she wore a brown mask covering her nose and mouth, he could make out an intense look on her face that matched her voice. Grim realized she was probably one of the orcs from Lukav's clan.

"Now!" she yelled.

"Okay, okay!" Grim replied. "I'm Grim. I'm a traveler from a foreign land. That is Lukav, a member of your clan."

The orc's eyes widened, and she gasped. She looked down at Lukav, turning his head a bit to get a better view of him. "Lukav?" she asked in a gentler voice.

Lukav groaned and said, "Hello, Vumira."

The female orc let go of Lukav's arm and pulled him up. She removed her mask, revealing a look of shock and a button nose and freckles. "What are you doing here? Where did you go, and why have you brought this outsider near our home? And what happened to you?" Vumira asked with fear and awe in her voice.

"It is alright," Lukav said with his palms out, trying to placate the female orc. "This is Grim. He is a mage I ran into out here."

Grim sighed quietly in relief. He was glad Lukav didn't tell her about him being a Progenitor, not knowing if they would respond in a hostile manner to that information.

"He used his magic to fix my body! We were going to the village to get some information and let you know we found a gnoll nearby."

Vumira notably tensed and immediately started scanning her surroundings. "Gnoll! Where?"

"We found a lone wanderer and managed to kill it before it could alert any others," Lukav said, gesturing to the newly decapitated split head by his feet.

Once she saw the head, Vumira grew more composed. Grim noticed she slightly loosened her grip on Lukav, showing obvious care for him. The female orc then let out a short, quick whistle.

Out of the forest behind her appeared a badger the size of a large dog. She picked up the head and let the creature sniff it, then it took off toward where they'd left the body. Once the animal disappeared among the trees, she started speaking again, but this time, it was a distinct, grinding language.

This is Orcish! Grim quickly realized. What really surprised him was that somehow, he understood what they were saying. He quickly assumed it must be because of his bond with Lukav.

"You know our rules! No outsiders. For all we know, he could be a spy sent here to bring about our demise," she said, gesturing to Grim.

"He is not a spy, Vumira," Lukav responded in Orcish. "He saved my life and rid me of my curse." He said the last part with raw emotion while looking at his hand. "I owe him a great debt and have pledged my service to him."

A heavy silence hung over them for a moment.

"I should have you both killed on the spot," Vumira said

with disappointment in her voice. "If my badger returns with evidence confirming your story, we shall take you to the council. If not, we will do what we must to protect our people."

Grim was not a fan of the second option. Fortunately, they didn't have to wait long before the large mammal brought back the rest of the gnoll's body.

Vumira examined the body, then nodded to the figure still holding something sharp at Grim's back. He felt the pressure of the blade ease off and a shirtless male orc wearing a wolf pelt like a cloak stepped up beside him. The large orc sheathed his dagger, then threw the head in a pouch on his waist.

Vumira said, "Go forward," and pointed her spear in the direction she wanted them to move. "If you try to run, you die."

Grim looked at Lukav, who silently confirmed to him that they should trust the orcs as he started walking. They traversed through the forest for about an hour, when Grim noticed the trees were getting larger and the vegetation more dense. By dusk, they came upon a large pine with a hole at its base big enough to fit them all. Vumira said they would camp there for the night. Lukav and Grim were given some water, then were bound with rope and had their weapons taken. Grim didn't like the idea, but the orcs hadn't done anything to harm them so far. He also took the chance to Analyze their escorts.

Vumira (LVL 22)

Race: Orc

Health: 220

Manna: 20

Stamina: 310

This orc is the Head Hunter of what remains of the Blood-Shield Clan. She has become a true expert of the wilds in the Spine of Zulnixia. Many beasts have fallen to her spear.

Kremoto (LVL 8)

Race: Orc

Health: 160

Manna: 10

Stamina: 155

This orc is a Hunter of the Blood-Shield Clan.

Congratulations! Analyze has reached LVL 2!

You can now gain basic information (Health, Manna, Stamina) from a distance of five feet or less. You will now know a target's resistances when performing this skill while making contact.

These two are no joke! She could probably kill us by herself! he thought. Analyzing those two confirmed something else for Grim too. When he had used Analyze on Lukav and his undead rabbit, it showed a lot more information compared to the gnoll and these orcs. He realized that those who are loyal or have attempted to pledge loyalty will reveal more information than others.

They made a small fire, and under its light, Grim was able to examine Vumira's spear. Even from a distance, he could tell it was much more than just a simple weapon. It was around seven feet long with a dark wood handle. Its tip was a light green metal with jagged edges for more damage. On both flat faces of the tip were intricate carvings. It didn't take Grim long to realize they were runes. Then he noticed a rune carved in Kremoto's dagger too.

Kremoto saw Grim looking at his dagger and gave him a scowl.

"What did you do to Lukav?" Vumira said, interrupting the tense moment.

"It's hard to say," Grim answered. "Essentially, I imbued him with magic that caused his body to morph."

"So you are a healer?" Vumira asked.

"No. I was able to activate magic inside of him. He had enough Affinity, so I was able to impart on him an extra ability."

Both orcs widened their eyes and looked at Lukav.

"You can use magic?" Kremoto asked incredulously.

Lukav nodded, smiled, said a word of power, and conjured a Death Orb in his right hand.

The two gasped, and Lukav willed the orb to dissipate.

Nobody said anything for a bit, and the only sound was the badger chewing on an antler it had found.

"You see that we could have broken out if we wanted to," Grim said, hoping they'd realize he was trustworthy.

"Death Magic!" Vumira whispered. She looked at Grim with fear and concern in her eyes, then at Kremoto and said in orcish, "Gag them."

Grim had just enough time to say, "Oh, come on!" before he and Lukav were gagged. His gesture of trust obviously had not worked.

After that, Vumira said sternly, still in her native tongue, "I've heard multiple stories of Death Mages. All of them ended badly." She gave Lukav a serious look before averting her gaze.

"I suggest you get some rest, Death Mage. Tomorrow, it will be decided if you can ever rest again."

Great! Grim thought. In his game, most Death magic users in the storyline were antagonistic, so he wasn't shocked that this world appeared to have the same viewpoint. He did wonder what that said of Zordell, though. He closed his eyes and thought about his situation. He couldn't help but smile. *You know, even though I'm a prisoner, I'm a fucking mage now! Twenty-four hours ago, I was a janitor with a flabby body. Now I have muscles, an enhanced body, a follower, and a purpose. This is awesome!* At that thought, with his body exhausted from the day's labor and events, Grim drifted off to sleep.

CHAPTER 9

The Clan

Grim was awoken by Vumira poking him with the blunt end of her spear.

"Ow!" he said. He blinked away his grogginess and realized he was no longer gagged and bound. He was given a piece of jerky for breakfast and then ushered with Lukav in the direction of his clan's home.

Grim tried to ask a few questions on their journey but was given no response from the hunters. Lukav answered some of his questions but, after a threat from Vumira, quickly hushed.

It took only a few hours for the group to get to the village's boundary. It appeared to be a wall of stone. Grim was confused until he watched Kremoto press against a small stone that jutted out of the wall. The stone sunk in partially, and a loud click was heard. A large slab of stone slid down out of the wall, revealing a doorway. Vumira led the way inside, followed by Lukav and Grim, with Kremoto bringing up the rear. They entered a dark cavern scantily lit with sconces that reminded Grim of where he'd met Zordell, except it was smaller and the sconces had regular fire instead of the purple glow. Ten feet ahead of them, two orcs clad in fine leather armor stood guard on either side. They had large sheathed swords hanging from their waists. One sword seemed like a scimitar while the other looked like a katana.

Both guards put their hands on the handles of their weapons, ready to unsheathe. "Who goes there?" one of them asked.

"I am Vumira, Head Hunter of our clan. With me is fellow Hunter Kremoto and my badger. On our hunt, we found our lost villager, Lukav, and a trespasser. We are bringing them before the council. Go tell Thrain what has happened."

The two guards eased. One put his hand to his heart and said, "Yes, Head Hunter!" and took off down the cavern. The other stepped to the side, allowing the group to pass.

Grim took the chance to try out his improved Analyze while passing the guard.

Mudún (LVL 6)

Race: Orc

Health: 195

Manna: 0

Stamina: 135

Resistances: Cold 15%

Soul Magic 25%

Nice, he thought. He used Analyze on Vumira and Kremoto too, finding they all had the same resistances. He figured it was either an orc thing or something with this clan.

Once they made it through the cavern, they came to a small valley about the size of four football fields, shaped like an L, and surrounded on all sides by rocks like it was a bowl. They had come out at an entrance on the far right side. Thick green grass up to Grim's ankles had a light amount of frost on top. There were a mixture of wooden shacks and large tents spread throughout. Well-manicured dirt paths crisscrossed the terrain, allowing for easy passage across the valley. A small stream flowed across the valley horizontally, somehow coming out of a hole in the rock wall on one side and disappearing through another at the other side.

Grim's taking in of the scenery was interrupted by Kremoto pushing him forward, saying, "Move!"

Walking through the valley, Grim saw more orcs. Children hid behind their mothers. They passed by a blacksmith working on an axe; a group practicing sword-forms in unison; a male orc with a wild Mohawk, tanning the hide of a deer; a feminine archer shooting arrows at targets; and three what looked to be monks in a meditative stance, sitting at an edge of the valley with their legs crossed. Most stopped or looked up to examine the helmet-wearing human intruder and his mutated ally in their home. Many gave scowls or looks of discomfort, the exception being the monks, who did not open their eyes at all. As the group came to the more vertical part of the L-shaped valley, they saw an upward ramp on the right side. The left side was flat and looked to have held crops during warmer weather. On the ramp were different shacks made of rock and wood spaced out diagonally. They went up the ramp until they made it to the top and another cave entrance was directly in front of them. The path turned to the left and ended where multiple orcs were sitting on stone stools in a semicircle. The path had a twenty-foot drop-off to the flat farmland seen previously.

Vumira bowed her head, placed a fist to her heart, and took a knee. In Orcish she said, "Council, I bring before you Lukav, who left our village without permission. He claims his reason was to undergo a pilgrimage to better our clan. With him is a human who calls himself Grim. He is a Death Mage and has imbued Lukav with Death Magic, changing his form." She gestured to Lukav, who responded by openly showing his new arm and foot to the council.

Some of the council members reacted with exasperated and concerned expressions, but multiple orcs remained stoic.

Grim examined the group sitting before them. There were seven in total, three females and four males. Many had scars and were musclebound. All of them appeared to be quite old except for the one on Grim's far right. He was a young male and wore an ornate headdress that was a mix of wood and leather and only revealed his face while covering his entire neck and shoulder with feathers flowing down from the top of it.

"Were they alone?" asked an orc with a brown goatee and a large facial scar that went through part of his upper lip and cheek, leaving a permanent snarl.

"They were," Vumira responded.

"Why did you decide to bring them back?" another council member asked angrily in a harsh voice. She had a large horizontal scar across her face and nose and two gray braided pigtails. "You know the rules of our village. For all we know, you have compromised our entire clan!"

Grim realized that this clan had a xenophobic "shoot first, ask questions later" kind of attitude. It did make him glad he was at least with Lukav.

"I know, Zapar, but then they told us about this." Vumira gave a look to Kremoto, who then pulled the gnoll's head out of a bag attached to his waist.

At this, even the more composed figures' eyes bulged. All except for the middle orc. The council began whispering with each other, growing louder with concern. The noise came to an immediate halt when the middle orc threw up his hand in an open palm gesture. All others looked to him with respect and fear. Grim bet he was the chief.

The center orc was extremely muscle bound and wore only metal wristguards and scaled metal pants. Grim could see runic carvings on them too. He had a ring of tribal-looking tattoos that formed a circumference around his neck. There was no hair on his head except for a braided gray ponytail that reminded Grim of ancient Egyptians and a long gray beard but no mustache. He was sitting with his legs crossed and had braided ropes wrapped around both his arms and legs that served as some sort of tribal bracelets. The orc had a look of intense yet calm focus.

He looked at Grim and said, "Vumira says you are a Death Mage named Grim. Is that true?" He had a deep masculine voice that was completely stoic and devoid of emotion.

"Yes," Grim replied.

"What do you know about our clan?"

"Only what Lukav told me," Grim replied. "He said you are the Blood-Shield Clan. He also said you have been at war with the gnolls here."

"Did he also tell you that no trespasser has ever seen our village and lived?" The chief's expression remained stoic, contradictory to the threatening statement he'd just made.

Grim paused, thrown off by his question.

Before he could answer, the chief continued. "Tell me, Grim, how did you end up with Lukav and that?" He nodded toward the gnoll's head. "Also, why should we spare you? Answer well. Know that I will not ask twice." He cracked his knuckles loudly.

The younger orc on the council smirked.

Even though the orc's tone had been calm, Grim felt a chill

run up his spine. He swallowed, took off his helmet, and proceeded to explain. "I am traveler from a world called Earth. I was unintentionally transported here and know of no way to return. I met Lukav right before he was about to be attacked by the lion he's now wearing. I was able to kill it and save him from a grisly end."

The chief looked to Lukav, who nodded in affirmation.

"Afterward, Lukav pledged himself to serve me. As I am new to this world, I wanted to learn more about it. Lukav suggested we visit your village to do so. On our way, we ran into the gnoll. It attacked us, but we were able to defeat it. Shortly after, we were ambushed by your people and brought here."

The shaman-looking orc interrupted. "This is absurd! This human has confirmed nothing. He could be working with the gnolls and setting us up for a trap." He voice was slightly deeper than Lukav's but with much more anger.

The chief sharply looked back, finally breaking his visage by glaring angrily at the younger orc. The shaman pursed his lips and bowed his head in respect and fear of his leader.

The stoic look of the chief returned as he looked to Grim and said, "Continue."

"Er, um, yes. Well, that's about it for my time here. I've literally only been in this world for about a day. As for why I should be spared, well, Lukav also mentioned that your clan hold the ideals of truth and freedom above all others. I have told you the truth and have committed no harm against the freedom of your village. If you are still cautious, I understand. I do ask that if you still have concern, you please give me an opportunity to prove myself. Also, that you spare Lukav. He has proven honorable in the time I've known him. You are his people, and I believe he can be of great use."

The shaman let out a mocking chuckle in clear disagreement.

Grim was not a fan of the orc douchebag from the little time he had seen him.

The extremely muscle-bound orc did not look back at the younger one this time. He stood up and walked to about three feet from the human. The orc was easily the biggest one Grim had seen so far, standing at least seven feet tall. He squinted his brown eyes to focus on Grim. Somehow, Grim could feel him concentrating. The orc's breath was visible in the cool air, and Grim felt it brush against the hair on his skin.

After a few uncomfortable seconds, the orc's tension eased a little. He stood a little taller and said, "Very well. We will give you an opportunity to prove yourself. I, Thrain, Chief of the Blood-Shield Clan, challenge you to undertake the Trial of Nalgex. If you pass, you both shall gain your freedom. If not, you both will die."

A prompt appeared.

Quest Unlocked! The Trial of Nalgex

Chief Thrain of the Blood-Shield Clan has invited you to undergo their ritual trial of truth. If you succeed, both you and Lukav will gain your freedom. The chief has made it clear that failure will result in your demise. Refusal of this quest will most likely end in your death as well.

Reward:

Both you and Lukav will be spared from certain death

Acceptance by the Blood-Shield Clan

Neutral Relationship with the Blood-Shield Clan

Do you accept?

Yes or No

(Would you really say no?)

I guess I really don't have a choice, Grim thought, then he said, "I accept." After the quest prompt disappeared, Grim cast Death Ward on himself to prepare for whatever he was about to face. His hand glowed purple, and he slapped his chest. A pulse of Death Magic coursed throughout his body, ensuring prevention from certain death one time in twenty-four hours. He did not realize the act of a known Death Mage casting an unknown spell would spark fear in almost everyone around him.

Almost every orc took a defensive stance and grabbed weapons in preparation to attack. Even Thrain went into some karate stance with his fists poised to strike.

Grim quickly threw his hands up in a placating manner. "Whoa, there! I'm sorry! I was just casting a spell on myself to get ready."

Lukav rushed between Grim and Thrain and pleaded, "Please, forgive Grim, Council Members! He is unfamiliar with the ways of the clan. Please overlook this offense."

Slowly, everyone composed themselves.

"Also, I wish to participate in the trials as well. I owe my life to Grim and cannot allow him to put his life in danger again on account of me," Lukav said with much more resolve.

Thrain replied, still stoically, "The trial is one that must be undertaken alone, but it speaks well of your new master that you are willing to join him." He turned to the two hunters who had brought them to the council. "Take them to the monks. The snow-skinned human is the only one who will participate. Lukav may watch. If the human uses any magic, kill him."

Grim had just enough time to think, *Snow-skin?* before he

93

was forced back the way he'd come. They were heading down the hill when a loud horn sounded throughout the valley. Another deep horn replied. Their pace did not change. After the second horn, a low drumming started. Soon, a melodic rhythm resounded through the valley, definitely adding to the "ritual trial" feel. Duum, dum, duum, duum! Duum, dum, duum, duum! Duum, dum, duum duum! Duum, dum, duum, duum!

As the group passed by, every orc in the village stopped what they were doing and fell in behind Grim's party to follow them. Eventually, they came to the outside of what looked to be a circular fence composed of wooden spikes so close together that you could not see through them. When they stopped at the only noticeable door, the music stopped. Grim stood examining all the orc's faces looking back at him. There was a mixture of excitement, fear, and curiosity. About a minute later, the shaman Grim was not a fan of came up with a look of malcontent toward him. Right behind him, Thrain addressed the crowd with more emotion than Grim had seen him show so far.

"Our clansman, Lukav, underwent an illegal pilgrimage. Normally, the penalty is death for putting our clan at risk, but he came back stronger and brought a human mage with him. So far, they have upheld our values of truth and freedom, and I have found no ill will toward our people. I will not, however, allow a serpent into our midst. The human has agreed to undergo the Trial of Nalgex to prove he knows what true freedom is. Let us commence."

The shaman pulled out a small clay vial and forcefully shoved it into Grim's chest. "Drink!"

Grim grabbed the vial and did as commanded. The fluid was gritty like it had coffee grounds in it and tasted bittersweet.

Fortunately, it went down smoothly. Within a few seconds, Grim lost all feeling in his hands, then fell to his knees and lost consciousness.

CHAPTER 10

THE TRIAL

GRIM DREAMED HE WAS A polar bear with red eyes and a cub. They were hungry and being fed by some orcs. Before anything else happened, he woke up lying on a dirt floor, in a not-so-small puddle of drool.

"What happened?" he said as he started to stand while blinking the blurriness out of his vision. As his vision was starting to clear he realized he had a notification.

> You have ingested Potion of Nalgex.
>
> Effects:
>
> 100% Manna Drain for 24 hours
>
> 50% Stamina Drain for 24 hours
>
> Unknown

Grim looked at his Manna and Stamina bars with a sinking feeling in his gut when they matched his notification. His shocked feeling was quickly replaced by concern when he noticed a single orc standing twenty feet away, in front of a door. The green-skinned being wore only simple boots, pants, and some sort of white tribal mask. He was large and muscle-bound with black tribal tattoos that covered both arms from shoulder to wrist. They were in a ten-by-forty-foot hallway that was slightly curved to the left. There was no ceiling, just an open view of the blue sky above. The floor was made of dirt, and the walls were made of wood that reminded Grim of the fence he had seen earlier before drinking the potion.

The orc started speaking to Grim. "Many pursue freedom but do not know what it really is. Because they do not know the truth, they are never free. Can you find freedom from this place?" The weaponless orc barreled toward Grim.

Grim exclaimed, "Oh, crap!" and tried to grab his great-sword but found nothing there.

By the time he'd grasped his situation, the orc's fist had landed against his sternum, knocking the air out of him and sending him flying. Pure adrenaline helped Grim roll to the left before the orc could stomp on him. With all his might, Grim swung his arm behind the orc's leg and tripped him. The orc fell onto his back. Grim rolled and slowly stood, taking only a couple steps toward the door before the orc had tripped him in return. Grim landed ungracefully on his back with a moan and blurry vision. Even though his game had been realistic, it had not trained him for the pain he had encountered so far!

The orc stood ten feet away, focused on Grim. "Have you found where freedom is?"

"No!" Grim whined.

"Then continue your pursuit through that door!" the orc replied while gesturing for Grim to enter the door he had previously been guarding.

Grim slowly got up and made his way toward the door, thoughts spinning through his head. *Okay. What is freedom, and where do I find it here? What do they mean "the truth of what it is"? Uhhh, umm, freedom is…freedom is…* He reached the door and, to Grim's surprise, found the space beyond was exactly identical to the room he'd just come from. The door forcefully closed behind him from the other side.

Two more mask-wearing orcs appeared from a hidden door under the dirt floor. They both turned to face Grim and said in unison, "Many pursue freedom but do not know what it really is. Because they do not know the truth, they are never free. Can you find freedom from this place?"

Both orcs ran toward Grim at full force. Grim was able to get a couple light punches in before they quickly beat him to the ground. He could feel blood flow from one of his nostrils and was sure he had a broken rib.

Both orcs stopped and asked Grim, "Have you found where freedom is?"

Grim struggled to stand, closed his eyes, and in a low voice said, "No."

"Then continue your pursuit through that door," they replied.

I wish I could have chosen what kind of trial this would be. A simple essay would have been nice, Grim thought. *Wait, choice! Freedom is choice, but where do I find it? From inside me?* He looked at the two orcs and said, "I find freedom from within." He thought it sounded good, and hey, it beat getting the piss beat out of you. He definitely did not want to keep fighting the masked orc-ninjas.

The two orcs looked at each other, then to Grim, and shook their heads in disapproval of his answer. They turned away from Grim and said, "Continue your pursuit through that door."

This process repeated a few more times until Grim had the

bright idea of investing his stat points. He put three points in Vitality and two in Endurance while increasing his HP by ten. He also invested his level point into Heavy Armor as it seemed to be the only skill that could benefit him at the moment. While it was nice to have increased health and stamina, the relief was only temporary. Fortunately, three orcs were the most Grim had to face as he went through door after door, entering the same room over and over again. It would always be the same question and then orcs beating him up. His face had swollen up so much that he could no longer see from his right eye. On his way to the sixth room, though, Grim had a realization.

Freedom is choice, but I'm never given a choice. I'm always told which way to pursue freedom. It's not my choice! Though it caused him some discomfort, Grim smiled. He had finally found his answer.

In the next room, instead of trying to fight the orcs, Grim curled up in a ball. The orcs were perplexed by his action but did not spare him the beating. He used the obviously timed beat down to gather a handful of sand and allow some of his Stamina to regenerate. When he reached the next room and the door in the floor opened, Grim used all his might to sprint toward the door with reckless abandon. As the first orc was about to intercept him, Grim threw sand at the orc's face. The sand startled the orc, throwing him off balance. Grim used his forward momentum to tackle the orc through the door, rolled off his attacker, and stood up to fight again, but the masked orcs did not attack him nor did they ask him any questions. They just looked behind him.

Grim turned around, and a flash of light shone in his eyes. He once again felt like he was dreaming. He was the red-eyed polar bear with its cub in tow in the midst of a battle. They looked different, though. They were bigger, stronger, and admittedly scarier. Their bodies were more muscular, and both their teeth and claws were longer and black. Both Grim and his cub were protecting the orcs that fed them from a large hyena. Over time, the two bears were able to pin and kill the large beast. The orcs began to cheer, and Grim's vision went dark again. He then woke up on a small dirt floor, again in a large puddle of drool. He slowly sat up, this time finding the chief, council, hunters, and Lukav standing around him about ten feet away.

It was a dream? he thought, taking in his surroundings. They were inside the circular wooden spiked walls he had seen earlier before he drank his potion. Instead of a never-ending hallway, though, it was an open flat arena around 100 feet in diameter. Grim found that he had his weapons back. He felt his face and found no bruising. In fact, he was in no pain at all!

Chief Thrain said in his usual neutral manner, "Grim, you have learned the truth. Freedom is being able to make your own decisions. The truth is that many forces will try to impose on you, and you may not even realize your decisions are not your own. While it is important to take council, one's freedom should never be controlled by another." The chieftain reached his hand toward Grim and helped him up off the ground.

"Uugh! What was that!?" Grim asked groggily.

"That was the potion of Nalgex," Thrain replied. "It puts you in a dream-like prison and gives you a vision. If you can escape, you may gift the world with your vision. If not, you are forever stuck in that prison until you die."

"Shit!" Grim exclaimed at the full realization of his previous predicament.

Stepping closer, Lukav asked him, "Are you alright, Grim?!"

"I'm okay," Grim replied. "It just really took a lot out of me."

"What did you see!?" the orc asked with excitement.

The rest of the orcs leaned in, equally interested as Grim explained about seeing the red-eyed white bear and the cub. The orcs were attentive. Some were perplexed. Thrain kept his usual visage.

After Grim finished telling his story, Lukav said, "Well, that is…interesting."

"Yeah. I don't know exactly what it means. Any ideas?" Grim asked Thrain.

Thrain looked at him seriously, but Grim saw something else. There was a light in his eyes. He looked hopeful. The chief then said, "Vumira. You, Lukav, and Grim come with me. The rest of you are dismissed. The prisoners have proven themselves."

The other members all left, albeit with a few members grumbling.

A notification appeared to Grim.

Quest Complete! The Trial of Nalgex

You have successfully escaped the dream prison and ascertained what true freedom is. You have also unlocked a vision to gift the world. You can choose whether or not to share your vision. Be warned that sharing your vision can bring about good or bad results.

Reward:

Sparing of both you and Lukav
Acceptance by the Blood-Shield Clan

101

> Neutral Relationship with the Blood-Shield Clan
>
> Bonus Reward:
>
> A spiritual vision

Grim wished that notification had appeared before he'd blurted out his vision to a number of strangers, especially with that shaman who had seemed to want to kill him before he could even prove himself. He knew he couldn't change the past, though, so he exited with his group not long after the others had left. When they exited the wooden corral, all the orcs of the village were standing there looking toward them, waiting in expectation.

Thrain addressed them in orcish, projecting his voice but keeping his calm tone. "Our clan member, Lukav, and the human, Grim, have proven themselves worthy. They shall not be executed." He scanned their faces before continuing. "Many of you remember Lukav and scoffed at him. He has come back from his pilgrimage stronger, thanks to Grim. Let this be a lesson to never doubt that anyone in our clan can be of worth no matter how they appear!" The chief had raised his voice to punctuate his point and stared seriously at the crowd.

Some villagers bowed their heads in shamed response.

"Also, this human is considered our ally. He has helped our tribe, and we shall help him in kind. There shall be no discrimination or harm to him." Thrain took a breath. "I believe with time, these two will help us win this war. So prepare a feast!"

The crowd of orcs shared looks of excitement with each other, then began to cheer.

Grim looked over to Lukav, finding him smiling with tears welling up in his eyes at the approval of his clan. That, more than anything Thrain had said, really had an effect on Grim. On Earth for most of his life, he had been lazy. He'd rarely applied himself and, if he was honest, had considered himself a loser with little to give. Just when he'd finally found a calling, it was ripped away from him, but he'd been given a second chance. He was no longer weak. Here, he had power and the ability to help people. And he felt incredible to have been able to give Lukav purpose and reunite him with his people. Even though he'd had a rough start, Grim knew he was where he was supposed to be and helping others was what he was supposed to do. His main quest to destroy the seals nagged at the back of his mind. He needed to find them. Who knew what Zordell could do to him?

Putting the thought aside, Grim smiled and then looked to Thrain as he walked ahead and gestured for Grim, Lukav, and Vumira to follow. They went back up the sloped ramp, but instead of turning left where all the council members were, they went straight ahead to the cave in front. Inside was a large cavern with a large bed against one wall and a small fire in the center with cut logs around it that Grim presumed were stools. There were banners hung on the stone walls, each red with a white shield in the center, and the shield displayed one large red droplet. It made sense with the name Blood-Shield Clan that it would be their banner. There was a large fur rug on the floor and a weapons rack along one wall with ornate and well taken care of weapons. Even though the lighting wasn't great, Grim could see runes carved in the rack and on all the weapons. Thrain sat on one of the stools by the fire, and Vumira, Lukav, and Grim followed his lead. Vumira's badger, Grim learned, was named Consin, was consistently by her side, and sat at his master's feet.

103

"I am sure you have a lot of questions," Thrain said, looking back and forth between Lukav and Grim. "Allow me to explain. What Lukav told you about our clan is correct, but that is not the whole story. In ancient times, our clan was known throughout the Ashen Plane for our skilled warriors and our enchantments. Long ago, our chief at the time was blessed with ancient arcane knowledge. He was gifted with the information and abilities to use runic enchantments. For generations, the knowledge was ceremoniously passed from chief to chief. With our runecraft and elite warriors, only a handful of soldiers from our clan could turn the tide of a battle. We could topple armies and kingdoms alike." The orc actually said the last statement with calm pride in his voice and a small smirk but quickly returned to his stoic nature as he continued.

"No one knows how, but a hundred years ago, our clan lost the ability to make runic enchantments. Our chief, who was also our runesmith, went out hunting one day, but his party never returned. When we went out searching for him, we found his entire group dead along with a number of slaughtered gnolls. The chief was nowhere to be found, though. That sparked our century-long war with the gnolls that we are still fighting today. Ever since, our clan has faced difficulty and hardships. While strong, we are not invincible, and the gnoll threat has grown more dire. Over the span of this conflict, we have even lost the location of our clan's original sacred burial site."

"Oh," Grim replied. "May I ask? Why are you telling me this?"

The orc chieftain took a big breath and continued. "Because our old shaman gave us a prophecy. It was about a dying white bear with red eyes and her cub being cared for and fed in our village. Once both were strong enough, they were able to protect our clan from certain doom in repayment for the kindness they received. I believe that from the vision you gave us, you, Grim, are the white bear, and Lukav is your cub. I believe you two will help us end this war."

Vumira nodded in agreement. "Not only do you have skin as white as snow, but when you used magic earlier, your eyes glowed red," the hunter said.

The dots seemed to connect for Grim. It made sense to him since Zordell's eyes had glowed red as well. He looked to Lukav, who returned his gaze with a flabbergasted expression.

"So what do you want us to do, exactly?" Grim asked.

"While we believe that you two are the key to our victory, it is obvious you both need training," Vumira said as both she and Thrain stood up.

Grim tensed at first, not knowing what they were going to do next.

Then they took a knee and bowed their heads to Lukav and Grim.

Thrain said, "We wish for our clan to survive. Not just that, we wish to thrive once more, like we did in the past. We promise to increase your strength, if you promise to use it to save our people."

Quest Unlocked! War Games

After hearing your vision, Thrain and Vumira are convinced you and your greater vassal Lukav are the key to ending the Blood-Shield Clan's war with the gnolls of the Cracked-Tooth Tribe. Thrain has offered to have both of you trained in exchange for helping them in the war effort. Will you help end the bloodshed?

105

> Reward:
>
> 50,000 EXP
>
> Training with the Clan
>
> New Skill(s)
>
> Friendly Relationship with Blood-Shield Clan
> Unknown
>
> Do you accept?
>
> Yes or No

Flabbergasted, Lukav asked, "So you believe Grim is the white bear and I am the cub?"

"Yes," Thrain answered with his head still down.

Lukav turned to Grim. "Grim, I know this is a lot, but please. My people need this! We can get training and help them!"

Though in no rush to fight in some war, Grim honestly couldn't think of a reason to say no. Well, except for his obligation to Zordell's quest. He reasoned that he needed training as well as an understanding of the world around him if he was going to find the seals keeping the Arch Necroid confined. He also figured there would be those who would try to oppose him. Obviously, whoever originally imprisoned Grim's patron was very powerful. Theses orcs could be the answer to helping him prepare for a larger battle ahead.

"First, I want you to know something," Grim said to the kneeling orcs. "While I am new to this world, I already have my own quests and goals. And there are probably those that will try to kill me for what I wish to do. I do not want to put your tribe in any more danger than they already are. If you have some way to conceal my location and help me find what I'm looking for, I'll do it."

After several moments of silence, Thrain stood up and walked over to Grim, taking a ring off of his pinky finger. The chief gave it to Grim, saying, "We accept your terms, Grim Snow-Skin. Take this ring."

Quest Accepted!

War Games

Congratulations! Commerce has reached LVL 2!

-2% cost for any purchases

+2% for overall better deals

The orc did not let go of the ring in Grim's palm but instead closed his eyes and willed the information about it to Grim.

You have found Ring of Certain Scry

Durability: 25/25

Weight: 0.1 kg

Rarity: Rare

Quality: Above Average

Properties: Can either consistently transmit or block your location (up to LVL 100 Scry). Even others in your service will not be able to find you unless you will it.

Grim smiled and to everyone's surprise said in orcish, "It's a deal." He put on the ring, then smiled at his friend Lukav.

Thrain then asked, "Now, what is it you are seeking?"

CHAPTER 11
THE FEAST

GRIM EXPLAINED TO THE TWO orcs in the firelit cave that he was looking for seven stone seals with a seven-fingered hand symbol on them. He did not bother to explain fully why, deciding to keep the knowledge of Zordell and that he was a Progenitor to himself. Both Thrain and Vumira pondered but could not recall any information about the seals. They said they would investigate and get back to him if they discovered anything, then led everyone back out to the valley for the evening meal.

As the group began filing out of the cavern, Lukav asked Grim about his apparent linguistic ability. He appeared content when Grim explained how he'd gained it from making the orc a Greater Vassal.

Grim took in the scene as they descended the sloped ramp. It was almost dusk, and multiple torches were already lit throughout the village. He could see that the entire village had gathered in celebration. There was a slight chill to the air. He guessed the great wall surrounding the village kept most of the wind chill out. While grateful for this, he imagined summers could get bad.

Their trek ended in the middle of the village where everyone had gathered around several large fires. Large cooking pots on a couple of the fires gave off the delicious aroma of beef stew. At Grim's request, one of the cooks put a leg of venison over the fire because he hadn't forgotten his living-dead status and didn't know how eating anything other than meat would affect him. He decided to risk having a drink, though, wanting to try the ale the orcs had brewed with local berries. To Grim's relief, no status debuff indicating a negative side-effect appeared.

Once food had been given out, Thrain addressed the people once more. He explained the vision from the previous shaman, described how Grim and Lukav fit into the picture, and told them how the clan would finally win the war. There were some mixed reactions, but after some questions and clarifications, none openly opposed. The feast commenced, definitely a joyous celebration. As Grim and Lukav looked for a place to sit with their wooden bowls of meat in hand, the orc explained that the morale of the clan had been down for a long time and some expected them to permanently die off here, so the celebration was long overdue.

Grim and Lukav sat down in a circle with Thrain, Vumira, the female archer he'd seen earlier, and the heavily scarred orc on the council he'd nicknamed Scar. Grim used the opportunity to practice his Analyze skill on the orcs at the feast, almost choking on his food when Scar's name actually was Scar! *These orcs are pretty on the nose*, he thought. The archer's name was Xumi and, on closer inspection, he noticed she looked similar to Vumira. *On the nose indeed.* She had a lot of similar features as Vumira. She had a button nose and freckles under her cheeks. Her hair was a lighter brown color than Vumira's and even had a slight red tinge to it, and she wore it in braids tied up in a ponytail. Her eyes were a slightly darker green than her skin. Each ear had multiple piercings with a feather earring on each lobe as well as a ring through her nose septum. When Xumi sat in between Thrain and Vumira, Grim put two and two together. *She's their daughter!*

Grim asked Thrain about his clan and the Ashen Plane, thinking that since he was the chief, he might possess the most information. Thrain was very informative about the clan. There were thirty-seven members in total, not including the children. That also did not include Lukav, whose original job had been assistant to the smith. They were a tight-knit community where people worked hard. They lived peaceful lives in a hunter/gatherer society, trying to stay in harmony with nature. The chief also mentioned there were certain orc clans that were extremely warlike in nature, and Grim should not assume all would be as welcoming as them.

At that statement, Grim chuckled internally. He had been bound, interrogated, and forced to fight for his life just to not get killed by the Blood-Shield Clan. If Thrain thought that was welcoming, he might just stay away from intruding into other orcs' territories at all. After shaking himself out of the uncomfortable thought, he looked around at the people feasting. The clan reminded Grim of a mixture between barbarian and Buddhist monk cultures.

When Grim asked about the Ashen Plane in general, the orc was not as helpful but still gave some good information. According to myth, the Ashen Plane was the former battleground of the gods. Their disputes had led to radical landscapes and formations. And they were on a western continent called Frassisi with multiple kingdoms dotting the vast landscape.

Orcs finishing their meals livened up the celebration, dancing around the fires as others beat drums. Grim could see many people watching his group with intrigue. He even noticed Lukav and Xumi exchanging flirting glances with each other. It was really more Xumi chuckling and Lukav looking nervous. *I want to get the scoop on this!* Grim thought, but serious conversation resumed.

"Thrain," Scar said. "We need to address their training."

Vumira nodded. "I agree. We need to know what path to set them on so they have the greatest chance to survive."

Grim didn't like how morbid that sounded, but he'd heard the mountains were dangerous and was a big fan of surviving. "What are our options?" he asked.

The orcs looked to Thrain.

The chief, in his usual calm demeanor, addressed Grim. "There are a few different paths. You may train as an armored warrior under Scar, learn archery under Xumi, follow the path of a hunter with Vumira, learn the basics of magic under Potor, or train as a monk with me."

At the last option, Lukav's eyes widened, making the path he wanted to follow pretty apparent.

"Wait, who's Potor?" Grim asked.

The chief nodded toward an orc in another group. It was the shaman in a headdress from earlier. Grim remembered the orc had been pretty eager for his death.

Grim fixed his gaze on the orc until Potor gave him a harsh look in reply.

"What's his deal?" Grim asked.

"He distrusts outsiders, but do not worry. He will do as his chief commands," Thrain replied.

Grim thought about which path he should follow. He had amazing magical abilities and skills. Those definitely had to be

111

nourished, and he did not want to be a one-trick-pony. If for some reason his magic was countered, he wanted to be able to handle his own fate. Grim was not a fan of being a glass cannon either—he smiled as he recalled the gamer term from Earth that meant being able to deal a lot of damage but not take much.

"Lukav, what would you like to do?" Grim asked.

The orc looked down at the ground as a series of emotions transformed his facial expression. "I had always dreamed of becoming a monk, but my body had prevented me from truly pursuing that path. Now, with this second chance, I would like to become one!"

Thrain nodded to the orc in respect and approval.

"Good! Well, I would like to split my time between Scar and Potor. While I do possess magic, I do not want to rely solely on that. Also, if we could get a map of the terrain and knowledge about the creatures from you, Vumira, that would be advantageous."

Thrain nodded in agreement. "Very well. Scar, go inform Potor of his new responsibility. You will have mornings to train young Snow-Skin. At midday, you will transfer him to Potor to train in magical arts until nightfall."

Scar nodded, got up, and left to go speak to the shaman.

Thrain continued. "Once the evening meal has been had, Vumira, you will inform Grim about the basics of our land."

The group seemed to be content with the status quo. Conversations and music filled the air until an angry shout rang out.

"Never! I will not!"

CHAPTER 12
THE CHALLENGE

ALL MUSIC AND TALKING SUDDENLY stopped. Grim quickly turned his head toward the angry shout, seeing Potor standing face to face with Scar and staring angrily. The shaman turned his glare toward Grim's group with nostrils flaring, looked at Grim and then to Thrain, and started a fast-paced stomp toward the chief. Thrain just calmly watched the shaman approach.

Anger and disgust obvious on his face, Potor started yelling the moment he reached the circle of orcs and stopped right in front of Thrain. "I am the shaman of this village! I am the only one who truly discerns what our ancestors desire. Our predecessors were great conquerors who forced their enemies into submission. They took what they wanted and feared no one! I do not acknowledge your vision. Our ancestors would never want this human outsider piece of filth or this deserter to gain our power. If you want us to become weaker and give our knowledge and training away so he can gain what's rightfully ours, *I refuse!*"

Thrain had waited patiently for Potor to finish his rant, then the calm-looking orc chief swiftly hopped to his feet with a loud stomp that made Grim's heart skip a beat. The two orcs stood a few feet apart, Thrain a good head taller and more muscular than his younger counterpart. Tension seemed to build rapidly as they glared at each other.

With the threatening, even tone of an experienced warrior, Thrain said, "Shall I take it that you are challenging me, boy? If not, you will do as ordered or face the consequences."

Potor stood stock still, breathing heavily for a moment. He turned his head slightly and his posture relaxed as if he was about to concede, but then he saw Grim. He turned back to the chief, defiantly squaring his shoulders and puffing out his chest, and said the ritual words. "I challenge you, Thrain, for leadership of this clan by rite of combat. I believe in my view of truth and freedom more than yours. Once I win, I will lead our tribe out of these lands to conquer all, spilling their blood along the way, starting with this human and his lackey!"

The chief nodded in acceptance of the challenge.

"Father, no!" Xumi said.

Vumira stuck her arm in front of her daughter, stopping her from going to the chief, as she said, "He must. Believe in him."

The whole atmosphere of the village changed. At first everyone was silent and still. Then the drums beat in a faster rhythm as all the orcs backed up, leaving about a fifty-foot circle for the two orcs and the bloodshed about to commence.

Lukav grabbed Grim and emphatically said, "We must move!"

"Wait. What's going on?" Grim asked.

"Potor challenged Thrain to become chief. If we do not move out of the way, we could get hurt or killed from their fight."

Potor turned his back to the chief and walked to the other edge of the circle. He was handed two large hand axes with sharp tips extending out from the tops. Thrain untied the ropes he was wearing. They dropped to the ground with an audible thump. Grim thought each of them had to weigh at least twenty-five pounds. Everyone's gaze was fixed on the two combatants. Both orcs stretched and popped joints until the drums abruptly stopped.

At the sudden silence, Potor charged Thrain. The chief went into a fighting stance as Potor jumped in the air with both his weapons held high above his head. He slammed the axes down, but Thrain dodged just in time. A small cloud of dust rose around the shaman. Potor continued his attack, furiously swinging his weapons at the chief. Thrain showed remarkable precision and grace, easily dodging and blocking the blows from the weapons with just his bare hands. He moved out of the way of one weapon, then blocked the other by hitting the flat part of the metal. Though Potor displayed trained technique, his form was far from the level Thrain was showing.

Grim asked Lukav, "So, Potor is a shaman, right? Why isn't he using magic?"

Lukav gave him a confused look but then remembered Grim was unfamiliar with their customs. He replied, "This is an ancient rite of our clan. We can challenge a chief for the authority to rule. It can be a challenge to the death too. In this challenge, though, you cannot use magic or enchanted weapons. You can only use skills and abilities."

Satisfied with the explanation, Grim turned back to watch the fight.

Thrain's form was defensive, but he was obviously at an advantage. Eventually, he blocked both weapons at once, leaving

Potor wide open. The chief headbutted the shaman in the face, breaking his nose. Potor backed up and grunted in pain as he held a hand to his face. Thrain capitalized on the distraction and kicked his feet out from under him. As soon as Potor fell on his back, the chief went for a finishing blow with a stomp to his face. Potor managed to roll away and jump to a kneeling stance, finally getting a hit in that scored a minor cut on Thrain's leg. Seemingly unfazed, the chief went on the attack. Thrain spent the next few minutes giving Potor a beatdown. The fight seemed completely one-sided until Thrain suddenly paused midattack and fell to one knee, his eyes closed and a hand to his stomach. He appeared to be in a great deal of pain.

Seeing that the chief looked nauseous, was covered in a ridiculous amount of sweat, and was pale, Grim asked Lukav, "What's going on?"

"I don't know," his friend answered. "Something is not right, though. Thrain would never go down this easily!"

Grim nodded to Lukav, then watched Potor smiling maliciously over his kneeling enemy.

"What is the matter, Chief? Can't take a small scratch?" The shaman began recklessly swinging his weapons at the chief with renewed aggression.

Thrain managed to dodge but was slightly hunched over and lacked the grace he'd had before. He couldn't block any more of the hits, just avoided them. The chief looked thoroughly exhausted and was breathing heavily, though he still had the look of determination on his face that he'd had at the beginning of the fight. He then fell to his other knee and had to catch himself with one hand on the ground. The chief put his head down, exhaustion consuming him.

Grim started to panic. "Lukav, if Thrain loses, we have to make a run for it."

Lukav's face instantly distorted to a look of terror. It was as if a kid realized their favorite superhero could actually die in the movie. "Mmmmph," he groaned uncomfortably at the thought but then relented. "Okay. If he loses, we sneak through the crowd and run for the nearest exit."

Grim nodded in approval, then returned his attention to the fight with intense focus.

With a look of smug satisfaction, Potor casually walked to the chief and lifted both axes, preparing to swing down toward Thrain's head.

Before he could swing down, the chief threw a handful of snow and dirt he'd secretly grabbed while taking a knee and threw it at the shaman's face.

Potor took a step back, disoriented by the surprise tactic.

With the moment of respite, Thrain closed his eyes. A glowing circle appeared on his chest, then enveloped him completely. As quickly as it had come, the glowing disappeared and the chief looked noticeably better.

"I thought they weren't allowed to use magic?" Grim said to Lukav.

"It is not magic," Lukav replied. Then with fanboy excitement, he said, "Thrain is not only the leader of the village, he is the leader of the monks. He possesses a specific monk ability to self-regenerate. It is awesome!"

Grim chuckled at the orc's glee, though he did agree that it was awesome. The ability to deal major damage with his bare hands and restore himself made Thrain the definition of badass in Grim's book.

Right as Potor wiped away the dirt from his eyes, the chief

117

stood up and went for the killing blow in the one place that's the insta-kill spot for all guys. He went for the nuts. Thrain forcefully grabbed Potor's testicles with his left hand. This was a fight to the death, but he would exhaust every weak point of the shaman before letting it go that far.

Potor squealed in extreme pain, sending chills down Grim's spine.

Thrain did not let go.

In desperation, the shaman swung both axes at the chief's head, hoping to decapitate him.

Thrain responded by grabbing both of Potor's wrists and stopping them midswing. Now the look of terror Lukav had earlier was plastered over the shaman's face. Thrain headbutted him once again, further shattering his nose. Potor let go of his axes, then was knocked unconscious by a flurry of blows from the old chief.

Once Potor had been defeated, the valley fell quiet as everyone stood in awe of their chief. Then, all of the orcs stuck one arm up in the air with clenched fists in a sign of respect and approval that he was their leader.

Still tired from the fight and huffing to catch his breath, Thrain looked to the crowd and yelled in orcish, "Who is the chief?"

The clan responded with their fists pumping in the air, "You! You! You!"

"Who do you follow?"

"You! You! You!"

If Grim hadn't thought Thrain was a badass before, he definitely did now.

"My chief, should we execute the challenger?" said Scar.

"No," Thrain replied. "The wilds have provided for us. Let us provide for them. Throw him out."

"Yes, my chief," Scar said, kneeling with his fist against his chest.

Two orcs with weapons then came and dragged the barely conscious shaman away.

Thrain turned his back to the exiting shaman and addressed the crowd in his familiar stoic manner. "You may go back to the festival." Then he gave Vumira, Xumi, Lukav, Grim, and Scar a serious look and said, "Come with me."

The group followed Thrain back to his cave. As soon as the chief rounded a corner and was out of sight of the villagers, he collapsed. "Vu…mira," he gasped, sweat pouring from him again. Then he grunted as he grabbed his leg in obvious pain.

"Quick, support his head!" Vumira commanded.

Xumi reached down to hold up her father.

"Vumira, his leg!" Scar said.

The hunter bent down and examined Thrain's leg, seeing that the cut he'd received from his fight with Potor had turned black and veins of necrosis were spreading outward from the wound. "Poison!" she spit in anger.

Now the battle made sense to Grim. *Potor's weapon must have been laced with some kind of toxin!*

Vumira reached inside a pocket while cursing in orcish. She took out a small wooden cup with a pale yellow powder and applied it to his wound. The orc immediately looked relieved, though not yet 100%.

"Scar, water!" Vumira commanded.

The warrior pulled out a canteen from his side and gave it to the chief, who drank it readily.

Thrain coughed, then thanked the group.

"Should I go get the healer?" Grim asked, wanting to contribute.

Lukav put his hand on Grim's shoulder and gave a sympathetic look. "Potor not only served as shaman but was the village healer as well."

Vumira nodded. "Fortunately, I know enough about herbalism to make poisons and antidotes. Though not as strong as Potor's, it should heal him. It will just take time and regular applications."

The chief groaned and coughed as he came out of his semiconscious state. "It appears that I will be unable to train you, Lukav, and Potor is no longer an option for you, Grim. Scar, go inform monk Iro that he will be training Lukav in the ways of the monk. You will still be training Grim till midday. Xumi, you now will be training Grim in the magical arts."

Lukav and Scar looked at Xumi in shock.

"You know magic, Xumi?" Lukav asked.

The young orc looked away embarrassed by the new attention.

Thrain answered for her. "Xumi has awakened Soul magic. Vumira and I have been letting her practice here in private. We did not let anyone know because we did not trust Potor or want him to spend any time with Xumi privately." The chief took a deep breath, fighting his exhaustion, then continued. "Now is not the time for secrets. If we really want these two to help us, we need to help them first." The chief coughed again before dismissing the group.

Scar departed from the group once they went down the hill, presumably to go inform the monk Thrain had previously mentioned. Xumi guided Lukav and Grim to a large tent not far from the celebration. Lukav nervously tried multiple times to say something to her on the way, but she kept dismissing him, seeming angry at the orc for some reason.

Once they reached the large tent where the duo would stay, Xumi quickly said, "Goodnight," and turned away.

Though it was clear she did not want any more conversation, Lukav still attempted. "Xumi, wait! What's wrong? Um, did something happen?"

She paused for a good moment, tension evident from her stance and clinched fists. "While I'm glad to see you back, Lukav, something did happen." She turned and yelled right at Lukav, "You said you would never leave without me, but you did!" Tears building up in her eyes, she then stormed off.

"Xumi!" Lukav said as he reached out for her, but then he stopped, defeated by her words.

Grim put his hand on his friend's shoulder to comfort him. "You okay, man?"

Lukav stared after Xumi, silent and unmoving.

"Why don't we go inside where it's warmer and you can tell me about Xumi?"

Lukav sighed, then followed Grim into the tent. "Xumi and I have a complicated relationship. She believed in me despite my appearance, and we wanted to be mates."

"So she's your girlfriend?" Grim asked.

Lukav looked confused at the question. "Xumi is not a girl. She's a woman!" the orc said with great emphasis. "While we are friends, I would consider us more. Well…maybe we are not now," he said, scratching the back of his head.

"So, what happened? I mean, she looked pretty pissed at you," Grim said.

"Our relationship was a secret. She would be mated to whoever Thrain deemed worthy. When my mother died, I realized

I needed to become stronger in order to win Xumi. Both she and I had promised to leave the village to do our pilgrimages in secret, but I did not want her to risk her life for me." Lukav then chuckled as if trying to comfort himself. "Guess I messed up, huh?"

Grim sat down next to Lukav and put a hand on his shoulder. "It's okay, bud. At least you have a chance to make up for it."

Then the two companions became aware of an assault on the senses brought on by being in a smaller, confined space. They stunk.

Lukav guided Grim to the bathing area. There was a natural hot spring in the valley that the clan made good use of. The nice part was since he was a new ally of the clan, they didn't have to pay! He knew of spas where he was from that charged an arm and a leg for their services. Once Grim had taken off his armor and clothes and sat in a bath, his mind was flooded with joy and relief. He could feel all the stresses of his new circumstances washing away. There was a small wooden wall that cut the hot spring into sections, allowing multiple people to bathe at once without intruding on their privacy. Lukav had splashed into another section to Grim's left. The fence was thin enough that they could chat while relaxing.

Grim also took the moment to teach his friend some of the language and phrases he was more familiar with on Earth. He thought Lukav could definitely learn some new terms to help decrease confusion between them. By the time they were done, Lukav was well-versed in the terms dude, bro, brah, man, brosef, gnarly, nice, that sucks, boyfriend, girlfriend, one-night stand, thumbs up, knuckle-bump, other terms and phrases, and of course, all the cuss words. What good is it to shit-talk your friend if they can't give any witty banter back? Lukav even came up with a new "bro" pun, a "brorc." While it wasn't the best, Grim thought it was an admirable first attempt. Afterward, Grim was pleasantly surprised when a female orc came and set some new clothes for them on a nearby rock.

You have found a Rough-Spun Clothes Set!

Armor: +0

Durability: 5/5

Rarity: Common

Quality: Average

Weight: 0.2kg

Rough-spun was some sort of wool-like material that was okay but not the most comfortable. Once he had put on his clothes, he went around the corner to Lukav to see the orc just finishing putting on his pants. There was an audible rip as the orc's mutated right foot shredded through the bottom half of a pant leg. Lukav was a little frustrated at the struggles of his new body but continued on with his shirt. As he slipped his larger arm into a sleeve, that section of the rough-spun shirt tore completely.

Once he finished, the kindhearted orc laughed nervously and said, "I guess I will have to be more careful with my new muscles."

"Is there anything else we need to do? Would you like to visit your mom's grave?"

Lukav shook his head from side to side and smiled slightly. "Our people once had an ancient burial ground, but unfortunately, it has been lost. We now cremate those who have passed on."

"You said your mother was important to you? What about your father?" Grim asked.

"I never knew him. He was a hunter with Vumira. Best in the clan, my mother told me. He died while on a trip before I was born, so I guess that's why Vumira, Thrain, and Xumi have always taken a liking to me while everyone else remained skeptical."

Grim nodded in understanding. "You're an honest orc who really wants to help his clan. I think your parents would be proud."

Lukav smiled in response, then said, "Thank you. I think we should get some sleep now. If our training is anything like what I have seen them doing while I grew up here, we'll need it."

CHAPTER 13
TRAINING

GRIM WAS IN THE MIDDLE of a nice dreamless sleep in his tent when all of a sudden something loud stirred him. He awoke to see Scar's visage right in front of his face.

"Wake up!" the orc yelled from so close that Grim could smell the ale on his breath from the night before.

"Uh...yes, sir!" Grim said as he quickly hopped out of his fur pile.

"Put on your armor. Now!"

Grim did so, looking over to see Lukav drearily blink his eyes after being startled awake. Then Scar looked in Lukav's direction.

His friend then asked, "What is going on?"

"It is time to begin young Snow-Skin's training," Scar replied.

"This early?" Lukav asked while rubbing his eyes.

"Yes! You're welcome to join if you have a problem with that," Scar said angrily.

"Oh! No, sir! Sorry, sir!" Lukav replied as if he was some sort of army cadet not about to argue with his superior.

Even though Grim knew Scar was not Lukav's designated trainer, he was still disappointed that his supposed "servant" was so quick to bail on him.

When Scar focused back on Grim, Lukav mimed, "Sorry."

Though Grim knew Lukav meant well, he still felt like the orc was leaving him out to dry. Once Scar and Grim left the tent, the orc led him to the edge of the valley. It was still dark out, so Grim assumed it was early morning. He was just thinking he needed to find a way to tell time in his new world when a digital game clock appeared in the upper right corner of his vision, notifying him it was 5:25 a.m. Though still so early, Grim felt great, like he had slept a full ten hours when that wasn't the case. Grim attributed it to his "living-dead" status.

When they had reached the stone wall encircling the village, Grim noticed a large square shield that had been propped against the stone wall. Wooden with a metal frame, the shield also had the carving of a smaller shield with a droplet of blood that Grim had learned was the symbol of the clan.

Scar picked up the shield with relative ease and shoved it at Grim. "Put it on."

Once he let go, Grim almost dropped the surprisingly heavy object right on the orc's feet. Recovering quickly, he strained under the unexpected weight and focused on the item. A prompt appeared.

> You have found a Wood and Iron Square Shield!
> Defense: +25
> Durability: 50/50
> Rarity: Uncommon
> Quality: Average
> Weight: 26kg

Grim had just dismissed the information when Scar commanded, "Run the border of the valley."

"With this?" Grim asked, struggling to hold the newly equipped item higher to make his point.

"Go!" Scar yelled angrily at the human.

Grim took off. Though the shield had slits for one arm to hold it, it definitely weighed down one side of his body, making it difficult to run. He looked behind him and saw Scar following him.

"Never look back!" the orc barked. "Forward always! Always forward!"

He was then struck on his right shoulder by what felt like a wooden club. *Ow! Fuck!* he thought. Grim spent the next few hours circling the village with Scar close on his heels.

One thing made apparent to both of them was that Grim's strength and cardio both needed serious improvement. The weight of his armor and shield put a serious hamper on his speed. A couple of times, Grim tried to carry the shield with both hands, but that was followed promptly by Scar whacking him on an unarmored part of his body with his club. They did take some breaks to let him catch his breath, and Grim was allowed to switch shield arms then. The human noticed that even though running was challenging, he wasn't tired from lack of sleep. By the time they finished, the sun had just risen. Many of the villagers had a look of surprise when they exited their homes and paused to watch the interesting sight during their morning meals.

When they stopped, Grim fell to his knees, took off his shield, and lay on his back breathing heavily. "Do all your warriors train like that?" he asked, exasperated.

127

"Yes," Scar said without nearly as much strain as Grim. "And they do better than that too."

That comment irritated Grim. "Are you serious?"

The orc went and stood over Grim menacingly. "War is not a game, Snow-Skin. My soldiers know that. Thrain has informed me on how you will be helping our people defeat the gnolls somehow. If I do not get you strong enough, it is likely that our people will die out here. So, yes, I am serious, and I suggest you be as well." The orc then walked toward a large pot at the center of the village, calling over his shoulder, "Get some food while you can. We have combat training next."

Though the chastisement made Grim angry, it also struck a chord with him. This was not just a game, and it was not just his life at stake. Scar was right. He did need to take it seriously.

Having recovered some, Grim stood and dusted himself off. He went over to the cooking pot, grabbed a ladle and bowl, and poured himself some meat stew. As he was walking to find a spot to sit and eat, he picked around the stew to just consume the meat from it like a kid avoiding their vegetables. He walked by a number of orcs. Most of the them were in small groups chatting to each other, sitting on wooden stools by tiny fires keeping them warm. They had essentially formed a circle of groups around the serving pot. Though they had accepted Grim, they were still wary of him. The tribe hadn't had an outsider visit in over fifty years. Grim thought about it and remembered Thrain had actually said they hadn't an outsider visit and live. They conversed in Orcish, assuming Grim didn't understand, which made it easy for him to hear what they said since they didn't whisper, and he actually did understand the language thanks to his making Lukav his Greater Vassal. A number of them were concerned about him doing more harm

128

than good. Multiple members remarked about his abnormal appearance from what they had recalled or heard of humans.

"That's the human Thrain let in."

"I heard he is training with Scar."

"I heard he knows magic!"

"What if he betrays us?"

"Why is he all sweaty and gross?"

"Are humans usually that pale?"

Grim thought it best to use this time to gain more knowledge, so used Analyze on a number of them. Most of the villagers were level three or lower, not very high in his book. He assumed that combat and quests led to more experience and levels versus just simply working in a village, since hunters like Vumira and Kremoto who fought dangerous monsters for a living were distinctly higher in level than those who were noncombatants. He noticed a large female orc stirring a cooking pot to the side of the eating orcs, adding some sort of seasoning, and directing the other cooks as if she were in charge. She looked to be in her thirties and half her head was shaved. She had multiple chins and ear and eyebrow piercings. Grim used Analyzed and found out her name was Riga.

"Hello there," Grim said as he walked up to her.

The orc female looked at him and gave a grunt in greeting.

"I am Grim. What's your name?"

"Hmph, I am called Riga." She had a scratchy voice that sounded as if she had been smoking for many years.

"Well, it's nice to meet you, Riga. This stew has some good meat in it."

She just kept stirring the pot, not too interested in the conversation.

"I discovered these seeds out in the forest that helped increase the flavor of some venison. Do you think you could use them?" Grim said as he handed her the remaining hanzos he'd looted off of the gnoll.

The cook's eyes widened at the gift Grim was offering her. She looked at him, then back to the seeds, then back to Grim. "Where in the forest did you get these?" she asked.

"Off of a dead gnoll about a few hours outside the village."

"Hmm. Hanzos are uncommon and hearty seeds that add saltiness to a dish. How did you know?" she asked suspiciously.

"I was told that they are salty, and I have the culinary skill," Grim said. "I'm betting that's how I figured out it could be used for food. I'm also betting that the head cook of this clan, with skills such as yours, could hopefully make good use of them."

She smirked at the comment.

With Riga's ego properly stroked, Grim continued. "Actually, I was wondering, could you show me how you make this stew?"

"So you fancy yourself a cook, aye?" She laughed. "Well, I have a proposition for you, Grim. You get me ten more hanzo seeds, and I'll show you how to cook this venison stew. Better yet, I'll teach you five different recipes if you can bring a hanzo bush here to the village. It's been a while since we had a steady supply of these seeds."

A prompt appeared in Grim's vision.

Quest Unlocked! Riga's Recipes

Riga, the clan's cook, has agreed to teach you one of her recipes in exchange for 10 hanzos. This is a repeatable quest.

Optional: Bring back to Riga an intact hanzo bush for five new recipes.

130

Reward:

Riga's venison stew recipe

50 EXP

Increase in the culinary skill

Friendly Relationship with Riga

Optional Quest Reward:

5 new recipes

Steady supply of hanzos for village

Do you accept?

Yes or No

Grim accepted the quest. This was the third time he had seen a change in relationship as a reward since coming to the village. Back in his game, relationships could be very powerful factors for a player. One could get discounts, protection, and even quests unobtainable otherwise. It also showed that while he had a neutral relationship with the overall clan, it did not represent every individual within it. He was glad to have another avenue for gaining allies inside the village.

"Sounds good to me," Grim said. "What can you tell me about hanzo bushes? Any idea where I should start looking?"

"Hanzo bushes have very prickly leaves and branches. They secrete a numbing serum that will temporarily take away feeling in anything it touches. They also cannot stand sunlight. If any part of the plant is exposed to it for at least five minutes, the plant will start to die. So, I'd start looking in dark places."

"Okay, thank you," Grim responded.

Riga nodded her head and went back to focusing on her stew.

131

Grim looked around, wondering where Lukav was as he hadn't seen him since the orc had left him to his own devices this morning. He was rewarded by seeing Lukav in some obviously uncomfortable pose, as if he were doing yoga, while being supervised by one of the monks. Grim supposed the abnormal distribution of the orc's body mass could make it more difficult for balance. Grim heard the monk say that Lukav needed to keep good form or he would not eat breakfast. His friend pursed his lips and narrowed his brow, appearing frustrated at that ultimatum.

Lukav looked over at Grim, watching him eat his stew with obvious desire for the food.

Grim mimed, "Sorry."

A look of defeat washed over the orc's face at the karma he'd just received.

Not long after Grim's morning meal, Scar suddenly appeared and put his large hand on Grim's shoulder. "Time for combat training," he said.

"Alright!" Grim replied, definitely excited to actually practice some fighting.

"Grab your shield," Scar commanded.

Grim said nothing but just let out a subtle sigh. He set down his bowl on a nearby rock, rose up from the ground, and picked up his shield. The two walked to a pressed-down field of grass that served as the village's training ground. Grim had noticed the area when he and Lukav first entered the village. He had also jogged by it a number of times while being chased by Scar around the village border earlier that morning.

"Leave your shield equipped. Set the rest of your weapons on that rock," Scar said, gesturing to a four-foot-tall stone to Grim's left.

132

Grim did as instructed and then moved back to stand facing Scar, who was holding his large stick that Grim was all-too-familiar with.

"Okay, so…what—"

"Defend yourself!" Scar leaped at him with his wooden club.

Grim spent the next few hours protecting himself, sometimes poorly, from the pounding force of Scar's blows. The orc would call out commands for Grim to defend himself from a certain direction. If he didn't do so correctly, with enough force, proper angle, or adequate speed, his attempt to protect himself would result in his being hit or falling to the ground. Sometimes he was knocked back or fell forward from a bad attempt to block. Occasionally, Scar tripped him as well.

After hours of practice, Grim's endurance was low—only 10% left. He was panting, dirt covered his body, his helmet had fallen off, his long black hair was sticking to his sweaty head, and he could not hold up his shield as well as before. He was bruised from head to toe and a small amount of blood trickled from his mouth.

"Is that all you can do? How can you expect to defend others when you can't even defend yourself?" Scar yelled at his student.

After hours of frustration and Scar's taunts, Grim had had it! "You want to see how much I can do? Well, come on then! I'll show you!"

Scar swung his club at a downward angle with his right hand. With the shield in his left hand, Grim moved his shield to the outer edge of the club and redirected it. That block led to Scar continuing his swing off-balance. Not wasting the op-

133

portunity, Grim swung at the orc's face as he let out a battle cry. The shield hit Scar, knocking the orc back a couple of feet.

Yes! Grim thought. His initial feeling of elation switched to "Oh, shit!" when Scar gave him a look that promised retribution.

Fortunately, that look changed to a smirk. "Good, Grim," Scar said. "You have some fight in you! As you can tell, you cannot always directly block blows from an opponent with greater strength." The orc then stood up. "A superior warrior must always asses their strengths and weaknesses versus their opponent's and use them to their advantage. They will always use their brains over their fists. Your training with me is done for today." Scar started to walk off, calling over his shoulder, "Go and rest. You have more to do with Xumi after the midday meal."

Filled with joy and fatigue, Grim went to the rock where his weapons were and rested against it.

Not long after, Lukav walked up to Grim. He was slightly limping and heavily panting. He stopped when he was standing right by the still sitting Grim. "Hi," he said nervously.

"Hey," Grim replied.

The orc was no longer in the tunic shirt he'd worn the night before or the fur poncho. He was wearing an orc's sleeveless leather vest stained a dark red, and his larger hand was wrapped with strips of white cloth under a fur wrist guard.

"Listen, sorry for not saying anything this morning."

"It's okay, man. I don't blame you. Honestly, I probably would have done the same thing! Sorry for kind of being a dick earlier with the morning meal."

"It is okay, Grim." Then Lukav chuckled. "I may have deserved it. I knew the path of a monk was tough, but this was, as you say, intense! I did get a new skill, though. What about you?"

Grim realized he might have used the word intense a little too much in his conversations with his friend. He then wondered about any distinct developments in any of his own abilities, soon noticing an exclamation mark inside a box indicating there was a notification pending. He focused on it.

> After intense training with Scar, your
> body and mind have grown!
>
> +1 Strength
>
> +2 Endurance
>
> +1 Mind

> Skill gained! Shields LVL 1
>
> This ability allows you to use shields of varying sizes.
>
> +5% Defense
>
> -1% Movement Penalty
>
> Augment Gained! Shield Bash
>
> Turn defense into offense by hitting your opponent with your shield, causing a 3-second stun. (This is an augment of a shield skill.)
>
> Cost: 10 Stamina
>
> Damage: 10-25
>
> Cooldown: 1 minute

Nice! Grim thought. It was definitely enjoyable to see the universe actually give him quantitative rewards for his hard work. Shield bash was a cool augment and pretty standard in Grim's book. In most MMORPGs, shield bash was a very common ability for many warrior classes. To Lukav, he said, "I learned the shields skill as well as an augment!"

The orc gave him a thumbs-up sign with his new giant arm.

Grim hadn't taught Lukav everything about pop culture and common expressions, but thought the orc was making progress. "You remember we can see each other's status pages, right?" Grim asked.

Lukav looked away, cheeks blushing from the embarrassment.

Grim laughed, then said, "Go on…tell me your new skill."

"The thing I learned is Pressure Points. It is a subskill of Unarmed Combat that allows me to hit certain parts of a body to stun an enemy for two seconds. The next thing I'm supposed to learn is another subskill called Deflect Projectiles. I can block enemy ranged weapons like arrows. If I level it up enough, I was told I can even redirect them!" he said with his usual fanboy excitement when it came to anything monk-related. The orc was clearly enjoying the fruits of his training so far. "Uh, you want to go get some food?" A little embarrassed by his own giddiness, Lukav scratched the back of his head while trying to change the subject.

"Nah. I'm good, man." Grim's living-dead status seemed to be kicking in with his 50% decreased need for sustenance. "I think I'm going to catch some Zs until Xumi is ready to train me."

Lukav gazed at Grim with a confused look.

Grim sighed at the realization that his Earth expression didn't make sense to the orc. "I'm going to take a nap until it's time for my next round of training."

Lukav nodded in understanding, waved goodbye to his friend, and then went on to grab some food.

136

Grim slipped his helmet off and lay back against the stone, enjoying the crispness of the air around him as he closed his eyes.

Grim felt something knock against his leg.

"Wake up!" Thud! The force was noticeably sharper the second time. "Wake up!"

Grim blinked his eyes at Xumi standing above him. Grim could see why Lukav liked her. He could admit she was cute for an orc. The orc archer was adorned with furs and leather and had a bow on her back.

"It's time to train," she said with a serious look on her face, then walked toward Thrain's cave.

Grim propped himself up on the rock and re-equipped his weapons, then followed Xumi to Thrain's cave. He saw the chief sleeping in his bed and was about to say something to him when Xumi stuck her arm out and stopped him.

"In addition to the powder he has been getting to stop the poison, my father was also given a sedative for pain. He will be in a deep sleep and not wake unless an extremely loud human would make a foolish mistake," she threatened.

"Okay, then. Where do we start?" Grim asked, avoiding the threat.

Xumi glared at him and gave a frustrated sigh.

He didn't know what exactly was going on or why they were in Thrain's cave if he needed to be resting, but could tell she had a problem with him. He decided to go with the direct approach. "Are you all ri—"

"We will be training in manna manipulation," she interrupted.

Well, that answered that question, he thought. "What's manna manipulation?"

137

Xumi sighed and rolled her eyes at him. "I do not know much about magic, but I have learned how to change the course and consistency of the physical manifestations of my spells. That is manna manipulation. For example..." Xumi said a word of power and did a gesture with her right hand.

A glowing translucent orb appeared.

Grim knew immediately that it was a Soul Orb.

Xumi quickly performed another spell, changing the orb into a small arrowhead before Grim's very eyes, and then launched it directly at Grim.

Grim reflexively put up his new shield to defend himself and closed his eyes, prepared for the impact to come. The arrow went right under the shield and hit him straight in the stomach, knocking him to the floor. "Guuh!" he grunted as he reeled from the impact. He didn't feel much physical pain but felt more tired than he thought he should. He remembered that Soul Orbs drained stamina, so it made sense to have such a big effect if that was an upgraded version. "Thrain was right. I see you clearly have some ability at this," he said jokingly as he stood back up.

Xumi crossed her arms, clearly ticked off by his statement. "Humph. *Some* ability? My father told me that no one in my clan has ever had such innate understanding of Soul Magic since our first chief! The village would be in awe of my magic, but I wish to keep it secret for now. Allow me to show you my *ability*," she said with clear disdain in her voice. Then she quickly conjured not one but two Soul Orbs, one above each hand, performed the spell to change each of the orbs to arrowheads, and threw them in succession at Grim.

Grim blocked the one that came from his left but staggered under the hit to his right shoulder by the other arrowhead.

Xumi conjured another orb but then said different words of power and put a hand on the top and bottom of it. Pressing against it like it was a piece of dough, she transformed the orb into a spear. Then she swiped her upper hand through the air in a karate chop motion, sending the spear toward Grim.

The magic weapon launched with such speed that Grim was unable to block it with his shield and was hit straight in the sternum.

Just like before there was not much physical damage, but Grim felt something new instead of feeling drained. He had a headache. While it was not overwhelming, it was distinct and sudden and made him lose focus.

He closed his eyes and put his hand to his head. "Ow! Okay. Point taken. I'm sorry. It was just a joke," he said grudgingly through the new pain in his head. He looked at his interface to see that his manna had dropped in half instantly from that one attack. "That was awesome though! Can you teach me how to do that!?" he asked, now understanding what was going on. Apparently instead of physical exhaustion that comes with stamina depletion, mental exhaustion was a result of the decrease in manna. This world, unlike in his game, had real-life checks and balances when it came to energy usage. He literally felt the actual damage to his body, unlike when he used up all of his manna in his game and there was no recoil.

Xumi interrupted his musings. "Teach you that?! Pfft!" she scoffed. "I am an initiate in manna manipulation. First, you have to be able to properly handle connecting with your spells."

"Sounds good to me! Wait. What do you mean 'connecting with your spells'?" Grim asked with renewed interest. If he could learn how to manipulate magic like she did, he could come up with a whole slurry of new spells to conquer his foes!

139

Xumi moved closer to be about five feet away from Grim. With obvious frustration in her voice, she asked, "Can you conjure a Soul orb?"

Grim did so for the first time, he realized. He had known the spell but never actually conjured it. He had the translucent orb floating above his hand. The new deficit on his manna did not help his head, and he squinted slightly.

Xumi looked at the orb, showing no indication that she was impressed by his ability. "Do you notice how you are able to keep it floating without having to strain or forcefully think about?"

"Well, now that you say that I do!" Grim replied, surprised by the realization.

"Good. So, you may not realize it, but you are actually connected to the orb. You are keeping it afloat subconsciously through tendrils of manna extending from your hand."

Grim recalled the knowledge about general magic intricacies he'd obtained from Zordell and realized that was true, though he had one question. He checked his manna bar to confirm before asking, "So if I'm keeping it afloat through manna, why isn't my overall manna decreasing as I hold this?"

Xumi shrugged and said, "I do not know, but that doesn't matter. What matters is if you want to focus on manipulation, you need to focus on your connections to the spells."

Grim didn't like the answer but bit his tongue about that for the moment. "Okay. So how do I do that?" he asked.

"Focus your attention on the area in between your hand and the orb. Imagine a thread connecting you to it. Put your concentration on that thread until it appears," she said as she herself conjured a Soul orb. Soon afterward a flowing tendril of magic appeared, connecting her palm to the magic ball. "Once you have successfully manifested it, you will have truly begun to understand manna manipulation." Xumi then dispelled the orb and walked toward the cave's entrance.

140

"So that's it?" Grim asked, confused and frustrated.

"Indeed," she replied. Xumi then left the cave.

Grim spent the next few hours in Thrain's cave, conjuring Soul orbs and trying to focus on the tendril of manna connecting him to the spells. He tried meditating and attempted to actually hold the invisible thread, but nothing worked. When Vumira came in with medicine for Thrain, he left the cave, frustrated at his lack of progress. Reaching the usual village gathering place, he found everyone tending to cooking fires and sharing the evening meal.

Grim took a kabob of meat from Riga, found Lukav sitting alone, and joined him. "So Xumi hates me," he said.

"Yeah," Lukav replied. "I am sorry. She won't talk to me either. What has she said to you?"

"Nothing much," Grim replied. "She has been all about business...not much of a Chatty Cathy, you would say."

"What? What business, and what's a Cathy?" the orc asked.

Grim sighed. "I mean she gave me basic instructions and nothing more, then she left me to practice by myself."

"I am not sure why she dislikes you, but it probably has something to do with me," Lukav said.

"Any ideas on how to get on her good side so she'll train me better?"

Lukav shook his head. "I know she likes sweets, but I do not know any recipes for them. If it makes you feel any better, she hasn't spoken another word to me after yelling at me." The orc then adopted a melancholy look. "It's hard seeing the one you love not acknowledge you. I'm sorry for my part, Grim."

"It's okay, man. I'm sorry too," Grim replied, in that moment deciding that learning a recipe from Riga should be higher on his priority list.

After dinner, the two new trainees went to bed.

The next two days were more of the same. Scar woke Grim before dawn and worked on his overall strength and endurance, then beat on Grim with his club while the trainee tried to block with his shield. Though the growth wasn't as strong as the first day of training, Grim still gained a few skill levels and a couple of stat points. Training with Xumi was less productive. In fact, he gained nothing at all. After midday meals, she came to Grim and asked if he had manifested the connection yet. Grim would tell her no, and she'd walk off, saying to come find her once he did. He tried hard to form the connection, but it did not come about. When Vumira arrived at the cave to tend to the chief each evening, Grim would call it quits. When he asked Vumira why her daughter seemed to dislike him so much, her answer was vague but at least pointed Grim in the right direction.

"Xumi leads with her heart, and right now, her heart is hurt," she said while petting her badger.

So her heart is hurting? he thought. *It probably has something to do with Lukav, but what exactly?* Grim needed to figure out what was going on, so he talked about it with Lukav that night.

Lukav said, "Xumi and I were going to sneak out of the village and do our pilgrimage together. I knew she would be upset about it, but I wanted to keep her safe. I did not want her dying for some cripple like me...like I was."

Grim put a hand on his friend's shoulder and said, "I think that may be what love is, man. Caring so much for someone that you're willing to put your life on the line for them." Grim was no Casanova, but that sounded right in his head. "You still love her, right?"

The innocent orc blushed and looked down at his hands clinching his pants. "Uh...yes," Lukav responded nervously.

"And you would die for her if needed?" Grim asked.

"Yes," Lukav answered with more certainty in his voice.

"Back when she yelled at you, she said you left her after you said you wouldn't. Now, while I believe it's honorable to not risk your loved ones, I believe it is just as important to keep your word. Isn't that what the clan is all about anyway? Truth?" Grim asked.

There was pregnant pause as Lukav chewed on his friend's words. "I think you are right, man," Lukav replied as tears formed in his eyes. "How do I apologize to her for that? How do I show her that this was for her?"

"While I wouldn't consider me a love expert, I have seen *Hitch* a number of times, and it has some good quotes. I think we can figure something out," Grim said, comforting his friend while ignoring the fact that Lukav hadn't seen the Will Smith classic.

The two went about chatting easily as if they'd been long-time friends while helping with after dinner cleanup before going to bed for the night.

CHAPTER 14

SLIME

GRIM COULD SEE NOTHING, NOT even his own body. All of a sudden, four glowing red eyes appeared, followed by a skeletal equine face appearing not two feet from Grim. It was Zordell!

Grim tried to control his breathing but was still breathing fast. Having been stabbed twice the last time he saw Zordell, he had no idea what the unpredictable Arch Necroid would do.

Zordell's eyes flashed for a moment, then the creature ominously said to Grim, "You are Death." The large being conjured a Death Orb in his skeletal hand, and soon after, a tendril of magic appeared, connecting his palm to the orb.

Grim looked at the Arch Necroid, wondering what he meant. Before he could ask any questions, his vision went white.

Grim jerked awake with a gasp. *Was it a vision?* he thought. *What did he mean exactly by saying I am death?* His musings were interrupted by a familiar sight, though this time it was Vumira instead of Scar.

The orc hunter approached Lukav and woke him up, then explained to them both, "You will not be training with your instructors this morning. Instead, you will be accompanying Xumi and me on a mission. We are almost out of a special grass that is needed to treat the poison in Thrain's body. We will be going out to a small tunnel where we can find some more. It will take a good part of the day to get there and back. Lukav, get ready. Someone will deliver some supplies here. Grim, come with me."

A prompt appeared before Grim as the hunter left the tent.

> Quest Unlocked! That's some good grass!
>
> Vumira, the clan's head hunter, has assigned you and Lukav to join her and Xumi on a mission. You will be collecting a rare grass that should help Thrain heal from his poison. This quest cannot be refused.
>
> Reward:
>
> Herbalism Skill
>
> 100 EXP
>
> Increase Relationship with Vumira
>
> Penalty for failure:
>
> Death of Thrain
>
> Distrust Relationship with Blood-Shield Clan

Well, no pressure there, Grim thought as he followed the hunter.

She took him to another tent and gestured for him to come in. When Grim entered, he saw a bald, muscular male orc in a tunic shirt and pants standing by a wooden chair, holding scissors and a straight razor in his hands. Tattoos covered his body, and his thick brown, imperial-style mustache was very distinct.

The orc looked remarkably well groomed, with not a wrinkle in his clothing or a hair out of place.

As she entered the tent behind Grim, Vumira said, "You cannot go back into the wilds looking like you do. Your hair is wild and unkempt. You cannot go out and hunt in this inefficient manner. If your hair gets in front of your eyes, that could provide a moment of distraction. Distractions lead to death in this land," she said sternly.

Grim agreed with her, even though he felt embarrassed at being chastised in front of a stranger. It was like being scolded by his mother to get a haircut when he was a kid.

"This is Grogmar. He is the village barber," she said, gesturing to the mustached orc.

"Greetings," he said, nodding his head. His much more formal and proper tone was not what Grim had become used to from the tribe so far.

"Uh, hello," Grim replied.

"Shall we begin?" Grogmar asked, gesturing for Grim to sit down.

"Okay, then," Grim conceded.

The grooming visit was remarkably well done and very reminiscent of old-school barbers back on Earth. The orc showed extreme precision and professionalism. It honestly was the best haircut Grim had had in either world! He had most of the hair on the sides of his head removed, leaving only the hair on top of his head thick and long. It was braided and put in a tight ponytail. His beard was also trimmed so that it was full but nicely manicured fairly close to Grim's face.

"This is great!" Grim exclaimed. "Thank you!" He definitely felt a new surge of confidence when he saw his new look. He felt like a badass hipster.

146

"My pleasure, sir," Grogmar replied.

A notification appeared.

Status Effect Gained: Hunter's Haircut

"Did you get a haircut? No, I got them all cut."

+10% Movement Speed when moving
in wooded areas for 24 hours.

+5% Stealth when moving in wooded areas for 24 hours.

"Is this more efficient?" Grim asked Vumira after dismissing the notification.

The head hunter examined him with trained focus and gave an approving nod, then said in her usual sharp and choppy manner, "Go back and equip yourself with your items and armor. I also had some extra furs placed in your tent that you and Lukav should put on. It will be cold."

Grim thanked them both and left the barber's shop, heading back to the tent. He found Lukav already wearing one of the capes with thick fur and spinning around to admire his new attire while doing some shadow boxing.

When he noticed Grim watching him, the introverted orc stopped and chuckled, nervously scratching the back of his head. "Um, we have these new fur capes," Lukav said.

"Looks cool, man," Grim said.

"Oh, no! They are actually quite warm!" he said enthusiastically.

Grim shook his head and sighed. "I mean it's stylish and looks impressive." He realized he needed to do more work in training his friend with idioms.

"Thanks!" Lukav said with genuine appreciation.

Grim then turned to his bedroll and found the fur cape Vumira had sent to the tent for him.

> You have found a Wolf Fur Cape!
> Armor: +5
> Durability: 15/15
> Rarity: Uncommon
> Quality: Above Average
> Weight: 1.1kg

Vumira was right. This thing is warm, Grim thought, pleased with his new item. He equipped himself with his heavy iron armor, which consisted of a helmet with horns on it, chest piece, bracers, greaves, and boots. It provided great protection, but definitely met the "heavy" qualification. He then sheathed his iron greatsword, three iron-tipped javelins, his wickedly sharp Daria's dagger, and the square shield he had been training with. He looked at his shield. While it was thick, it had lost ten points of durability during his training with Scar. He would have to see if anyone in the village could repair it. The shield was still functional, though, which he was happy about. Grim completed his attire by putting on his new cape.

The two, fully equipped, left their tent and found Vumira, Xumi, and Consin waiting by another tent about twenty feet away from them. The two huntresses were talking to each other quietly while the badger chewed on a femur bone. After they approached, Vumira gave Grim and Lukav each ten herbs. Five would restore health while the other five would restore stamina, each by fourteen points over ten seconds. The group left the valley as the sky began to brighten.

The beginning of the trip was rather quiet. Grim could tell he, with his heavy armor style and lack of training, was definitely not as quick or as stealthy as his traveling companions. Vumira's and Xumi's footsteps gave off very little noise compared to his lead feet trudging through the snow. Even Lukav and the badger were quieter than him, though admittedly, Lukav had light armor on just like the two hunters. Grim's tracking skill came in handy, though, showing multiple tracks of different animals with a faint purple highlight that illuminated the snow. Vumira, noticing Grim's struggle, guided him in stealth through the forest.

Apparently, how you place your foot—whether stepping down ankle to toes or just flat on the ground—made a difference. She also showed Lukav and Grim the tracks of different creatures as well as explaining the migrating patterns of them. The most common herbivores hunted by the clan were deer and a dog-sized rodent that hops like a frog, called a *woohig*. The female orc was a wealth of information.

Grim noticed Vumira had her higher quality spear with her and asked, "So, Thrain said that your clan lost the ability to create enchantments. If that's the case, how do you have that spear?"

Vumira looked up at the tip of the weapon in her hands, then back to Grim. "That is true, but we still have this one. It is passed down from one head hunter to the next."

"Do you mind if I look at it?" he asked, knowing he was pushing his luck.

The hunter looked back at her weapon, then to Grim. "You have proven true so far. I trust you will not stop now," she said as she handed the spear over to him.

As Grim accepted the weapon, he expected the orc to let go. She did not, however, instead closing her eyes. He remembered this was what Thrain had done when giving him the Ring of Certain Scry.

149

Information appeared in his field of vision, and Vumira let go of the spear.

> You have found the Orichalcum Spear
> of Beast Slaying (Exquisite)!
> Damage: +22-25
> Durability: 101/110
> Rarity: Fabled
> Quality: Masterwork
> Weight: 2.3 kg
> Properties: +2 Damage
> +6 Damage to Beasts
> Requirements: 20 Strength, Hunter Vocation

"Nice!" he proclaimed in appreciation of the weapon. It was the first time he had seen requirements on an item, making him think that was because he hadn't met any requirements yet. He assumed the orichalcum was the light green metal that made up the spear head. "I can see how you're the head hunter."

The stern hunter nodded, then took her weapon back.

The group continued their path until they were about twenty yards from the tunnel. Vumira put her hand up in what Grim knew was the universal gesture for halt. The others immediately stopped and crouched to the ground. Consin went up to her master, hair standing up on her back in obvious tension at the area where her master was looking.

"What do you see?" Xumi asked in a hushed tone.

"Something is not right. The land around the tunnel is dead, and there are no animal noises," Vumira said without taking her eyes off the area.

Grim peeked up to see that her assessment was indeed correct. The mountainous forest around them consisted of many coniferous trees, and the ground was covered with a light amount of snow. The area around the entrance to the tunnel was just a circle of dirt. The ground was noticeably dry and had holes the size of cantaloupes interspersed randomly. There were no trees in its immediate vicinity, but there appeared to be two dead husks of trunks nearby.

Vumira readied her spear with both hands and with the sure tone of a leader said, "Keep your guard up." The hunter then proceeded cautiously toward the opening with Consin close behind.

The other three looked at each other and then followed their leader. Not long after Vumira crossed into the dry circle of land, the ground started to shake. A light, almost highlighter-green ooze started to emerge out of one of the holes in the ground. The group backed up quickly and poised their weapons, not sure of what was to come. The ooze came out slowly at first, but then surfaced quicker and quicker, building up on itself. And it was not just the gelatinous substance emerging. Grim could see bones! Soon enough, a snake-like figure formed out of the green plasma. The upper third of it had vertebral bones that were visible through its translucent body, giving the semblance of a neck. The line of neck bones ended in a grotesque, mutated-appearing skull with four eye sockets in a horizontal line. It possessed abnormally large upper and lower canine teeth that extended outside of the slime body. On top of the neck was a large singular slime tentacle that towered above the group at twelve feet high. It roared at them, reminding Grim of what a dinosaur should sound like.

151

"Oh, crap!" Grim exclaimed as he drew out his greatsword and used Analyze on the creature.

Slime Abomination (LVL 12)

Race: Monster

Type: Slime

Health: 301

Manna: 10

Stamina: 150

Slimes are the result of magical forces coming into contact. They do not have much in mental capacity, usually just waiting for or wandering aimlessly for prey. This abomination has somehow managed to evolve past the base instincts of its predecessors.

Just as Grim gathered that information, the slime's tentacle launched toward him. Quickly, as if on its own accord, his shield raised up to defend against the abomination. Grim looked at his own shield in surprise at his rapid response. Vumira and Consin hopped backward, then the whole group spread out to encircle the creature. Xumi fired two arrows in quick succession. The momentum of both shots stopped dead in their tracks, not bothering the abomination at all.

At the same time, Lukav threw a punch that was ineffective and resulted in his arm getting stuck in the creature. Freaking out at his predicament, the orc flailed the claws of his enchanted right arm, trying to free his arm.

The slime roared in pain at the claw attack, letting Lukav go. It turned its head and tentacle toward the creature that had hurt it.

Grim used the new distraction to quickly share some information he knew about slime monsters from his D&D experiences. He didn't know if it was accurate in this world, but it was worth a shot. "It's resistant to most physical attacks and poison! It also can absorb things and probably has some sort of acid attack." Then he tried to swing his greatsword at the slime, but it was notably unwieldly in his grip, and the attack was slow. When the sword made contact with the slime's body, it just stopped as if suddenly stuck in really hard molasses. The attack did no damage to the abomination, which was focused on reaching Lukav.

The large slime swung its tentacle at Lukav. The orc's training with the monks and his new body had improved his dexterity enough that he was able to dodge three such attacks. Unfortunately, the abomination used the momentum from its third swing to continue the attack past Lukav. It swung the tentacle around the entire circumference of its body in an area-of-effect (AOE) attack. The creature hit Xumi in her chest, knocking her into a tree.

Grim was able to block the creature from advancing farther, though it still caused him to stumble back and lose his grip on his weapon that was still stuck in the abomination's body. Both Vumira and Consin managed to retreat out of range of the attack.

"Xumi!" Lukav exclaimed as he saw his beloved get knocked into a semiunconscious state.

The slime capitalized on his distraction and lashed its head toward Lukav like a snake, managing to clamp its teeth down on his upper left arm.

Lukav screamed in pain while writhing and flexing against the bite to prevent the creature from tearing through him.

"Vumira!" Grim said as he unsheathed Daria's Dagger. "Let's use our enchanted weapons! The magic inside them should be able to damage the creature."

The hunter nodded and gave a quick command to her badger to stay back since it couldn't harm the monster. The two attacked the creature a few times, and Grim noticed a lot less resistance from its body against his blade. The slime threw Lukav as it unclenched its jaws, then let out a roar in defiance. It let loose another AOE attack with its tentacle orbiting around its body, managing to trip both Grim and Vumira so they fell on their backs.

"Ugghhh!" Grim groaned as he started to get back up. As his vision refocused, he saw the abomination charge toward the dazed Xumi, jaws wide open for a killing blow.

"Nooo!" Lukav said as he charged from the slime's right side. He leaped in the air, dipping his right shoulder, and hit the monster in the temple.

To Grim's surprise, the physical attack worked! The slime was knocked over to its side and let out a deep groaning sound. Lukav also fell to the ground after passing down his momentum to the creature.

Xumi, no longer dazed, gasped and rushed over to help Lukav stand up. Once she had accomplished that, the knocked-over abomination started getting back up. Xumi stuck her arm out, putting Lukav behind her in an obvious attempt to protect him. She then started to conjure a Soul Orb in each palm. Grim saw what she was doing and decided to copy her magical assault. He threw down his damaged shield, sheathed his dagger, and started conjuring Death Orbs. Both Xumi and Grim started to pepper the monster with long-distance magical attacks while Lukav and Vumira watched with hope in their

154

eyes. Xumi's Soul Orbs were draining the slime of stamina while Grim's Death Orbs were taking away its health. Their plan was working wonderfully because the slime did not seem to have any way to attack foes from afar, until the abomination did something unexpected.

The slime stuck out its lower body and threw its head up in the air. A large dark green bump traveled up its body. Before the bump reached its mouth, the monster quickly lowered its head, opened its mouth, and released a surge of frothy green acid at the attackers. Xumi and Lukav managed to hide behind a nearby tree. The slime then turned its large stream of acid toward Vumira.

Grim stopped conjuring, grabbed his square shield, and started running toward her, yelling, "Shit, shit, shit, shit, shiiitt!"

She, paying attention to the fight, ran toward Grim as well, knowing that his shield would provide cover.

Even though the slime was slower, Grim realized he wasn't going to make it in time. To his surprise, Consin jumped out of the tunnel where she had been hiding to protect her master. The animal appeared suddenly behind Vumira and used her momentum to push the hunter forward enough to get behind Grim's shield. Vumira fell to the ground behind Grim, not sure of how she'd made it right before the large stream of acid engulfed her pet. There was a loud shrill of pain right before the acid attack made it to Grim's shield. The force of the blast reminding him of the strong hoses firemen used, Grim pressed his feet firmly on the ground. Though he was successfully blocking the attack, he was still being pushed back. Small droplets of acid were reflecting off his shield and spraying around them. He could hear a sizzling sound from the acid starting to

155

dissolve the shield. Fortunately, after a few more seconds, the attack stopped.

Vumira managed to get up and poised to strike back, then looked over to her side and was immediately shaken. "Consin! Nooooo!" the hunter wailed as she ran over to what was left of her pet. The hunter knelt down by the animal and let out a barely audible sob.

Grim spared a glance and saw that the badger's body was partially dissolved.

"Crap!" he said in sorrow-filled frustration. *I could have prevented this if I had only cast Death Ward earlier!* Grateful it had been a quick death, he turned back toward the abomination as it charged toward Vumira.

She was distracted by her anguish, so Grim beat his shield and yelled to get the attention of the slime. "Hey, Ivan's Ooze Reject! Come get some!"

The abomination was clearly not a fan of the classic *Mighty Morphin Power Rangers,* because that was enough to draw its attention away from the exposed hunter. Within seconds, the monster was on Grim, launching its mouth at him in an attempt to rip the Progenitor asunder. The large jaws of the creature clamped down on both sides of the shield. Grim heard the screech of metal bending, then the splintering sound of shattering wood. He could feel the wood giving way as splinters launched against his face.

Lukav and Xumi had come from around the tree once they heard the acid attack stop. Lukav yelled, "Grim! Get out of the way! Its tentacle is coming!"

Grim felt a surge of adrenaline. He knew an attack was coming but didn't know from where. Also, he felt if he tried to move away and escape the tentacle's attack, the monster's teeth would just finish the job.

What to do!? he thought urgently. Out of options, he attempted the only thing he could think of and activated Shield Bash. The augment actually worked, pushing the slime back, dealing some damage, and stunning it temporarily. After seeing Lukav hit the slime in the head with nothing but his shoulder earlier, he was perplexed as to why all of a sudden a regular physical attack worked. He assumed the partially exposed skeletal head was susceptible now and noticed his sword still stuck in the slime. "Yes!" he said.

An angered Vumira jumped high in the air behind Grim, spear in hand, and slashed down at the monster. Immediately afterward, she activated an augment called Skewering Thrusts. The hunter stabbed her enchanted spear into the monster over and over again in quick succession, keeping constant focus and composure. It could not retaliate because of the speed with which she was plunging her weapon in and out of it.

Grim thought it looked like someone spamming a move in a video game and smirked at the irony. By the time the hunter was done, she had stabbed the monster at least twenty times. *That must require a remarkable amount of stamina!* he thought.

Lukav then flanked the abomination and did a semi-awkward kick and claw swipe at it with his magic appendages. Xumi threw two more Soul Orbs at the creature.

Grim noticed the monster was distinctly slower and no longer moving outside its immediate area. He used Analyze and saw that it only had fifty health and twenty stamina. He pulled out his dagger and said, "It's almost down! The head is the weak point!"

The group pressed the attack and quickly overcame the slime abomination. Grim got the final blow in by stabbing it in the stomach with his dagger. He felt the familiar pulse from the weapon that he had experienced when he'd killed the lion. The slime shook, then broke down into a large puddle of ooze on the ground. Grim looked at the dagger once again, but no information appeared in his vision to indicate what had happened. He looked at his team. Even though they'd experienced a loss, he was proud of their accomplishment. Then, notifications appeared in his vision.

You have killed Slime Abomination LVL 12 +278 EXP

Level Up!

You have acquired enough EXP to reach LVL 3!

5 Stat Points are available to distribute
for your race: Human

Do you wish to distribute them now?

Yes or No

Congratulations!

Your use of heavy armor in combat has increased your Heavy Armor skill to LVL 4!

+4% Damage Protection

-4% Movement Penalty

Congratulations!

Your use of a shield to successfully defend in combat has increased your Shields skill to LVL 2!

+6% Defense

-2% Movement Penalty

Congratulations!

In killing the Slime Abomination with your dagger, Short Blades reached LVL 2!

+2% Damage

+2% Attack Speed

Grim selected No to adding his stat points, then dismissed his notifications. He would allot points after he got back to the village.

CHAPTER 15
HERBALISM

AFTER THE CREATURE DIED, VUMIRA went to Consin's body. The tough exterior of the hunter broke down and tears rolled down her face as she sobbed.

Xumi went to comfort her mother, and Grim went to check on Lukav.

"You okay, man?" Grim asked.

"I'm alright," Lukav said, clutching his left arm.

"Let me take a look," Grim persisted.

The orc agreed and slowly moved his hand off his upper arm to reveal four puncture marks from the slime's canine teeth. Fortunately, though they were distinct, they were not terribly deep wounds and were not bleeding much. Grim grabbed some icicles dangling off a tree branch and placed them on each of the wounds to stop the bleeding. He then cut a few strips off the edge of his cape and wrapped them around Lukav's arm as makeshift bandages.

The orc smiled and said, "Thank you. I do feel better now. Plus, I gained a level!"

"That's great, man!" Grim replied. "What are you going to invest your stat points in?"

"About that," Lukav answered. "You are my master, and I have dedicated myself to serving you. I will invest in whatever you want me to. Unlike humans, we orcs gain four statistic points per level with an extra plus one automatically assigned to Strength and Vitality. While I can do magic now, every monk must learn a skill called Channeling."

"What does that do?" Grim asked, as if waiting for the other shoe to drop.

"It allows one to transfer their health, manna, or stamina points to another. So, if one is low on health, they can transfer their manna into their health bar to regenerate themselves. You saw Thrain do it when he fought Potor," Lukav answered.

"That's awesome!" Grim exclaimed. "Do you have it?"

"Not yet," Lukav said nervously. "It requires you to cut one of those three stats in half permanently."

Grim's eyes widened, and he nodded in understanding.

"So, I have waited to learn the skill until I talked with you about it. Most monks reduce their manna, as they mainly learn physically related skills."

"And you want to do the same to invest in your statistics accordingly?" Grim asked.

Lukav bowed his head slightly and respectfully said, "Yes."

"Honestly, bro, I don't have much idea of how to become a bad-ass monk like Thrain. If you think you know how to optimize your stats and capabilities, go on ahead. I trust you. If something does come up where I need you to invest elsewhere, I'll let you know," Grim said in reply.

Their moment of bro-bonding was quickly cut off when Xumi returned.

"Lukav, may we talk in private?" she asked in a much kinder tone than Grim had ever heard from her.

161

Not wanting to be a third wheel, Grim made like he was going to talk to Vumira and then hid behind a tree to listen in on his friend's conversation. He definitely hoped the young orc wasn't going to get slapped for saying something dumb to the female!

"What's going on?" Lukav asked his beloved.

Xumi looked down, discomfort evident in her expression. She was experiencing a turmoil of emotion and having difficulty processing. "Um, when you left, I was upset. We had promised to do our pilgrimages together, and you went back on your word."

"Xumi, I—"

She held her palm out, signaling that she wanted to continue without his interruption. "I've loved you for who you are, Lukav. You did not need to change to become worthy of me." Tears started forming in her eyes. "I thought you were dead, alone in the wilderness without me. Then you came back! While I was originally elated to see you, I soon became upset. You had changed dramatically, and it seemed you had replaced me," she said. "I thought the mage had perverted who you are, that you no longer cared for me, but it appears I was wrong."

Lukav's eyes swelled with tears too.

"You put your life on the line to protect me of your own accord. Thank you," she expressed with loving gratitude.

"Xumi, I made a mistake in leaving without you. I am so sorry. I love you, and if you will have me, I will never betray your trust again. Life is not the number of breaths you take but the moments that take your breath away."

At that, the archer walked toward Lukav, grabbed him by the shirt, smiled, and said, "That actually doesn't make any sense, but you better keep my trust, silly." Then she kissed him.

162

Grim fist-pumped the air in celebration. *Wingman success: 100%!* He started to softly sing *All I Do Is Win* as he walked away, then saw Vumira sitting with her badger's dead body, tears streaking her face. He focused back on the situation at hand and approached her.

"I'm sorry about Consin, Vumira," Grim said.

The hunter's visage was pained but still had a fierce strength to it.

"He died a warrior's death, worthy of a true hunter," she said, not taking her eyes off her pet. "Come, we need to collect wood."

"What for?" Grim asked.

The head hunter turned and gave Grim an angry look. Through gritted teeth, she said, "To cremate her remains."

Grim facepalmed himself, then apologized for sounding ignorant. He had learned early on that apologizing to women for your mistakes quickly was much better than letting their anger toward you boil. It had saved him from a lot of trouble more times than he could count.

The group spent the next hour gathering wood, patching up wounds, and looting what was left of the slime monster. As per clan tradition, the lead hunter, which in this case was Vumira, had the choice of the loot. She collected five vials of the remains as well as an iron dagger, telling Grim the slime could possibly be used for increasing weapon damage. Xumi collected her arrows, Lukav found a steel wrist guard, and Grim collected thirty-five gold coins and the skull. He didn't know what he was going to use it for but even if it was just a trophy, he thought it would be cool.

Once the group had collected enough wood, they cremated the remains of Consin. It was a simple ceremony with Vumira singing an orcish burial song that was strong and proud but still had distinct melancholic tones to it. When that was finished, Vumira gave Grim a small satchel and went down the tunnel while Xumi and Lukav stood guard at the entrance, to which neither of them objected.

The tunnel was not very large at about ten feet tall and wide. Planks of wood were interspersed as support beams and columns. Grim wondered why they hadn't brought a torch, but as they descended down the tunnel, it started to glow. A phosphorescent fungus hanging above them and on the sides was guiding them on a certain path as the tunnel branched off. Vumira informed Grim that the tunnel was part of an ancient herb garden the clan now used to grow low-light plants. Enemies would try to sneak in using their torches, not realizing they were preventing the glow from appearing for them. They would go down the wrong paths, getting lost and dying and becoming fertilizer for some of the more dangerous plants in the underground garden.

"Phew!" Grim replied in relief. "Glad I have you here."

After about half an hour, she led him to a small outlet that led to a dead-end. Once they were close to the end, Vumira stopped them. "Look down," she said.

Grim did and saw rows of carefully placed plants, herbs, and fungi on the ground. He looked on the walls and saw shelves carved into the stone. "How is this possible?" he asked. "I know some plants need only a little light, but this is insane! They don't get any at all. Also, how do they get any water?"

"This tunnel was made by a Mighty Burrower Salamander. They live underground, coming up once a year to mate. The creatures secrete a mucous that permanently moisturizes the ground. It makes it fertile and great for growing. The plants here do not need any sunlight."

"Cool!" Grim remarked. "Wait, is that large salamander still in here?" he asked looking around in concern.

"No," Vumira replied. "The one that made this left many years ago, before our clan originally descended the mountains." The hunter then bent down and gestured for Grim to do the same. There was a small strange grassy plant in front of them with three spiraling branches, each with one leaf on them. "This is a Prefortiba. It is a rare grass and very potent antidote for many poisons. You have to be careful when extracting it. You do not want the blades or the stems, but the spiraling branch instead." She began collecting as she explained to Grim what she was doing. "One first breaks the blade off the stem, then the stem off the branch. You must also leave one intact branch at all times or else the plant will die." She then tilted her head and gestured for Grim to try.

After collecting a branch like she'd shown him, notifications appeared.

Skill gained! Herbalism LVL 1

This knowledge allows you to find and know at least one use of most plants and herbs.

+1% Herb Effectiveness

+1% Chance of finding useful herbs

You have found Prefortiba Branch!

This can be used in a tea to cure a wide variety of toxicities.

Weight: 0.1kg

Rarity: Epic

165

"Thank you," Grim said to Vumira as he handed her the stem. "I now know the Herbalism skill."

"It's a useful skill. I advise you to increase the skill's level as it could save your life one day," she replied.

"Um, I don't know if there are any here, but do you have any hanzo bushes? I heard they grow in darkness. Riga asked if I could get her one," Grim said.

Vumira smirked. "She has been trying to get one of those for years. Unfortunately, we only have one here, and Thrain has deemed it too risky to move any of these plants outside of the tunnels. They have been at odds about it ever since. I cannot give you a whole plant, but I can allow you to pick some hanzos off the bush."

"Sure! Thank you!" Grim said. "But why don't you just plant one of the hanzos in a dark area?"

"A good question," Vumira replied. "Hanzos are considered the dead seeds of the bush. On rare occasions, they produce a large, viable seed for planting, but no one knows when that is." The stern hunter then showed Grim the bush.

It reminded him of a small bonsai tree. There were four distinct branches with bushes at each end. The hanzos hung off each of the smaller bushes. By the time Grim was done, he had eleven of the tasty seeds, enough to learn a new recipe from Riga. They continued picking valuable herbs and plants for the next twenty minutes, Grim leveling his new skill two more times in the process. The two then headed back to the tunnel entrance with full satchels.

By the time they made it back to fresh air, it was midafternoon. Grim chuckled when he saw Lukav and Xumi sitting in close proximity to each other and backing away immediately when they spotted Vumira, like a couple of dating high-schoolers embarrassed when a parent spots them. As they sat down to eat travel rations, Vumira made sure to sit in between her daughter and Lukav. Grim took a moment to examine his damaged shield, finding its durability was now only 10/50, while the defense it provided had markedly been reduced to just +5. While kind of frustrating, he was not shocked to see its reduced stats.

After their meal, the group made their way back to the village after Grim cast Death Ward on everyone. They went at a faster, much less cautious, pace. Vumira made it clear they did not want to be out at night if they did not have to. All four of them made it back to the entrance right around sunset. When they made it into the hidden valley, Vumira halted the group. She looked at each of them firmly, then said, "You did good today. All of you." She put her hand on her daughter's shoulder, and they touched foreheads. She also gave Grim and Lukav an approving nod, then whispered something in Lukav's ear to which he responded with bulging eyes and frantic nodding. After that, the head hunter went off to Thrain's cave.

"Dude, what'd she say to you?" Grim asked.

Lukav looked to Grim, then Xumi, back to Grim, then to the ground, all with a nervous expression on his face. Not making eye contact with either one of them, he said, "She said she would emasculate me if I ever hurt Xumi and asked if I understood what she said."

Both Grim and Xumi chuckled, then walked with him toward the area where the community evening meal was being served. On their way, the trio each received a prompt that they had completed their quest.

Quest Complete! That's some good grass!

You have aided Vumira in obtaining the rare poison antidote needed to treat Thrain.

Reward:

Herbalism Skill

> 100 EXP
>
> Increase Relationship with Vumira
> (Current Relationship: Friendly)

Nice! Grim thought. His new experience points reminded him of another quest. He took off ahead of Lukav and Xumi, saying, "I'll see you later." Approaching the main cooking fire, Grim called out to the portly cook, "Riga!"

She looked up and gave a small smile. "Ah, well, if it isn't my favorite human cook. Did you find me a hanzo bush?"

Grim shook his head and held out ten seeds. "I'm sorry I couldn't get a bush for you, but I did find some hanzos!"

Upon seeing the seeds, Riga's eyes widened. Then, quicker than Grim thought possible, she took them out of his hand.

The cook's quick motions startled Grim, and he took out his dagger in a defensive response.

Riga didn't even notice as she looked down, counting the seeds.

Embarrassed by his overreaction and concerned by his rapid ease at drawing a dagger against a friend, Grim quickly sheathed the weapon before Riga looked back at him.

She said, "Good, good. I'll show you how to make my stew."

Grim spent the next half-hour learning Riga's recipe. It was, fortunately, not too complicated. He only needed water, a pot, a fire, raw venison, a couple of spices, some random cave moss, and the Ashen Plane's equivalent of a black bean.

> Quest Complete! Riga's Recipes
>
> You have brought ten hanzos to Riga, so she will teach you a recipe. As this is a repeatable quest, you may bring

her more for future rewards.

Reward:

Riga's Venison Stew Recipe

+50 EXP

Increase in the Culinary skill

Friendly Relationship with Riga

(Current Relationship: Friendly)

Recipe Discovered!

Riga's Sweet Venison Stew

You have discovered how to cook venison in boiling water with spices and mountain beans.

Ingredients: Frassisi Mountain Beans (varying amounts), Raw Venison (varying amounts), Salt (varying amounts), Sweetened Cave Moss (varying amounts)

+4% to taste

+2% to cold resistance

+1% to morale

Congratulations! Culinary reached LVL 2!

+2% positive benefits to your dishes

+2% to taste

Satisfied with his progress, Grim sat down to eat his stew in the company of his new friends. It was a nice evening with plenty of laughter shared between the three until they were interrupted.

A large, bald shirtless orc wearing tan leather pants stomped toward them. "Why are you still here, weakling!?" he said to Lukav.

Everyone in the area stopped talking. Only the crackling

of fire could be heard as everyone's attention went to the large brute.

"You should do us a favor and go die along with this puny human you dishonor us with!" the bald orc said angrily.

Lukav took a moment to compose himself and not let his nervous nature take over. After he let out a calming breath, he said, "Borril, Thrain has approved both me and Grim. He wants us both to be here to help defeat the gnolls."

Borril laughed. "Defeat the gnolls? You, who could barely walk a month ago, and this pathetic, sickly looking human? Not long ago you would have to piss yourself if you did not have your cane! You may have fooled the chief, but you did not fool Potor, and you do not fool me."

Unwilling to let this thug bully them, Grim quickly equipped his shield and stood up to face the seven-foot-tall brute. "Hey, Mr. Clean wannabe!"

Borril looked down at Grim, partly confused and partly angry.

Grim looked the large orc straight in the eyes. "If you want to hurt my friend, you'll have to go through me." For some reason, he again experienced an overwhelming desire to fight with his dagger, like it was outside of his control. His hand instinctually half-drew the dagger.

Borril snarled and put his hand on his holstered mace as a smooth voice interrupted.

"If you touch them, you defy the chief and therefore defy the clan."

Grim looked to his right and saw Grogmar, the mustached barber, had stood up. He had a butcher knife in one hand, pointing toward Borril, and a straight razor in the other. Grim

170

looked around to see that a number of orcs had stood up and appeared ready to engage the large brute.

Borril huffed. He stepped closer and leaned down to within inches of Grim's face, then said, "This is not over." He stormed off.

Quickly after he left, the orcs went about eating their food, conversing loudly, and playing drums, bringing back the liveliness the area had previously had.

Grim looked down at his hand still gripping the dagger's handle. His hand trembled, and it took too many uncomfortable seconds to let go. Once he did let the weapon slide back in its sheath, he sighed in relief and then looked around. Fortunately, no one seemed to have noticed his previous discomfort. He then walked over to the barber.

"Thanks," Grim said to Grogmar.

The orc waved it off as no big deal. "You have brought my sister great joy. She told me what you did for her. I have not seen her this happy in a long time, sir."

"Sister? Wait, who's your sister?" Grim asked.

The barber turned a little and motioned toward Riga, who was smiling and seemed distinctly more cheerful than when Grim had first met her.

"Riga's your sister!?" he asked incredulously.

"Yes, sir," the polite orc replied.

Grim's mind tried to find the similarities one would expect of siblings as he looked from one to the other and back again. Grogmar was the definition of prim and proper while Riga was unkempt. He was pretty sure there had always been some dirt on her cheek.

"But you're so...so..." Grim said.

"Different?" Grogmar replied. "My sister is more of a free spirit. I help keep her in line."

Grim looked again at Riga to see that she and her brother did resemble each other...somewhat. "Well, thanks again," he said before walking over to Lukav.

After talking with Lukav, he learned that Borril had been a childhood bully and had been very close to Potor. No one had heard of the shaman since his exile from the clan. Lukav was also surprised that the angry orc hadn't left with Potor.

"Okay, man. I'm gonna head to bed. As for Xumi, make sure you use protection," Grim said, then he started walking to their tent.

"Protection for what?" Lukav asked.

Grim just kept walking with a smirk on his face.

Lukav asked again but louder to his friend, "Protection for what?"

Grim entered his tent and sat on his cot. Before he could lie down, his vision became skewed by darkness again. He tensed, gripping the edge of his cot while trying to gain his bearings in the darkness. His surprise made him not even realize that he was no longer sitting but standing instead.

"Wh-where am I? Hello?" Grim called out.

A chilling voice replied, "Hello, Grim!" Zordell chuckled as his skeletal, unicorn-like face suddenly appeared out of the darkness, towering over Grim. His four large red eyes focused on his Progenitor as the rest of his body emerged out of the darkness, the chains connected to his bindings rattling as he moved.

"Zordell!? What are you doing here? Where are we?" Grim asked.

"Physically, we are in different places. This is an isolated

172

area where we can mentally communicate. There is no way to track when we can have these times to converse, but this one came at an opportune moment."

A wave of concern surged over Grim. "What do you mean?" he asked.

Zordell jerked forward so that his face was inches away from Grim's, his chains clanging as he moved. "Why have you not destroyed a seal yet?" the Arch Necroid demanded.

Grim gulped, realizing his decisions were coming back to haunt him. The familiar smell of necrosis permeated his nostrils. "I can explain. I'm doing exactly what you told me to do. I'm getting stronger! I have gained the trust of an orc tribe and already acquired a Greater Vassal!"

Zordell looked surprised as his gaze examined the pale human up and down. "Indeed you are, and you say you've unlocked a Greater Vassal already? Was it the weak orc I sent you to?"

Grim nodded.

Zordell then let out a creepy smile that could be the stuff of nightmares. "Good! Good! Very well, my Progenitor. I will trust your plan for now. I will do my best to help you in the meantime. Do not forget, it is not only my freedom at stake but your life as well."

The large skeletal being then snapped his bony fingers, and Grim's vision flashed white.

Grim blinked and found himself back in his tent, back on his cot. He took a few deep breaths and processed what he'd just been through. He lay down on his bed with revived motivation. Knowing that he would have to answer Zordell wherever he might go impressed him with the seriousness of his situation. He must keep getting stronger. He had no choice...

CHAPTER 16
GRINDING

WAKING BEFORE DAWN, GRIM AND Lukav started their normal training routines. After the previous evening's surprise visit from Zordell, Grim worked with renewed vigor, not wanting to disappoint his undead patron. Scar examined the shield and asked Grim what had happened. Grim explained the battle with the slime abomination that led to its heavily damaged state.

"Good," Scar said in approval. "You've learned how to successfully defend. Now I will teach you how to attack."

"Yes!" Grim said.

He'd been looking forward to some payback for taking Scar's beatings and not being able to hit back. Grim equipped himself with his greatsword and picked up his shield. Scar held the wooden club Grim was all too familiar with and a square shield casually, then struck with speed and precision. The orc was much stronger than Grim and able to swing his thick wooden club quicker.

Grim took a majority of the hits during their sparring session, making his retribution not nearly as good as he'd hoped. Getting frustrated at the continual beating he was receiving,

Grim almost completely unsheathed his Daria's dagger to give the orc a piece of his mind. Once he realized what he was doing, though, Grim forcefully resheathed his weapon. The dagger was enchanted and could do some real harm if he wasn't careful! Grim did not like the fact that he was so ready to use it, and it was so hard to put back. Unfortunately, since he was focusing on putting away his dagger and not on the orc in front of him, when Grim looked back at his opponent, he was swiftly met by a club to the temple, resulting in unconsciousness.

Fortunately, once Grim regained consciousness, Scar did take the time to show him proper feet placements and the correct way to grip and swing his weapons. Although awkward at first, practice was making a difference for Grim's skill level.

Their sparring session completed, the Progenitor approached Scar. "Hey, Scar, I have a question."

"What is it, Snow-Skin?" the orc replied.

"Well, I have five stat points to allocate, and I didn't know if you had any recommendations."

The orc stroked his chin for a moment, then said, "Hmm, well, it depends. You are a mage, so Intelligence and Mind are important, but you're also a capable fledgling warrior. You've also shown a brave, headstrong approach, like that of a fighter on the frontline."

Grim smiled. It was only the second time Scar had ever complimented him, the first being when he'd first used Shield Bash.

Scar, a little uncomfortable with giving a compliment, quickly changed his tone. "Hmph! That said, you have a long way to go if you do not want to be battle fodder. I would recommend investing in Strength and Vitality. That should allow

175

you to take hits and return them. Also, don't forget Agility! Your moves in combat are too slow and predictable."

Grim appreciated the in-depth analysis, and the suggestions definitely coincided with the approach of developing himself as a tank with magic capabilities that he'd been considering. "Thank you, Scar," he replied.

The gruff orc just nodded in reply and went to grab some food.

Grim quickly took his advice and invested two points into Agility while putting one each into Vitality, Strength, and Intelligence. Even though his magical capabilities were just at the beginning stage, he knew that binding his soul with an extremely powerful being of death would eventually come into play.

His training with Xumi started off differently than before. Instead of the cold disposition he was used to, the young orc had a bright smile on her face as he walked into the cave. Her reconciliation with Lukav had brought about an obvious improvement in her demeanor. Grim was also pleased to see that Thrain was notably healthier and sitting by the fire with his daughter.

"Hello, Chief," Grim greeted. "It's good to see you up and awake."

"Yes, while Herbalism is not Vumira's favorite skill, you can see she is quite capable at it." The chief started to get up. "I will now oversee young Lukav's training starting today."

"That's good," Grim said. "I know he will enjoy having one so skilled as yourself training him."

The chief looked at Xumi, then replied with a more serious tone, "No, he will not." Then the orc left.

Grim could tell he wasn't the target of that last statement, but it still sent a chill up his spine. He didn't dare say anything until the chief left the cave, "What was that about?" he asked Xumi.

The archer shyly looked away from Grim and uncomfortably said, "My father is a bit…protective. I am to be the next chief, and he wants me to take a worthy mate."

"You don't say?" Grim replied sarcastically. "Well, I'm not an expert in true love, but from all the rom-coms I've seen, it always works out."

"What's a rom-com?" Xumi asked.

"Never mind," Grim said, realizing that maybe he shouldn't give any more advice based solely off movies he'd seen. "So, any new advice on how to manipulate manna?"

Xumi shook her head. "I am sorry. It is hard to explain. I was able to have such a deep connection with Soul Magic that it came naturally. When I learned the skill, it said that only those with a strong affinity or granted a blessing can learn it."

Grim thought about it, then had an idea. "Does one have to learn manna manipulation through Soul Magic?"

She shrugged. "I do not know."

Grim remembered his dream with Zordell showing him a Death Orb with a manna tendril attached to it and wondered what the Arch Necroid was trying to tell him. After several moments, it dawned on him. "I have an idea," he said.

Grim cast Death Orb, then focused on the orb, his palm, and the space in between where the invisible tendril was connecting them. When nothing happened, he imagined actually touching the orb as if it were a ball in his hand. Sure enough, a tendril appeared.

"Yes!" Grim exclaimed. His joy caused him to lose focus and the orb fizzled out, then a prompt appeared.

Skill Gained: Manna Manipulation LVL 1

Many magi have the ability to channel manna into known spells. You, however, have gained the extremely rare skill of being able to bend manna to your will, bringing new spells into existence. Only those who have a very strong magical affinity or who gain divine favor ever learn this skill. This skill is linked to the Mind stat. Increase the Mind stat to increase your skill's capability.

+1% Manipulation Speed

+1 Intelligence

"Nice!" Grim said as he dismissed the notification from his interface.

He realized that Xumi's affinity for Soul Magic must be high for her to learn this skill naturally, then spent the next few days working to increase his stats and skills. Unfortunately, he had some difficulty permanently changing a spell like Xumi could. The best he could do was momentarily press down on a Death Orb like it was a ball of dough. It would resemble the Soul Spear Xumi had created but then quickly disappear before it fully came to fruition. According to Xumi, Grim should be able to vary raw manna into new physical manifestations of spells, such as changing her Soul Orb into arrows. She informed Grim that the changed spells would likely gain new effects as well. Grim also took some time to increase his relationships with a number of the clan members. Both he and Lukav were even allowed to join Vumira on a hunt for woohig.

Outside of his Manna Manipulation skill, the most bothersome thing to Grim was Daria's Dagger. Ever since he'd used it to kill the slime abomination, he felt like it was trying influence him. On more than one occasion when he was holding the dagger, he'd felt a sudden strong desire to use it. To kill with it. Every time he'd sheathed it, he'd had to mentally force himself. He talked with Lukav about it, and they decided it was best for Grim to keep it on his belt so no one else would succumb to the weapon's power. They also decided that until they found an enchanter to evaluate the dagger, it would be best that Grim not use it again.

Lukav's training time, while productive, was a lot more strenuous than Grim's. First, he underwent the ceremony to gain the skill Channeling, which would officially allow him to join the monks of his clan. Unfortunately, it involved him standing naked before the monks and them striking at certain pressure points on his body to permanently hinder his manna pool. It also took the monks longer than usual to perform the ceremony because of Lukav's strange body. Grim made a joke about him getting frostbite on one of his "appendages" and was glad to see that the orc had picked up some of his humor when Lukav said that his arm and foot were not the only things that had grown when he was imbued with magic. Lukav learned not only the Channeling skill but the subskill Pressure Points as well. The second thing that made his time difficult was Thrain.

The chief was undoubtedly the strongest of the four other monks, but he was also Xumi's father. Vumira had informed Thrain that Lukav was courting their daughter, launching his fatherly instincts into overdrive. The stoic monk was relentless, barely giving his student any rest. He had Lukav practice forms over and over again and pummeled poor Lukav with information and his fists as well. By the end of his practice sessions, the best the young orc could typically do was limp over to his tent. After some meditation, though, Lukav took some time to work out. Ever since he had started training to be a monk, the orc had kind of become obsessed with working out. In their tent at night, he was frequently doing lunges or some other challenging activity before he slept. Grim figured having your body miraculously fixed might do that to someone and just shrugged it off; he was not going to complain about the orc wanting to better himself. Fortunately, on the eighth day, Vumira had convinced her mate to allow Lukav to join her and Grim on a hunt.

A lot less sore and more energetic that night compared to others, Lukav was unaware how much that was going to matter.

CHAPTER 17
DON'T CALL IT A COMEBACK

ON THE EIGHTH NIGHT AFTER Grim had been welcomed to the Blood-Shield Clan village, he enjoyed some of the snake meat from their hunt that day during the evening clan meal, sitting by a fire with Lukav, Xumi, and Riga. The place where the clan meals were held was in the center of the valley right by the small stream and bridge crossing over it. Grim's group was not too far from the water and edge of the bridge. While chewing the reptile meat, Grim remarked that it actually did taste like chicken. Riga was upset that Grim wouldn't try her grilled mushrooms, but he was not ready to take a risk outside of drinks with his living-dead status requiring him to ingest only meat and blood for sustenance. The idea of drinking blood just kind of freaked him out. Even on Earth, he liked to have his meat cooked more on the burnt side. Ingesting blood seemed kind of gross to him. Grim was busy explaining to Riga and his friends the concept and the pure bliss of fried chicken when it started to snow.

While he had seen snow before, it was the first time he had seen it coming down in the Ashen Plane. It fell at a moderate rate, collecting in people's hair, no different than on Earth. He

181

smiled and began thinking about his situation. He and Lukav had grown much in their short time together, and in just a week, the orcs of the clan had accepted him as a friend. Well, most of them had. Borril and his twin brother Torril had both made their distaste apparent but done nothing to challenge the decree of their chief.

He decided to look at his status page.

Grim Snow-Skin (LVL 3)

Race: Human (Living-Dead)

Strength: 13

Agility: 13

Vitality: 16

Intelligence: 12

Mind: 11

Endurance: 16

Charisma: 12

Health: 140

Manna: 105

Stamina: 125

Feats: Ogre Skin, Shrewd, Sapper

Skills:

Culinary LVL 2

Great Weapon Wielding LVL 6

Analyze LVL 2

Commerce LVL 2

Heavy Armor LVL 6

Shields LVL 3→Shield Bash Augment

Heavy Shields LVL 2

Short Blades LVL 2

Stealth LVL 2

Herbalism LVL 3

Tracking LVL 2

Manna Manipulation LVL 1

Death Magic LVL 3

Death Ward

Death Orb

Commune with Dead

Decay

Summon Undead

Soul Magic LVL 1

Fusion

Soul Spear

Soul Orb

Resistances: Death Magic 50%, Cold 25%, Slashing Damage 25%, Soul Magic 5%, Fire -25%

Languages: Common, Orcish

Titles: Progenitor of the Arch Necroid, Death Mage (Novice), Soul Mage (Novice)

Nice! he thought. For only being at level three, he had a variety of skills. His training had increased his stats without his having to level up, and he had a regencration rate for his health, manna, and stamina. He calculated that health was at 1.8 per 5 seconds, Manna at 1.05 per 5 seconds, and Stamina at 3.2 per 5 seconds. He was about to call it a night when a voice cut through all the conversations in the village.

"People of the Blood-Shield Clan, I have come to inform you of a change of leadership," said Potor from the nearest entrance into the village.

While the darkness of night prevented him from being fully seen, the lit torches on each side of the entrance behind him made his visage distinct. Grim could tell something was different about the orc. He appeared more...menacing.

"Why have you returned?" the deep voice of Thrain echoed over the valley.

Grim turned to see him standing at his cave entrance, at the other end of the valley, arms crossed over his chest. The tension was palpable.

"To allow those who wish to follow me the chance. I certainly do not wish your fate to befall them, Thrain," Potor replied smugly. Potor continued, "We once had a great power with our former chief, Gulag, but we all know he is not coming back. Instead of bringing our clan out of this accursed mountain range, you, Thrain, have kept us here. Not only that, you entrust the fate of our clan to a strange human mage and his mutated pet!

"You have led our clan on a path we should not have followed. We hide here like mere vermin instead of taking what is ours! Instead of becoming conquerors, we've become weaker and weaker! You have allied the fate of our clan to some human scum and his corrupted orc pet on the false hope that they can find that pitiful Gulag," he said, pointing at Grim and Lukav. "I do not believe we should wait for you to lead our clan to the slaughter. I'm offering a chance to kill and conquer like we orcs should do. First this mountain range, then the entire plane!"

"Enough!" Thrain's voice bellowed. "I will not have your pride and warmongering lead our clan to further despair! Guards, execute the traitor!"

Potor smiled and looked back to the tunnel entrance where he'd come from.

Out walked Borril, wielding a mace dripping with blood, with his face splattered red. "I stand with Potor," the large brute said.

"As do I," Borril's twin Torril said as he appeared through the other cavern entrance, also covered in gore.

"Anyone else?" Potor asked, looking at the crowd in front of him with his arms open as if he were some sort of cult leader.

No one spoke. The villagers stood fast, some snarling as everyone took a defensive posture. Some parents put their children behind them and picked up their clubs or axes.

"No?" Potor asked with obvious amusement. "Well, then, welcome my new tribe! They have been needing a meal! Time to *eat!*"

Hordes of gnolls rapidly emerged through the two entrances like ants out of an anthill. Chaos ensued. A number of orcs ran to confront the gnolls while the children and some of their parents ran across the bridge to the other side of the valley. Meanwhile, Thrain and the other monks were sprinting to join the defenders. Grim, Xumi, and Lukav quickly readied themselves. They were about to run into the fray when a nearby Vumira stuck out her arm and stopped them.

"No! We stay alive by staying together in formation!" she said.

The hunter then gathered some of the other orcs not already in combat and ordered them into a V-shaped phalanx with the trio in the center. Xumi and Grim would provide cover while

185

Lukav protected them from anyone breaking through the formation. Vumira positioned the group in front of the bridge to provide a barrier for the escapees. Once in formation, Grim looked at the orcs and gnolls fighting ahead of them and the flood of gnolls still coming in. The brave orcs were quickly overwhelmed by the larger creatures' sheer numbers. Grim looked on with horror as the gnolls ate dead brethren and enemies alike. A blue light shone from behind the gnolls as Potor conjured a spell with words of power and complicated gestures.

Grim only had a moment to think *Oh, crap!* before the shaman loudly clapped his hands together, ending his spell. Suddenly, a fifty-foot wall of large, sharp ice arose from the stream dividing the valley. Grim looked back to see that it even went through the rock wall circling the village. A large crack rang out as the rock wall to the phalanx's right broke off and started to shift away, revealing a large gap to the outside.

Right as Grim turned back, the group was beset by the monstrous creatures. Vumira was at the tip of the spear, fighting them off. Xumi fired her arrows while Grim cast Death Ward on all three of them, then pelted the gnolls with Death Orbs. They had only been fighting for barely a minute when Grim noticed it was not going well. The gnolls were just too strong. One of the orcs on the phalanx's right had her trachea ripped out. Lukav ran in to replace her, to keep the formation from breaking.

Grim spared a glance to the gap in the wall. "Vumira, this isn't working! I have an idea!" he yelled.

Without looking back, she yelled to him, "What is it?"

"That spell opened a gap to the wall on the right. It leads outside of the village!" Grim yelled back.

"Change point!" Vumira yelled in orcish.

186

The rest of the phalanx, outside of Lukav, yelled "Point change!" in response.

Vumira shifted back to join Grim while the two orcs to her left and right moved to cover for her empty space. She quickly ran to Grim and Xumi, then looked to the broken gap. The head hunter swiftly surveyed the battlefield, then grabbed a small pouch on her side and shoved it at Xumi.

"Take this and go!" Vumira said.

"What? No! Moth—"

"You must live, my daughter! That is an order!" Vumira interrupted. She then addressed Grim. "You and Lukav protect her with your lives!"

"You have my word," Grim replied hurriedly.

She then nodded and ran to Lukav. She grabbed him by the shoulder and threw him back, yelling, "Ruuuuun!" as she reengaged in the bloody mayhem.

Without much time to process events, Xumi and Grim helped Lukav up and began to run toward the gap. They were not unnoticed, though. Xumi stopped the group suddenly right before a bolt of ice shot across in front of them.

Grim looked over in time to see Potor already casting another spell. "Run!" he yelled.

The group made it inside the gap just in time for the next ice bolt to miss them. Rough rock was to their left and a wall of ice was to their right, so they rushed through single file, Xumi leading Lukav and Grim. They had almost made it out when suddenly the ground under their feet started to shake. The group stopped to stabilize themselves. Grim stuck his arms out instinctively to keep balance, accidentally cutting his hand on the sharp ice. Cracks could be seen emerging on the ice wall

187

beside them. They were about to take off again when the path underneath suddenly collapsed.

All three of them screamed as they plunged into darkness.

CHAPTER 18

CATACOMBS

GRIM AWOKE TO PURE DARKNESS, letting out a moan as he slowly pushed himself up from what felt like a hard stone floor. Minor aches and pains made themselves known through his body as he moved. "You guys there?" he asked.

"Ugh. Yeah, man," Lukav replied.

"Me too," Xumi said.

Grim stood up, willing his eyes to adjust but to no avail. He reached his arms out to find a wall and shuffled forward carefully.

"What are you doing?" Xumi asked.

"I'm trying to find a wall. Wait! Can you see me?" Grim said.

Xumi chuckled. "Oh! I didn't know you don't have dark vision," she said. Then she grabbed a small torch from her satchel and lit it. "There."

Grim looked around what appeared to be a small underground room around ten feet tall, littered with rocks of varying sizes that had fallen down with them. The ceiling appeared to be completely closed up by a mixture of debris from the cave-in. Rocks and chunks of ice protruding through reminded him just how fortunate the trio had been not to be crushed.

"Where are we?" Grim asked.

The trio took a good look at their surroundings. There was a carved-out doorway in front of them, and the walls on both sides of the space had shelves carved into them. Each shelf held a corpse in varying stages of decay, some completely desiccated and others still wrapped in linens. It was easy to reason they were in a tomb.

Lukav started speaking in slow realization. "Xumi…are we…"

"Yes," she replied with obvious fear in her voice. "We are in our in clan's original burial site. The Catacombs of Eternal Servitude."

"Wait, *the original burial site?*" Grim asked. "Like the one that the location was lost during your war with the gnolls?"

Xumi looked at the entrance and nodded in confirmation, her eyes wide with concern.

What is it with this clan and underground things? Underground herb garden, underground catacomb, and the chief lives in a cave, which is underground-ish, Grim thought. "So, what's the deal? Are there like undead protectors or something?" he asked.

"Shhh!" Xumi replied quickly. She then whispered, "This is the place where our ancestors are buried. The *deal* is that it has been warded to protect the secrets and dead of our clan. No one knows how, but legend has it that the dead themselves somehow still serve the clan forever by protecting the tomb."

Well, the name Catacombs of Eternal Servitude makes sense now, Grim thought as he looked at the dead bodies with caution.

"Xumi, babe, what do we do?" Lukav whispered.

190

"We don't have any choice," she said. "We are going to have to find our way out. While I don't know exactly which way to the exit, going up should lead out."

Grim reasoned that her logic was sound and nodded his agreement. He cast Death Ward on all of them before they left the room, ensuring their health would only drop to one instead of zero one time to prevent their deaths. Xumi took point while Grim held the torch behind her and Lukav took up the rear. They slowly walked out of the room, careful to be quiet with every step. The room they exited was part of a hallway. Looking left, they realized they couldn't go that way, as there was some collapsed rubble blocking their path. As right was the only option, they quietly proceeded in that direction. It was dark, and Grim couldn't see far ahead of the group. The air was warm and humid, not cool like the air the group was used to.

They continued in stealth, careful to make as little noise as possible. Grim was obviously less capable than his orc companions as his heavy iron armor made his steps much louder, but he did his best. Some of the pieces of his armor were dented, but nothing was broken. The only thing missing was his helmet, which he'd left in the village in all the chaos. Eventually, they made it into an open cavern. Grim couldn't tell much except that they were out of the tunnel and on some kind of platform. The group stopped to evaluate which way to go. The hallway entrance was behind them, and two stalagmites in front of them had shelves between them with skulls and candles decorating them.

Grim moved closer to look at them with his torch. Looking at one of the skulls, he realized it was hollowed out and had a candle inside. What he didn't realize was that his torch was too close to the skull candle next to the one he was inspecting and

191

had lit it. As he stood back up, he noticed the light source and the skulls and other candles on the shelves began to light up.

"Uhhh, guys?" Grim said, forgetting to whisper. His voice echoed through the cavern.

Lukav and Xumi, who had been surveying the area to figure out which way to go, quickly turned back to see the self-lit shelves.

"What happened!?" Lukav asked.

As he was talking, more candles and skulls decorating the platform perimeter started to light up. Then the stone floor began to glow like flames along its distinct cracks.

"I accidentally lit a candle, and now all this happened!" Grim explained.

"It doesn't matter. Form up back to back, now!" Xumi commanded.

The two, knowing the wrath of a woman, did as instructed. All three of them pressed against each other and looked around for potential danger. It did not take long for the entire cavern to light up. Statues with glowing eyes, magic sconces and candles, and what appeared to be ducts of fire illuminated the entire catacomb they were in so well that Grim could see just as well as the orcs. After several minutes, the group eased their formation.

"Grim, please be careful!" Lukav said with some annoyance, though obviously finding it difficult to reprimand the man he proclaimed to be his master and friend. "I know you are curious, but please do not forget we are in an enchanted catacomb made to kill intruders," he pleaded.

Grim put a hand on his shoulder. "I know, my friend. I'm sorry for my carelessness. Come on. Let's find a way out of here."

The group focused on their surroundings. The room they were in was around 200 feet wide. There was a large chasm in front of them, at least ten yards across and deep enough that no one could see the bottom. There were two pathways they could travel, both going up. One was to the right while the other went left. The one on the right led to a well-maintained wall that did not show some of the roughness and decay other parts of the tomb had shown. Magical light shone from inside. The door the left path led to was much different. It was literally a dark doorway carved into the natural rock wall that appeared much less grandiose to Grim's eyes. He was about to suggest going toward the well-lit path when a noise started to echo. It was a rapid clicking sound, like that of an insect, and it put everyone on edge. Shadows soon flickered across the walls of the lit room.

"Spiders! Move!" Xumi hastily whispered.

At the thought of having to battle giant spiders, Grim quickly moved toward the other room behind his friends, almost knocking them out of the way. As he entered the dark room, he saw a large, hairy leg of an arachnid on the other side of the cavern. All three of them crouched in the dark room, looking back into the chamber they'd left. A spider larger than Grim had ever seen emerged into view on the right pathway. It was the size of a full-grown Great Dane. It moved up to the platform they had just left, then turned back and left.

> Congratulations! Stealth reached LVL 3!
> +3% Stealth Speed
> -3% Chance of Being Detected

Grim dismissed the notification from his interface. "What do we do now?" he asked Xumi.

"Both ways go up. Right now, I suggest we continue this way," she said, gesturing deeper in the dark room they were in. "And turn back if we cannot find a path out."

The other two approved of the plan and followed her. They discovered the room beyond the dark doorway they entered was another crypt. It was as tall as the room they'd originally fallen into but much bigger overall. Multiple archways could be seen even though there were only a few sconces randomly interspersed, giving poor lighting. Multiple shelf coffins were carved in the pillars and walls, and all were filled with decayed orc bodies. The group slowly crouched their way across the room, keeping an eye out for any spiders. A strong musty odor assaulted their nostrils. Nearing the exit straight across the room, Grim heard a loud gagging cough followed by a soft moan.

"Hey!" Grim whispered, causing the others to stop. "Did you hear that?" he asked.

Lukav and Xumi nodded.

Grim focused on their surroundings. He was rewarded with the sight of an ancient orc corpse emerging out of one of the coffins. Its skin was gray and in an advanced state of decay, and it had unblinking white eyes. It began to stomp toward the group with a curved dagger in its left hand. After its second step, two more corpses stepped out of their coffins behind them, one to the left and the other to the right of the first one.

"We got company!" Grim yelled, equipping himself with his greatsword.

He and Lukav ran to the undead while Xumi backed up and took out her bow.

The undead were no match for the speed of the trio. Lukav jumped and punched the first zombie in the face, followed by Grim taking a wide swing at its chest. The blade cut across the undead's body. No blood came out, and the creature showed no sign of pain, but Grim was able to push it back slightly. It was still close enough that he could use Analyze on it.

Undead Orc (LVL 5)

Health: 100/205

Manna: 0

Stamina: N/A

Feats: Orcish Tenacity, No Pain

Skills:

Short Blades LVL 14

Unarmed Combat LVL 13

Resistances: Death Magic 25%, Soul Magic 25%, Fire -50%

Languages: N/A

This orc had been enspelled as a guardian of its tomb. As an undead creature, it was immune to stamina defects or physical pain. If proper damage was done to the skull or if the head was separated from the body, immediate death would come.

"Cut off their heads! They'll go down if we do that!" Grim yelled to the other two.

An arrow struck the undead in the neck, right in front of Grim. It let out a moan as it staggered back. Lukav was already moving to one of the other two undead behind them. He began to fight the creature on the right, and Grim noticed the other

195

undead turned to flank the monk. Grim kicked the undead closest to him in the chest and was able to knock it back into the one that was going to attack Lukav, stunning them both.

Grim did not waste time as he rushed forward with his greatsword, successfully performing a downward chop attack that Scar had taught him and cutting the undead's skull in half. The now fully dead creature disintegrated to dust, leaving no barrier for the other undead behind it. The creature had remarkable strength and quickly punched Grim in the face. His vision went white from the sudden surge of pain, and he took a few steps back. Before he could do anything, though, he felt a rush of wind go by his ear. He took a defensive stance and, as his vision adjusted, saw the undead now had an arrow in its eye. It was an insta-kill as the creature crumbled to dust before his eyes. Grim turned to Lukav as the once handicapped orc literally punched through the skull of the undead.

"Nice!" Grim said. He was glad to have the two orcs on his team. "Everyone alright?" he asked.

"I'm okay," Lukav replied.

"Me too," Xumi said.

"Good," said Grim. "Let's check the dust piles to see if there are any valuable items."

He and Lukav started to check the remains when Xumi yelled at them. "No! These are the remains of our ancestors! We cannot rob them of their possessions. I know we had to defend ourselves, but we should not desecrate their remains even more."

Lukav answered before Grim could respond. "Xumi, it is up to us to save our clan. It is up to us to get out of here, save our clan, and inform them of our burial ground. Our ancestors would understand that we have to do everything we can to survive."

"Well...I guess you're right," she admitted solemnly.

Xumi and the group looked through the remains of their attackers. Unfortunately, they found only a pile of dust and three crude iron daggers. There was nothing that they needed, but Xumi held onto the weapons just in case.

Grim had an idea. *I could raise some of the dead orcs and have an army escorting us!* After attempting to use Summon Undead on one of the still resting corpses, though, a notification appeared informing him that the enchantment of the catacomb prevented any dead body from being used for service outside of protecting the crypt. The trio then continued on to a tunnel that sloped slightly downward. At the end, they entered an open chamber. It was so large they couldn't see the top, and there was a pool of water in the middle with a large statue of an armored orc on an island in the center. There were crisscrossing stone pathways over the water, connecting to the center island. Each stone pathway led to a different exit. One led up to their location, another to some stairs going into another cave. The right one led to a rickety bridge leading to some creepy ruins. The final path led to what looked like nothing. There was also a large hole in the pool of water that had become a waterfall. Steam could be seen coming out of it, and rushing water could be heard. Finally, there was a tunnel where water rushing out was feeding the pool.

The group decided to make camp by the statue so that should any enemies come their way, they could see them from farther out. The three of them didn't realize it, but adrenaline had been fueling them since before they accidentally found the catacombs. With the new lull in their travel, the strains of the

197

night's events were hitting them hard. Once they reached the island statue, they quickly collapsed from exhaustion. They were even too tired to take guard shifts.

Grim was awoken by a thud against him. He saw that both Lukav and Xumi were already awake. Lukav was doing one-handed push-ups, keeping his strength up and passing the time. Xumi ate some travel rations, sitting against the statue and taking obvious pleasure in watching the muscular Lukav. Grim smirked at them, then looked around in the distance. He could see the silhouettes of bats sleeping upside down on a cave wall. No fire was present as there was no readily available source of wood in the large tomb. A thought then occurred to him.

"Where did you get those travel rations?" he asked.

Both Lukav and Xumi stopped eating, then Xumi tossed the pouch Vumira had given her to him.

Grim caught and examined it. It was a small, dark brown pouch with a thread tied around the top. It was very light. When he touched the bottom, it felt as if the pouch had nothing in there, but it definitely had weight to it. Wondering what was in it, Grim opened it and stuck his hand inside. To his surprise, a five-by-four square grid appeared in his interface. He realized it was essentially a small bag of holding. Bags of holding were a must for almost any MMORPG player! They were enchanted to be small portals to a pocket of space that was able to hold a certain number of items. What was cool about them was they would reduce the weight of held items, sometimes completely. Quickly Grim looked at the pouch and noticed a rune he had not seen before.

"Did you know Vumira had this?'" he asked incredulously.

Xumi shook her head. "No. I did not. I assume this was one of the enchanted items they were able to save."

Satisfied with the answer, Grim went back to looking at the grid. He saw that each square could only hold one type of item, but apparently the number per square was unlimited and the properties of the bag reduced the weight of each item to .01% of its original weight. There were healing and restoring herbs, potions, travel rations, rope, torches, a bear trap, the three daggers they'd picked up earlier, and two enchanted stones marked Opal Explosion Ward. Some information about the latter appeared when Grim focused on it.

> An opal enchanted to cause an explosion. Any pressure greater than 1 kg will trigger the trap. This is a one-time-use item.

Well, that wasn't very informative. While a little frustrated, Grim decided not to mess with the stones until absolutely necessary. He was not a fan of accidentally exploding. He grabbed a travel ration out of the bag by reaching in and thinking of the item, then tossed the bag back to Xumi. He checked the time on his display clock.

"Soooo," Grim said. "Which way do we go?"

Xumi pointed to the set of stairs going upward toward another tunnel. "I say that way. It is the only path here that leads up, and up is the way we need to go."

The other two agreed with her logic and, after taking care of some necessary bodily functions, began their trek in that direction. The tunnel was notably darker than other parts of the cave because there were no sources of magical light inside. Xumi took out a torch, lit it, and gave it to Grim. They proceeded in their usual manner, Xumi in front, Grim in the middle, and Lukav bringing up the rear. They cautiously walked for about ten minutes until a light could be seen from the other side. When they reached the end, they found a large cathedral-like room. Bright artificial white light shone from the top. There was a large, wooden, zigzagging bridge that led from one end of the room to the other with support beams interspersed underneath. Where there was no wooden path was a large drop-off. It was black and deep enough that you could not see the bottom. Both the left and right walls held hundreds of corpses. There were also large metal beams in the middle of unfinished pillars along the sides of the space, as if this were a grand mausoleum left in midconstruction.

"Whoa!" Grim said, partly in awe, partly in fear.

"Yeah!" Lukav confirmed nervously.

Grim could see that the exit at the end of the room led to a staircase that went both up and down from their level. "That appears to be the way out, but what about the—"

"Corpses?" Xumi interrupted. "They all appear to be too far away for them to make any jump toward us."

That eased both Grim's and Lukav's minds, but not by much.

The group carefully began crossing the wooden bridge. It was obvious that it was built long ago as there was much creaking and bending of wood. They stayed around five feet from each other to make sure they were not putting too much weight on each individual piece of wood. They went along for about ten minutes and got about three-quarters of the way across before Xumi held her fist up. Grim and Lukav immediately stopped. She then pointed down to a wooden square in the middle of one of the wooden paths that was notably darker than the rest. It was fairly obvious that it was a trap. She gingerly stepped around the trap, and. Lukav and Grim followed suit. When Grim had just made it around the trap, subtle haunting moans of the undead started to echo throughout the chamber. The group stopped and frantically began scanning their surroundings. Xumi used the time to take out and nock her bow. The large size of the room made it difficult to discern where the noise came from.

Grim noticed an undead hand appear from the right side of the bridge, and a surge of panic went through him. "We've got undead here!" he yelled. He reflexively took a step back to meet the new enemy, then felt his right foot sink slightly and heard a distinct click. Grim's panic then turned to dread as he looked to find that he had stepped on the trap. "Crap!"

A loud, metallic clicking noise echoed throughout the chamber. The room slightly shook as dust fell from the ground. Right as the undead orc had stood up, all of the metal beams dislodged from the pillars and began to fall. Noticing that one of the beams was coming right for him, Grim quickly rolled to his right. Multiple loud crashes of metal on wood could be heard. He felt splinters splash against his skin, and the wooden bridge shook and rocked from the new assault.

"Is everyone alright?" Grim asked as he stood and composed himself.

He looked to see the undead was completely smashed by the beam. Both Lukav and Xumi had dodged the beams and appeared no worse for wear.

"We are okay," Lukav replied.

As if in response, the subtle moans erupted into voracious roars and groans. They all looked at each other, then around the room. A large horde of undead were emerging from under the end of the wooden path where they were going. The ones in the walls began to emerge as well. Grim could see that they were walking down the large metal beams toward the group. There were too many of them. Grim and his friends would quickly be overrun.

"Go back!" Xumi yelled, quickly grasping the situation.

All three of them took off in a full sprint. Speed was in their favor, but the undead were about fifty feet behind.

While running, Grim realized there was no way to escape. There was no place they could hide or get away. *If there were only a way to block off this room.* Then an idea struck. "Xumi, give me one of the opals!" he said in between breaths.

"What!?" she replied incredulously.

"Just do it!" Grim yelled.

Still running, the orc archer managed to reach in her pouch, pull out one of the opals, and give it to Grim.

"Keep going!" he yelled while stopping and turning around. He placed the opal on the ground and a notification appeared in his vision.

> Do you wish to place the Opal Explosion Ward here?
> Yes or No

"Yes!" Grim answered with obvious desperation in his voice.

He felt stone embed itself in the wooden beam. With the horde just ten feet away, Grim took off toward his friends waiting for him at the room's entrance. After a few seconds, he heard a large BOOM! A wave of heat and force surged from behind him, launching him forward. He landed with a thud in front of the two orcs. Lukav helped his friend up, and Grim frantically patted down his cape where it was on fire.

"Thanks, dude," Grim said to the orc. He scrunched his face at the smell of burnt wolf fur.

"We should thank you," Xumi interrupted. "Without your foresight, I do not know how we were going to avoid getting killed."

Grim turned back to see a now 100-foot gap between the stone entrance they were at and the flaming wooden bridge and the hundreds of orc undead on the bridge and in the walls focused on them with a desire to kill. It was obvious that the trio would have met a gruesome end.

Notifications appeared in Grim's vision.

You have killed Undead Orc X 45!
Reward: 1,234 EXP

Level Up!

You have acquired enough EXP to reach LVL 4!

+5 Stat Points

+1 Level Point

+10 Health, Manna, or Stamina are available to distribute

Do you wish to distribute them now?

Yes or No

Skill gained! Traps LVL 1

Some prefer to charge at their opponents. You prefer to lie in wait.

+1% Trap Effectiveness

-1% Chance of Trap Being Detected

Congratulations! Traps reached LVL 3!

+3% Trap Effectiveness

-3% Chance of Trap Being Detected

"I leveled up!" Grim exclaimed.

"As did I!" Lukav said.

"Me too!" Xumi replied. "I guess killing all those undead gave us enough experience."

"Guess so!" Grim agreed. He decided to allocate his stat points later.

Since they could no longer go that route, the group went back to the statue where they had previously camped. Grim noticed there were more bats in the cave than he remembered. They took a break to recover from the morning's stressful events and shooed away the creatures from around them. One bat in particular did not like being disturbed from its resting place, and instead of flying away, it swiftly flew around the group and soon focused on Lukav.

"Ah! Get this thing away from me!" he pleaded.

Grim and Xumi chuckled at his expense. It was funny to see such a large and strong-looking orc so bothered by a tiny flying creature. Grim also wondered why Lukav couldn't hit it. With the orc's speed, it should have been a trivial task. His criticism of the monk was short-lived when the bat focused its attention on Grim. This time it was Lukav's turn to laugh.

"Gah! Eh! Get out of here!" Grim exclaimed. For a good thirty seconds, he swiped and ducked from the small mammal while it somehow masterfully dodged his attacks and managed to scratch Grim more than once. He had had enough. Knowing his greatsword was too bulky to catch the bat, he quickly pulled Daria's Dagger from his belt. He swiped it at a diagonal and managed to cut the bat slightly across the chest, causing it to fall to the ground.

"Grim, what are you doing?" Lukav asked with concern after seeing the dagger unsheathed.

Grim didn't hear him. He felt the dagger's familiar pulses steadily increasing.

Something echoed in his mind. *"Kill, Kill, KILL!"*

In one quick motion, Grim stabbed the hobbling bat in the chest, instantly killing it. After it let out its last breath, the dagger started to pulse wildly. Grim could feel the pulsing creeping up his arm, then through the rest of his body. He tried to pull it back, but it wouldn't move. He couldn't even let go of it.

"Grr!" Grim groaned as he tried to yank away from the dagger. His alarmed state took him out of his trance, and he finally heard Lukav yelling at him.

"Grim! Grim!! What are you doing! Let go!" he pleaded.

"I…can't!" Grim said, straining against whatever unknown force had him stuck.

His body was pulsing in unison with the weapon, somehow synchronized. Suddenly, the bat started to rapidly decay, seeming to be absorbed by the dagger. Once the animal had disappeared, the red jewel on the hilt changed to a slit eye.

The eye looked at Grim, and a deep, menacing voice rang in his ears. *"Yes!"*

"Ahhhhhh!" Grim exclaimed fearfully as he was finally able to let go of the dagger and crawl a few feet back to collapse in exhaustion. "What"—pant—"the"—pant—"fuck!"

"I was going to ask the same thing!" Lukav said.

The dagger began to vibrate uncontrollably. Its form then appeared to melt into a black ooze before their very eyes. As quickly as the weapon deformed, it reformed, but not into a blade. The ooze began to coalesce into an orb around the size of a basketball. The black color gave way to a bright green that appeared artificial. Then the orb began to change shape again. Claws, then legs, then a tail, then a head appeared. The creature was about half a foot tall and maybe twice as long. Its head and body had distinct feline features and a mane like a lion. It was covered in fur. The creature was bright green except for its mane, which was completely black. Two large bat-like wings emerged out of its back. Each of its claws and all of the teeth were sharply curved and solid black. There was also a barb at the end of its tail that looked like its claws as well. The most unsettling part of the little green thing was its eyes. It had two slitted red eyes just like what was on Grim's blade.

Quickly, as the being was forming, the group readied themselves, not sure of what to expect. The creature shook its head and seemed to gain consciousness. It started to frantically look around with a feral intensity. Then, it noticed the group and let out a deep snarl in defiance as it spread its wings out in an attempt to intimidate the party. After a couple of tense seconds, the creature locked eyes on Grim and noticeably calmed, tucking its wings back in. Grim also seemed to feel calm for some reason. Then the voice he had heard earlier returned.

"Hello, master," the rough, deep voice rang in his head.

"Huh? Did you just talk to me?" he thought to the bat-like creature.

"Yes, master," the small creature replied. It sounded as if Batman had a really sore throat.

Multiple notifications appeared in Grim's interface.

Secret Quest Complete!

A Familiar Weapon

Daria's dagger was so intricately enchanted that the weapon itself became alive with a high desire to kill. The strong magic in it allowed it to take on a new form as well. The first person to use the dagger and deal three

---

final blows within 10 days would be granted a familiar that possessed the traits of its victims. As such, you have been granted a unique familiar, the "Slime Manticore."

Reward:

Slime Manticore Familiar

Access to Full Information on Daria's Dagger

+3000 EXP

Congratulations!

You have gained a familiar! "Slime Manticore"

Familiars are creatures that bond with a being, granting boosts or abilities to one another most often by magical means. Your familiar possesses the capabilities to mentally communicate with you as well.

Note: Owing to the magical nature of your familiar and the way you have gained it, the familiar is soul-bound to you. It will follow you and only you for as long as you both shall live.

Reward:

+50% Affinity for Slimes

+10% Chance to Intimidate

Level Up!

You have acquired enough EXP to reach LVL 5!

5 Stat Points +1 Level Point +10 Health, Manna, or Stamina are available to distribute

Do you wish to distribute them now?

Yes or No

"What is going on, Grim?" Lukav asked uneasily. "Why did the dagger turn into a freaky green thing, and why has it stopped moving?"

The creature hissed at Lukav. *"Freaky?! Can I kill it, master? Oooh, please say I can kill it!"* it communicated eagerly to Grim.

Grim's eyes widened. *"No! No, you cannot. He is our ally!"* he thought back.

"But, master!"

"Do I make myself clear?" Grim asserted out loud to emphasize his point.

"Yes, master," the manticore replied, looking down after being admonished.

"Dude, can you please tell us what is going on?!" Lukav said with more frustration in his voice.

Xumi stood behind him, an arrow still nocked.

Grim stuck out his arms submissively to placate both sides he was now standing in between. "Whoa, whoa! It's okay. When the dagger changed, I was notified of a hidden quest. Apparently, it was alive and has now become my familiar. We can communicate with our thoughts."

"What! That is absurd!" Xumi said. "Our clan once had some of the best enchanters in all the Ashen Plane, and I've never heard of anyone making a blade capable of morphing into an animal! Let alone a highly intelligent one."

"Well, now you have," Grim replied matter-of-factly.

"Uhhh, okay, so what do we call it?" Lukav asked uncomfortably.

"Good question. Do you have a name?" Grim asked the manticore.

The creature looked a little perplexed at the question, then bowed its head and replied in Grim's mind, *"Hmm, I do not, master. This is the first time I have had complete awareness. As the one who has given me life, I entrust my name to you."*

Grim thought for a moment about the perfect name for the magical manticore. Then, an idea came to mind. "What about Manny? Yeah! Manny the Manticore. How does that sound?"

Upon hearing his name, Manny looked up with a slight smile, then hopped on Grim's right shoulder.

"I guess it's good. Manny, meet Xumi and Lukav. Xumi and Lukav, meet Manny," Grim said.

The orcs' tensions eased, and they nodded their heads at the manticore.

Manny responded in kind.

"Do you know what it can do?" Lukav asked.

Grim looked at his familiar. "What can you do, little buddy?" he asked.

The small creature looked to be in thought for a moment, then closed his eyes and a window appeared in Grim's vision.

Feats: This creature has gained feats and skills based on the three beings it killed as a weapon as well as its inherent magical abilities:

Starving Juvenile Dire Lion + Slime Abomination + Cave Bat

Slime Body: Has an extremely malleable body. Can go through cracks 1 cm and up. 100% resistance to nonmagical attacks owing to its slime nature.

Magic Teeth, Talons, and Tail-Bite and Claw Attacks do +1 Death damage

Enhanced Smell: Has ability to smell and track things from a kilometer away

Change Form: Can change into a Legendary quality

---

enchanted dagger and back again on command or when HP hits 0. *Note* If HP hits 0, it will take 24 hours before it can change back again. If HP and Durability hit 0, death will be permanent.

Mental Connection: Can telepathically communicate with its master and vice versa.

Skills:

Echolocation LVL 1: Emits a shriek that allows it to thoroughly survey its environment.

Flying LVL 1: Can use its wings to fly.

Sonic Screech LVL 1: Emits a small screech that affects all within a 10 foot cone with +2 sonic damage & 2 seconds of disorientation. The closer the target, the stronger chance it will happen.

Grim closed the interface, then explained about how Manny came to be and his abilities. He personally found it interesting that the small creature could have fur but yet could be a slime. An idea then struck him.

"I think Manny can lead us out of here. With his echolocation, he can find out which way we need to go," he said with some excitement.

Lukav readily agreed.

Xumi appeared slightly offended that she was no longer in the lead but quickly conceded as she admitted she had no idea which way to go anymore.

Grim thought the command, and Manny flew around the cavern letting out chirps and shrieks intermittently, then hopped back down to Grim's shoulder.

Manny then led the group back the way they had come because the tunnel and bridge did not lead upward. He also mentioned that the air appeared fresher back up the stairs. The group cautiously followed the green bat. Once they made it back to the cavern with the large hole, Manny flew around and surveyed the room. To their surprise, he noticed a small path they had not seen originally. It led slightly downward to a tunnel in the wall of the hole. Manny also warned them of traps ahead. With his guidance, they safely made it to the hidden path. The path led to a small tunnel, which eventually opened into a massive chamber that reminded Grim of a large abandoned library. Their journey was pretty uneventful except for fighting some large rats. Manny's ability proved invaluable, allowing them to avoid multiple encounters with the undead. It had taken them the better part of the day, but they finally found a winding staircase leading to an exit.

CHAPTER 19
GULAG

WHEN THEY REACHED THE TOP of the staircase, they found a stone doorway. Upon reaching the top, Manny turned into a dagger again at Grim's request. To the man's surprise, the white handle was now the same green as Manny's fur, and the red jewel was replaced with the familiar red eye.

When they looked at the doorway, they noticed some orcish words inscribed over it.

"Front antechamber," Grim read aloud. "Guess this is it." Grim pushed the door open.

They entered a small stone room about the size of half a basketball court. There were shelves that contained dead orcs in varying states of decay along the walls. What was distinct though, was at the center of the room. A large orc skeleton sat on a stone throne facing the group. There was a large, double-sided greataxe carved with runes leaning against the throne. Even from a distance, it was apparent that the bones were abnormally thick, and the skeleton had a large cut across the upper part of its left orbital bone. Somehow the skeleton still had a ring of unruly white hair around its head that traveled down to two long mutton chops. It wore only a kilt, boots, and a large red cape that was much more ornate than either Grim's or Lukav's. Right away they could tell something was different. As soon as they stopped walking to take in the room, the doors shut behind them with a THUMP!

A sense of dread came over Grim as they looked back to confirm they were trapped.

"Who dares trespass into our domain?" a deep haunting voice echoed from behind them.

They turned back and saw that the skeleton's eye sockets now possessed bright purple orbs of light, and it was looking right at them.

"We meant no disrespect," Xumi answered. "We arrived here by accident and are part of the Blood-Shield Clan."

The skeleton's jaw hung open as it appeared to examine each of the trio individually. Once it had finished, the jaws shut with an audible click. "You may be, but he is not," it said, pointing at Grim. The skeleton's tone then turned hostile. "You have brought an outsider in, dishonoring our clan, defacing our tomb, and destroying its protectors. You have disturbed the sanctity of the Catacombs of Eternal Servitude, and I, Chief Gulag and guardian of the upper level, will make sure you pay by becoming its thralls for all of time!" The skeleton stood up and stuck its arm out with palms facing upward. Its bone hands glowed the telltale purple of Death Magic. Then it raised them as if lifting some sort of weight. In response to its summons, four undead orcs arose from their tombs. Two held daggers, one a rusty sword and a buckler, and the last held a bow.

As the undead walked toward the skeleton, Grim addressed his companions. "Did I hear that right? Is this guy a former chief?"

"Yeah. What the fuck?" Lukav replied in disbelief at what they were seeing.

Even though they were in danger, Grim couldn't help but smirk at Lukav saying something he'd learned from Grim.

"Focus!" Xumi yelled, interrupting their thoughts as she released two arrows in rapid succession. Both of them hit Gulag, one in each of his eyes, and caused him to stagger backward, nearly falling back into the throne. "Get your heads out of your asses and get ready to fight!" she said.

Grim realized Lukav had been teaching her the phrases he had taught him. *I'm a bad influence!* "Right. Sorry," he blurted while equipping himself with his greatsword.

Lukav also readied himself in a defensive pose.

Gulag ripped the arrows out and groaned in pain.

"I'll focus on Gulag. You two focus on the others. Take care of the archer first, then the other three."

Xumi launched another arrow at Gulag, but with one hand the large skeleton quickly grabbed one of the dagger-wielding corpses and used its body as a shield. The arrow sank into the corpse's abdomen but did not faze it one bit. Then, a purple aura surrounded the orc corpse being held in the air. The undead rapidly decayed before their eyes and disintegrated to dust.

Gulag let out a sigh of relief and looked to be completely recovered. It pointed its bony hand at the group and vengefully yelled, "Attack!"

Grim ran out to intercept the former chief before he could do any more damage. He swung a downward chop, but Gulag had good reaction time and was able to grab the greataxe and block his attack. Grim used the close proximity to initiate Analyze.

214

Gulag the Ghul (LVL 15)

Vocation: Barbarian

Health: 505/505

Manna: 300/350

Stamina: N/A

Feats: Orcish Tenacity, Skeletal Body, Barbarism, Fleshless

Skills:

Short Blades LVL 20

Unarmed Combat LVL 8

Great-Weapon Wielding LVL 36

Death Magic LVL 10

Soul Magic LVL 25

Resistances: Death Magic 25%, Soul Magic 25%, Piercing Damage 50%, Slashing Damage 50%, Fire -50%, Blunt Damage -50%

Languages: Common, Orcish

This orc died inside the Catacombs of Eternal Servitude and has been enspelled to become a guardian of its tomb. As an undead skeleton, it is immune to stamina defects. If proper damage is done to the skull or if the head is separated from the body, immediate death will come.

Crap! Grim thought. The thing was level 15, the highest level creature they had fought together by far. Also, the slashing damage resistance was a real bummer. He wished he had a mace. Gulag then pushed Grim back with great force and swung its axe. Grim fell to the ground to dodge the swing, then swung his greatsword at Gulag's exposed abdomen. He felt a distinct resistance from the bones against his weapon. He turned back to face his foe, but he wasn't quick enough. Gulag had already swung the enchanted axe at Grim with an underhand swing, using the weapon's momentum to reposition. The axe connected clean against Grim's chestplate, cutting a definite groove in his armor and sending him flying through the air.

"Ooof!" Grim said as he landed on the other side of the chamber.

After gaining some distance, albeit unintentionally, from Gulag, Grim spared a moment to see how his companions were doing. He saw Lukav gracefully dodge the attacks from the two melee fighters moving fluidly toward the archer. Before the undead could shoot the monk, Xumi struck it in the chest with an arrow, disorienting it. Lukav took advantage of that. In one motion, he sliced his enchanted claws across the archer's throat, quickly wrapped his large hand around the injured throat, and squeezed. The undead archer was too slow to react before the vertebrae in its neck gave way with an audible crack, followed by it turning to dust. Grim heard a roar coming from another direction and turned to see Gulag jumping in the air with his large axe overhead, aiming directly for him.

"Oh, shit!" Grim yelled as he narrowly rolled out of the way. He got back up and swung his greatsword but was not a match for Gulag's strength.

The skeleton blocked his swing and knocked the weapon out of Grim's hands, disarming him. It then proceeded with a downward chop that Grim dodged. Backing up from the barbarian, Grim conjured a Death Orb in each hand. He felt the familiar sensation of Death Magic coalesce into spheres in each hand. Gulag faced Grim just as he threw the orbs. They connected, and Grim could see the white bones crack and give way slightly. It seemed to damage Gulag but not that much. The undead being stomped toward Grim. Grim kept backing up and launching Death Orbs at Gulag, trying to keep his distance. The skeleton did not even bother to dodge the attacks, taking them one after the other as it quickly made it to Grim, grabbed him by the throat, and lifted him up in the air.

"It will take a lot more than that to truly harm me!" the skeleton yelled at Grim.

Deprived of oxygen, Grim was trying to keep focus. He saw Gulag's eyes flash with intensity as a purple aura surrounded the barbarian, then him. Immediately he began to feel weaker as if the strength was leaving his body. He noticed the wounds and marks of decay on the skeleton had begun to repair and be healed.

He's sucking out my health! Grim thought. He looked to see his health bar declining quickly.

A voice rang in his head. *"Master! Use me!"* Manny pleaded.

Feeling like an idiot for not using his familiar earlier, Grim desperately grabbed his dagger from its sheath and used the pommel to hit Gulag in the face. The skeleton's weakness to blunt damage showed itself as Gulag let go of Grim and took a few steps back, cradling its face. Gulag removed its hand and growled at Grim, revealing that the section of bone that was hit had broken off.

"Say hello to my little friend!" Grim yelled in his best Pacino accent while throwing Manny in his dagger form.

Gulag positioned its greataxe to block the weapon, but Grim mentally triggered his familiar to change midflight, which changed the momentum and path. The manticore attack surprised the skeleton and occupied its attention. With the surge of adrenaline spent, Grim collapsed to his knees, exhausted. He

217

saw that his health, manna, and stamina were all around 25%. Suddenly, he felt what seemed to be small cube hit his chest at high velocity. After his initial surprise, he realized there was no weapon sticking in him and he didn't feel any pain from the strike. In fact, he felt rejuvenated! Grim looked to see his status bars refilling at a faster rate, then felt a comforting hand on his shoulder. He looked up to see Xumi smiling down at him. A streak of blood was across the left side of her head.

"Thanks for keeping it busy. You bought us enough time to finish the other two," she said.

Grim sighed with relief and looked back at the skeleton. Both Lukav and Manny had successfully drawn aggro from the barbarian, buying Grim some reprieve, but he could tell that it wouldn't last long. Gulag was just too strong for the duo.

Xumi noticed it too. "What do we do? You were busy fighting it. Did you find a weakness?" she asked

"Blunt damage and magic," Grim replied. "I don't think we're strong enough to outlast it, though, with the minimal damage we're doing. My Death Orb worked. If only I could make it into a spear, but my Manna Manipulation…" He thought for a moment. "I have an idea! Help Lukav and Manny! I need some time."

"This better work!" Xumi answered as she ran off to help the others.

Grim realized he hadn't allocated his stat or level points yet, and they might be the key to winning. He quickly opened his interface and allotted his two unused level points into Manna Manipulation, twenty points into Manna, and all ten of the unused stat points to Mind. Instantly, he felt more magically aware, intuitive, and confident.

"Part one done. Now for part two," Grim said as he conjured a Death Orb. Once it appeared in his hands, he began pressing it down like dough as he had seen Xumi do.

"Grim! Hurry!" Lukav yelled. The orc had been doing his best to dodge Gulag's strikes while Xumi and Manny harassed the skeleton from other directions. Gulag, though, was getting annoyed. Worse, it was becoming enraged. Suddenly, it let out a roar, stunning the three near him and surrounding itself with a red aura. With a new burst of speed, the barbarian spun and clipped Manny with its axe. The skeleton continued its spin and Spartan-kicked Lukav into Xumi, knocking them prone on the ground. Grim was intensely focusing on getting the orb to change. Still not getting much headway, he added a little extra manna to the construct and felt it give way.

"Do you think you can stop me with your petty magic and *our* monk training!? I was raised with it!" Gulag spat at the orcs. It raised its axe, about to cleave the monk and archer.

"Hey, asshole!" Grim yelled.

The skeleton turned its head just in time to see Grim launch a spear of Death Magic at it. The spell quickly soared through the air and connected, the force launching Gulag into the stone wall of the chamber and buying enough time for the rest of the party to get behind Grim.

He groaned as a headache from the rapid depletion of manna set in. "Errh! You two heal up. Manny and I got this," Grim said after his familiar hopped on his right shoulder. He grabbed his greatsword off the ground and charged at the recently stunned skeleton, red aura still around it, hoping to finish it off before it could recover.

"Sonic screech!" Grim mentally commanded.

The manticore flew off his master's shoulder and released a high-pitch screech aimed toward Gulag. The severely injured skeleton did not appear fazed and slashed its weapon at the familiar, bringing him to zero HP. Manny changed back into a dagger and dropped to the ground. Gulag caught Grim's arm midswing with its hand, stopping the blade.

Oh, crap! Grim thought as the red aura intensified.

Glowing red runes highlighted Gulag's bones as it activated the Barbarian talent Fury. It pushed Grim to the ground and relentlessly hacked at the Progenitor repeatedly. Grim's world became full of blood and pain. He could feel the greataxe piercing his armor and thick skin and reaching all the way to his internal organs. He screamed in pain. Grim coughed up some blood and could only curl up in the fetal position as he was overwhelmed. Strangely, he felt a moment of relief as his Death Ward activated and stabilized him. The relief was short-lived, though, as Gulag chopped once more at his abdomen while attempting to cleave him in two. His moment of pain once again gave way as his Ring of Death's Protection activated and restabilized him. It was all too much for him to take, and he was about to pass out when he saw Lukav jump through the air.

"Nooo!" the orc yelled as he rushed at Gulag.

The monk's right arm glowed purple as he somehow punched Gulag right in the jaw. There was a loud crack as he connected with his target. The lower jaw completely separated from its body, and the skeleton fell face down to the ground, stunned.

Grim felt his head lifted up and tasted something minty as Xumi helping him chew a healing herb.

Gulag tried to get back up but Lukav put his foot on its neck, stopping it.

"Grraa!" Gulag moaned against the stone floor.

Lukav looked at him with anger for hurting his friend. "You're done," the orc said coldly before curb-stomping the skeleton and shattering its skull. The rest of the skeleton appeared to crumble away, all except for a few bones. Lukav ran over to Grim. "Are you okay, brah?"

"I got the piss beaten out of me, but yeah, we won! That was awesome, dude! Xumi, you have one bad-ass lover!" Grim said after he drank one of the healing potions, then he winked at Lukav. While Grim wasn't always smooth with the ladies, he was a pretty confident wingman.

"I know," Xumi answered and smiled at the monk.

Lukav blushed and looked away nervously.

A notification appeared.

> Congratulations!
> You have defeated LVL 14 Barbarian: Gulag the Ghul
>
> Reward:
>
> +340 EXP
> Living Runic Inscription

"Runic Inscription? What is that?" Grim said aloud.

"I'm not sure," Xumi answered while reading the same notification in her vision.

A voice from behind them said, "Thank you."

All three of the group quickly turned around, ready for a fight, but there was no undead in front of them. Instead, it was Gulag! The orc was no longer a skeleton but a glowing spirit with a completely restored body. He did not appear hostile anymore either. In fact, the dead chief looked happy. "You have restored my spirit, and you must restore our clan. Now for your reward." The chief stuck out his left hand and three beams of white light shot out. Each one struck the group in the chest too quickly for them to respond.

Grim felt a surge of warm energy wash over him. It felt good, really good. The warmth sank all the way into his body, and he could feel it sink into his very soul.

> Gulag has cast Restore Allies on you.
> Health Restored to 100%!

Then there was a sharp pain in his right arm. It felt like someone chiseling into his humerus! After a minute, the pain left, and he felt knowledge and ability rush through him. His muscles had grown. He had become...more! Once the white glow disappeared, notifications filled Grim's vision.

> Hidden Quest Complete! Wisdom of a Lost Leader I
> You have found Gulag's remains and
> gained the skill Runesmithing.
>
> Reward:
>
> Runesmithing Skill
> 10,000 EXP
> Gulag's Remains

> A New Quest
> You have been inscribed with Kahn
> the Living Strength Rune!
>
> Reward:
> +5 Strength

Can wield two-handed weapons with
one hand without a penalty

Congratulations! You have learned the skill Runesmithing!
Requirements: Soul Magic + Inscription of a Living Rune

Congratulations! You used your wits and abilities to best a superior foe! You also withstood extreme pain and injury without succumbing to your wounds.

Heavy Armor +5

Great-Weapon Wielding +1

Short Blades +1

+1 Vitality

+1 Mind

Death Magic +5

A New Spell

Congratulations! Your ability to manipulate manna
has given you the ability to conjure a new spell!

You have learned Death Spear. Cast a spear of concentrated Death Magic at your enemies that will do +100 base Death damage. As you level up, benefits and improvements will come.

Cost: 70 manna

Duration: Detonate on impact

Cast Time: 3 seconds

Range: Up to 30 feet

Cooldown: 1 minute

Level Up! You have acquired enough EXP to reach LVL 6!

5 Stat Points +1 Level Point +10 Health, Manna,
or Stamina are available to distribute

Do you wish to distribute them now?

Yes or No

Congratulations! Heavy Armor skill reached Initiate LVL 10!

+25% Armor Bonus when wearing only Heavy Armor

-25% Movement Penalty when wearing Heavy Armor

+1 Strength

Quest Unlocked! Wisdom of a Lost Leader II

Gulag, the last chief of the Blood-Shield Clan with the Runesmithing skill, was mortally wounded in an attack by a golden wyvern while hunting. His party managed to escape but were ambushed by gnolls of the Cracked Tooth Tribe on their trek back. Before he could be killed by the wicked creatures, his allies sacrificed themselves and pushed him into their tomb nearby to protect his sacred knowledge. When he died inside, the Catacombs of Eternal Servitude's enchantment made him an undead guardian, preventing him from helping his people. Will you clear his name and avenge his and his peoples' deaths?

Requirements:

Kill the Golden Wyvern that attacked Gulag's hunting party or find evidence of its death

End the war between the Blood-Shield Clan and the Cracked Tooth Tribe

Inform the Blood-Shield Clan of Gulag's fate

Reward:

100,000 EXP
Unknown

Do you accept?
Yes or No

"Wow," Grim said. "Did you get all those messages?"

Lukav and Xumi acknowledged that they had received similar messages too. The two orcs were recipients of different living runes, and Lukav did not learn Runesmithing as he did not know Soul Magic. They also figured out that living runes actually enchant the person rather than an object.

Grim examined his body and marveled in amazement. Zordell had already granted him a very admirable body, but now he was massive! He could rival some body builders he had seen on TV! He was also pretty sure some of his clothes had ripped as his armor definitely felt more snug. His left upper shoulder was covered with the complicated living rune. What was also exciting was that even though his armor was notably tighter on his body owing to his increased mass, his armor actually felt lighter! He reasoned his Heavy Armor skill reaching Initiate Rank had something to do with that. After some of the wonder and excitement had settled down, they looked around and realized that the spirit of Gulag had disappeared while his equipment remained.

"How do we know what these do?" Grim asked. When he had seen enchanted items before, usually someone else willed the information to him.

"When you fully know your item's capabilities, you can share that information with anyone touching it," Xumi said. "If you don't, though, there are spells and items that you can use instead." The orc hunter started saying some words of power and did some intricate hand signs.

Grim soon realized she was doing an identify spell.

You have found Ring of Manna!

Durability: 9/10

Weight: 0.1 kg

Rarity: Uncommon

Quality: Above Average

Properties: +25 to total Manna

You have found Ring of Speed!

Durability: 10/10

Weight: 0.1 kg

Rarity: Uncommon

Quality: Above Average

Properties: +5 Agility

You have found Ring of Retribution!

Durability: 8/20

Weight: 0.1 kg

Rarity: Fabled

Quality: Excellent

Properties: Infused with the blood of a goblin witch doctor. It will mimic the largest amount of damage you receive in one attack and return it back as a surge of infernal force once every 24 hours.

You have found Kilt of the Ghul!

Durability: 10/12

Weight: 0.1 kg

Rarity: Exceptional

Quality: Great

Type: Light Armor

Properties: +5 Vitality, +2 Damage to all melee attacks

You have found Ring of Health!

Durability: 10/10

Weight: 0.1 kg

Rarity: Uncommon

Quality: Above Average

Properties: +20 Health

You have found Blood-Shield Greataxe of Leeching!

Damage: +25-34

Durability: 80/100

Weight: 10 kg

Rarity: Exceptional

Quality: Great

Properties: Wielder absorbs 5 HP from every hit

Requirement: 20 Strength

You have found Tome of Domination!

Durability: 11/12

Weight: 1 kg

Rarity: Rare

Quality: Fine
Properties: Contains the spell Dominate.

Dominate: Channel manna to literally kill the will of your target for 5 hours. Target must have a lower overall Intelligence & Mind sum than you. Any living beings affected by this spell will have their intelligence decrease by 1 every hour while under control. Once it reaches 0, the affected will devolve to become uncontrollable berserkers. Every time the spell is recast on a subject, they gain a 2x resistance. Can only be dispelled by caster or caster's death.

Maximum Number that can be dominated:
(Intelligence+Mind+Death Magic
LVL)/2 Current Maximum=19

Requirements: Death Magic LVL 15,
Mind LVL 25, Intelligence LVL 15

Cost: 40 manna

Duration: Permanent

Cast Time: 1 second

Range: Touch

Cooldown: 3 seconds

You have found Tome of Absorption!

Durability: 12/12

Weight: 1.1 kg

Rarity: Rare

Quality: Fine

Properties: Contains the spell Absorb

Absorb: Drain the Health of a target you touch at a rate of your Death Magic Level/2 every 2 seconds. Can be continuously cast.

Requirements: Death Magic LVL 2, Intelligence LVL 12

Cost: 5 manna/sec

Duration: 1 second

Cast Time: 1 second

Range: Touch

Cooldown: None

You have found Tome of Heal Allies!

Durability: 12/13

Weight: 1 kg

Rarity: Rare

Quality: Fine

Properties: Contains the spell Heal Allies.

Heal Allies: Use Soul Magic to heal all allies within a 20-meter circumference by 15 HP. Only will work on who the caster deems an ally & does not heal the caster.

Requirements: Soul Magic LVL 4,
Intelligence LVL 16

Cost: 20 manna

Duration: Permanent

Cast Time: 1 second

Range: 20 meters

Cooldown: 5 seconds

The Ring of Speed and kilt went to Lukav. Xumi received the Rings of Health and Manna, while Grim received the Ring of Retribution, which seemed useful but also something to be cautious of. He also received the Tome of Absorption and

Domination since he was the main Death Magic user, and he was pumped about that. What was also cool was that his Progenitor status automatically qualified him to learn the spells even though he didn't have the requirements! Something was bothering him though.

"For every skill rank you go up, like from Novice to Initiate, do you gain special bonuses?" he asked.

"Yes," Lukav replied. "I remember reaching level ten in Metal Cleaning and receiving a +25% bonus to cleaning speed."

Grim nodded thanks to his friend for the info. That provided a special incentive to level up his skills.

The Tome of Heal Allies brought some internal conflict for Grim. If he was being honest, he wanted to keep it for himself. Having a healing spell could be a crutch, but seeing as his Soul Magic level was only at one, he reasoned that Xumi would be the best choice. They needed every advantage they could get if they were going to save the clan. Despite the rough start, Grim had grown close to them and kind of felt like they were the family he'd never had. Thinking of gaining advantages, Grim had an idea.

"What if I could teach you Death Magic?" he asked Xumi.

She sharply looked back at him. "You are an associate or higher level mage?" she asked with obvious doubt.

"Well, if you don't believe me, look at Lukav. I awakened Death Magic inside him. Isn't that right, buddy?" he called over to his friend.

"He is right, Xumi. He can," Lukav said as he conjured a Death Orb.

The archer watched in shock. "Really? Can you?" she asked Grim in awe.

He nodded. "I'll make you a deal. If you promise to serve

230

me and have a high enough Affinity, I will awaken Death Magic in you. If it's not high enough, I guarantee I can still make you stronger. We need every advantage we can get if we want to save the clan." *This could be a win-win!* he thought. Even if Xumi could not become a Greater Vassal, giving her at least some resistance to Death Magic could provide an advantage in the fight to come.

Xumi looked apprehensive at the request, then shrugged her resolve. "You have shown honor and truth, and I trust you. If you promise to help me save my clan, then I will follow you." She then took a knee. "I, Xumi of the Blood-Shield Clan, pledge my fealty in service to you, Grim. In life and in death, for now and always."

A notification appeared in his vision.

Xumi the orc has pledged her service to you and your deity. As a Progenitor you may accept this offer or reject it.

Do you accept?

Yes or No

"I accept your pledge," Grim said.

As with Lukav, he glowed purple as a small thread-sized stream of purple magic reached out from his chest and touched Xumi, causing her to glow purple too. Momentarily, the glows and the thread of magic disappeared.

A new notification took up Grim's vision.

Devotion I

Current follower status (2/50)

Would you like to make this follower

> a Greater Vassal?
> Yes or No
>
> Note: Your follower must undergo an awakening of Death Magic in order to become a Greater Vassal.

Grim mentally selected yes, then thought of what he wanted to say before the ritual words. "The sharp-witted Xumi, become more." His hand shot out toward Xumi with the palm facing her. It pressed against her upper chest where the clavicles met the sternum. The Death Magic inside Grim extended out, searching for purchase. Unfortunately, her Affinity wasn't high enough, and he was unable to awaken a reservoir.

"I'm sorry, Xumi," Grim apologized.

"It is alright," she said, not seeming bothered. "It is very rare for an orc to be able to use magic at all. So, I am grateful for my ability as it is. Plus, I did get 5% resistance in Death Magic!" she replied.

Grim smiled, then went to assess the other items left over and check his status. He thought it would be best to let Xumi and Lukav have some time alone, and he wasn't a fan of being a third wheel.

CHAPTER 20
RUNESMITHING

GRIM TOOK OFF HIS ARMOR and found that Gulag had done a number on it. The durability on each piece had been reduced by at least 45% and there were some large gashes in his chestplate. Grim equipped himself with the rusted bronze buckler. It wasn't the best, but it was better than nothing. His Augment Shield Bash too could come in handy. Grim also noticed that his Commerce skill had increased a level. He stored his greatsword in the pouch of holding along with the two iron daggers and bronze cutlass loot from the undead. He found Manny on the ground and tried to mentally communicate with his familiar, but he did not get a response. Grim reasoned that he wouldn't get one for another day, remembering his notification about when Manny's HP goes to 0 he would revert to his dagger form and be unable to communicate for twenty-four hours.

Grim was checking his boots when he saw a crude, incomplete carving of the rune he'd seen in Zordell's tunnel. When he looked at it, it was much more rewarding than last time.

> You have discovered Mei the Slow Rune!
>
> Effect: 15% Chance to Decrease Target's Speed

Whaaatttt????!!!! he thought. Apparently, his crude carving was good enough to write a rune. He had the rune the whole time, but the only way he could have learned it was through the Runesmithing skill.

He showed Xumi the rune, which gave her the knowledge of it too. He then decided to read the tomes to gain his new spells. When he opened the first book, a notification appeared in his interface asking if he wanted to learn the spell. When he selected yes, the book floated out of his hands. Grim's eyes locked onto the book, and he couldn't look away if he wanted to. One page turned, then another, then another, then the pages turned faster and faster until it was a blur. When the tome was at its end, it crumbled to dust. Grim felt a pulse of magic surge through his body as a notification appeared.

> Congratulations! You have learned the spell Absorb!

Grim and Xumi repeated the process, both learning their spells successfully. Afterward, they frantically examined all the other rune-crafted items they had. Unfortunately, they kept getting notified that their skill level was too low to comprehend them. They kept the items, as they were extremely useful and they would at some point presumably reach the needed skill level. Once the group had recovered enough, they decided to leave the tomb. They opened a stone door to a whoosh of fresh air entering the chamber. They were at the side of a mountain, under a late afternoon sky. The door behind them had Orcish

234

carved into it, so they felt like they could find it later, but stacked some rocks by it just in case.

They were in a heavily forested area that sloped down. Before they left the tomb, a basic game plan was formed.

Step 1: Find out where exactly they were.

Step 2: Find out what had happened to the clan.

Step 3: Save the clan.

Grim would admit that it was easier said than done, and a lot of details were missing, but whatever. He had grown up an AmeriCAN, not an AmeriCAN'T. They would figure it out. The trio went down the hill until they reached a clearing and a big icy lake. Almost all around it the land sloped upward, giving clear indication it was a crater that had filled up. The only exception was a large strip of grassland interspersed with trees and bushes to the left of the lake. About 150 to 200 yards ahead of them was a large peninsula jutting up at an angle around fifty feet tall that almost separated the lake in two. A distinct tall, thin area of water falling off one of the tall cliff faces behind the peninsula glittered in the afternoon sun.

"I know where we are," Xumi said. "We are about a day's walk north of the clan. Mother has brought me hunting here a few times. I can't believe we missed the catacombs' entrance before now! Well, forward always, that is what Father would say."

"I heard Scar say the same thing," Grim said. "What does that mean exactly?"

"It is the mantra of the clan," Lukav answered. "In life, you must always go forward no matter what. There is no way to advance by standing still. That is why I snuck out before," he admitted as an afterthought.

"I like it." Grim smiled. "Well, let's make camp here tonight. That way we can hunt for food, have a fire, practice our skills, and prepare to scout and hopefully save the clan tomorrow. We will wait for Manny, as he can fly and scout the area for us." He didn't want to admit it, but he was getting hungry. He needed meat.

Fortunately, Xumi was a skilled hunter. She expediently found a rabbit and two squirrels for the trio to eat. Once they had cooked and eaten, Grim felt a pang of guilt. He realized that while being living-dead had a lot of benefits, such as decreased sleep and food requirements, there were also some real drawbacks. Becoming a savage, flesh-eating monster just because he couldn't have some regularly available meat was a real minus. He did not want to scare or harm his friends and was concerned that he may have had he not been fed.

"Um, I need to explain something," Grim said uncomfortably. He then began to explain to the two about his living-dead status and its benefits and disadvantages. "I'm sorry. I know nothing happened, but I wanted you to know that I'm not like a normal human. If my body ever lacks sustenance for too long, I'm concerned I could attack you," he said sincerely.

The two orcs nodded in understanding, not seeming too bothered by their leader's status.

"So that's why your skin is like snow! I should have examined your status more carefully!" Lukav blurted out in his usually enthusiastic way.

"Yeah, I guess being a creature of death might require me to be ghostly pale. Anyway…" Grim said. "While we're waiting for Manny to come back, we'll gather our resources and train." His gamer experience was allowing him to take control of the situation. "Xumi, you and I will practice enchanting and our magic. If we can free the villagers and equip them with

236

enchanted weapons, we may stand a chance. Lukav, practice your techniques and keep an eye out for gnolls."

The trio agreed, then began practicing.

Grim learned that the living rune Xumi was inscribed with gave a 15% bonus to all enchantments, so he had her practice solely on enchantments and teach him what she learned afterward. He practiced his Soul Magic, which he desperately needed to work on. With his improved Manna Manipulation skill, he thought it would make his work easier. At one point he contemplated having the group hide in the tomb, but then decided not to. He didn't want them to end up like Gulag.

The night passed by uneventfully. Concern for the village caused all of them not to sleep well, though, so they used their time to make notable headway in their skills.

Xumi had enchanted all her arrows, four daggers, and the rusty cutlass with the Meí rune, increasing her Runesmithing skill two times that night. She also taught Grim how to do it with his greatsword. It was quite complex. Whenever he wanted to enchant something, a screen would appear on his interface. Each weapon had a certain number of rune slots. All he needed to do was use a rune schematic he knew on the screen, and it would show him the effect. Once that was done, he just needed to carve it into an item and channel Soul Magic into it.

> Congratulations! You have enchanted
> Iron Greatsword of Slowing!
> Damage: +20-25
> Durability: 19/25
> Rarity: Common
> Quality: Above Average
> Weight: 3kg

Properties: 15% chance will slow target by 5%
for every successful hit for 15 seconds

"Awesome!" Grim exclaimed.

He had also managed to learn how to create a Soul Spear. The process was much like how he had discovered his Death Spear spell.

Lukav mainly meditated, and at some point during the night, enthusiastically informed the group that he had leveled his Channeling skill twice. In the daytime, to break the monotony and tension of waiting for Manny to come back, Lukav and Grim had a light sparring session.

Grim thought it would be nice to see how well he could do against the orc now in a fistfight. Seeing how Lukav's speed was more than double Grim's, he didn't stand a chance. By the end of the session, Grim had to go rest his ass after it had been thoroughly whooped. He decided to take a nap, but before that, he invested three points into Strength and the other two into Agility. He wanted to use his new greataxe, and his Agility stat sorely needed some investing. He also allocated ten points in Stamina and a level point into Death Magic, as that was the closest skill he had to reaching level ten. Feeling a little less exhausted, Grim fell asleep.

Grim heard a deep, low voice in his head. He couldn't make out what it was saying, but then it got louder. He jerked awake when Manny was almost yelling inside his head.

"Master! Master, are you hurt? What happened?" Manny projected.

"Hey, hey, hey! It's okay, buddy. We're alright. We won," he thought groggily to his familiar while looking down at his sheathed dagger.

Manny's red eye had returned to replace the jewel.

238

"How are you feeling?" Grim asked.

"I-I am angry! No one should harm you! I want to tear that thing limb from limb!" he said viciously.

"Settle down, buddy. It's okay," Grim thought soothingly. *"The bad guy's dead. I actually have a new job for you."*

"Do I get to kill something else?" Manny asked excitedly.

"Noooo," Grim thought back, put off by his familiar's bloodlust. He then relayed the plan to Manny, who readily agreed to help his master.

The group began their trek to scout the Blood-Shield Village. There was not much snow left on the ground, as it seemed that spring had just hit the area. Grim reasoned that he'd arrived in the Ashen Plane at the end of winter and, after only being there for ten days, there was already a change in seasons. With Xumi leading the way on foot and Manny scouting from the sky, the group was able to make good headway toward the village. A couple of times, Manny steered them clear of some deadly animals. Grim was able to increase both his Stealth and Tracking skills by +1. They made it to the edge of the village's domain by early afternoon.

They were at the edge of the small rocky hill overlooking the village, on some small raised ledges that stair-stepped down to the flat ground. There was a foul odor in the air, and the group quickly found the cause. Behind them, down a ledge, was a giant rotting creature leaning against the stone. Curious, they backtracked to inspect it. An ogre, the dead body had gray skin and many open, rotting wounds. There was a wooden spear jutting out of its round, distended abdomen. Flies surrounded it, and one eye was missing. Grim estimated the creature to be at least ten feet tall with a bald head, uneven stubbly sideburns, and a strong underbite. It wore no items except a loincloth.

There were three dead gnolls flanking it. One was half-crushed under the dead giant's body and the other beneath a giant wooden club bigger than Grim was tall. The odor was so strong that none of the group dared get too close.

Grim's familiar, conveniently of its own volition, decided to fly around and check out the village and surrounding area for them. The small manticore returned after less than fifteen minutes, his eager tone replaced with an uneasy one.

"What did you find?" Grim asked.

"It is…not good, master." The slime creature then relayed what he saw, and Grim interpreted it for the other two.

All in all, there were around forty gnolls still inside the camp. They had made two wooden watchtowers. Torril and Borril watched the prisoners and the village's entrance respectively. The creatures were using the orcs as slave labor to build some sort of demonic altar that was already littered with the corpses of dead gnolls and orcs alike. Potor and a larger gnoll were at the altar. The larger gnoll was female, with large scars across both sides of her face as if she were clawed by an animal. She stood slightly hunched over, wearing purple tattered robes with ornate patterns. Her mouth was in a constant snarl as she was missing a chunk of her upper lip. Her right ear had a multitude of piercings, but her left outer ear seemed to be completely missing. She was moving her hands in complicated patterns and chanting rhythmically. The two were surrounded by almost all the gnolls with their heads bowed and their hands waving around in some sort of ritual. There was a cage by the ramp going to Thrain's cave where they were keeping prisoners. Also, two figures were tied up to poles near but separate from the other prisoners. They looked bloody and beaten. One of the tied figures looked like Thrain while the other, surprisingly, resembled an ogre. Possibly, it could have been the dead one's ally that they discovered earlier. The only way in or out of the village now was from the side of the stone wall damaged by Potor's spell when they invaded. The information that made the group's blood boil was that the gnolls had obviously been eating the prisoners as evidenced by the bodily remains scattered throughout the village. Heads and strewn intestines of both orcs and gnolls were impaled on pikes by the entrance to the village. Apparently, feeding them the prisoners was how the traitorous shaman had been keeping them in check.

"What do you think?" Lukav asked the group.

"I'm not sure. Their numbers are too great. We're going to have to use stealth to get in," Xumi replied.

After some pondering, Grim had an idea. "I don't think stealth will do. I'm too bulky and not that good at using it. Their main strength is that they have significant numbers on us, but I have a plan."

A bloodthirsty grin crossed Grim's face as the purple light of Death Magic began to emit from his left hand.

CHAPTER 21

ARMY

THE GNOLLS WERE ANGRILY CHASING the little green creature who attacked them. Their queen's new mate, who gave them so much fresh meat, had told them to protect the camp from any aggressive creatures. And anything they killed, they could eat. What they couldn't understand though, was why their weapons weren't working. They just seemed to pass right through the annoying thing. Once they chased it deep enough into the woods, it had finally become cornered. The patrol's leader told his comrades to attack the creature, but nothing happened. When he turned back, he saw that his group was gone. The last thing he saw when he turned back was a glowing purple hand grabbing his face.

"Well, that was awesome!" Grim said to Lukav and Xumi.

Their plan had gone off without a hitch. They'd used Manny to bait the gnolls to a rocky dead-end deep in the woods, where they could ambush them. At that point, all they needed to do was distract them long enough for Grim to touch their heads and use Dominate. It was strange at first, but the process went quickly as he sent a pulse of magic into their minds. With the newly dominated servants, Grim's troop numbers went from four to seven in under a minute.

He looked at his new servants. Each had blood spatter around their mouths and stood obediently waiting for orders. If Grim focused hard enough, he could see a faint purple flicker in their eyes.

"Can you understand what I'm saying?" Grim asked them.

All three of them nodded.

"Good," he said. "Okay. I want you to return back to the camp and bring more of your allies back here. Don't tell them about us. Tell them there is a green creature that you could not kill. See if you can get one of the orcs to come too. Once you get them to this rocky corner, attack them."

At that last statement, the gnolls revealed maniacal smiles.

Grim didn't know how they did it, but after around ten minutes, the dominated gnolls were actually able to not only lure three others of their kind, but Borril as well! The orc appeared more annoyed rather than actually interested in killing something, which could not be said of the other gnolls, who were all drooling and laughing with that distinct hyena laugh. The group noticed that Borril looked different than when they last had seen him. He was adorned in thick leather armor that covered most of his body instead of just the greaves he'd had before. Xumi had to forcibly calm herself when she saw that the traitor was wearing a helmet with Scar's decapitated head on top.

"Where are we going?" the brute demanded from the group.

The gnolls chattered quickly in their own tongue, then one of Grim's dominated creatures looked back to the orc. He communicated in broken Common, "Creature...hee hee hee... Green...kill!"

Borril grunted, "Stupid creatures."

The group of seven proceeded down to the trap. The three dominated gnolls were in front of the other three, with Borril taking the rear, making a 3-3-1 formation. The dead end they were heading toward was really a shallow fjord formed from the two small mountains intersecting each other. Grim, Xumi, and Lukav were hiding behind some thick trees, making sure to be downwind of their targets. Manny waited, making sure to draw the others in.

Once the group made it into the trap, Manny let out a small roar. It was rather intimidating, like a full-grown lion, despite the manticore's size. The gnolls howled in ecstasy, thrilled at finding their prey.

Before they attacked, Borril barreled his way through the group to get a better look at their quarry. "This! This is the creature you could not kill?" the orc asked as he turned back to mock his troops.

His musings were interrupted by two figures descending upon him from above.

Borril tried to swing his mace reactively at one of them, but his forearm was shot by an arrow that changed his swing's trajectory and made him miss. He was quickly put in a sleeper hold. The arm against his neck was rough and dug into the flesh of his neck.

The brute seemed to realize he was stronger than the individual holding him and was about to break the hold, but he had not paid attention to the other figure who had landed in front of him. The figure swiftly kicked him in the crotch, causing him to moan loudly and become stunned. When Borril looked up, a glowing purple hand grabbed his head, and his will was no longer his own.

Grim quickly left his newly dominated puppet to help the others. His three gnolls had attacked the others as soon as he and Lukav jumped down on Borril. Fortunately, Xumi was raining arrows down on them too. With their combined efforts, Grim's group was able to subdue and dominate their opponents. They were now a combined force of ten. They had to kill one of them, unfortunately, because Grim's total manna was not sufficient enough to perform the spell four times in rapid succession. He needed to invest some of his stat points in Intelligence. On the bright side, they were able to get control of someone they could finally understand. Now fully submissive, Borril and the nine gnolls stopped fighting and focused on their new master.

Grim decided to get some information. "How many are inside the camp?" he asked.

"Not sure," Borril replied. "Maybe forty gnolls outside of the ones here. I do not know how many prisoners we have left, but they have been subdued."

"Are there any others?" Grim asked.

"We always have two patrols of three out at a time. They will all come back in at dusk."

"Where are Potor and Torril?" Xumi interrupted, barely able to contain her anger.

"Torril is keeping guard on the prisoners. Potor is with our new queen. They will be performing the ritual soon," he said.

"Ritual? What ritual?" Grim asked.

Borril began explaining that Potor's father had been Thrain's rival for chief but was killed by humans before he could fight for his spot. Since then, Potor had been focused on becoming

245

the chief and avenging his father's death. When Thrain kicked him out of the clan, he was desperate. The shaman wanted revenge. If Potor couldn't lead the clan, he would find a new one and kill all humans and enemies alike. So, he'd made a deal with the gnoll queen to defeat the Blood-Shield Clan in exchange for the demonic power she possessed.

Lukav, Xumi, and Grim looked at each other, eyes bulging in shock.

"Oh, crap! How long does the ritual take?" Grim asked with dread.

"Potor told me a couple of hours," Borril replied. "It is about halfway through, currently."

Grim turned back to his friends. "Okay, I had planned on thinning out their numbers slowly and then infiltrating their camp. With whatever Potor is doing, though, I suggest we stop it as soon as we can."

"How do you suggest we do that?" Lukav asked. "Even though we're stronger, I do not think we can handle forty gnolls on our own."

"You're right," Grim replied. "We need to find a way to take as many out as we can at one time. Any ideas?"

There was a pause until Lukav had an idea. "The opal!"

CHAPTER 22

COUNTERSTRIKE

POTOR GRUNTED AND PACED, IRRITATED. The queen was chanting while the rest of the gnolls smacked their spears and chanted in unison. When she'd promised him the power of a demon, she hadn't told him it would require building an altar and take days. He was ready to become stronger and kill that disgusting human and his weakling friends. He looked around impatiently.

There was a strange-looking gnoll hobbling toward them from a distance. Even though it was not close, Potor could see flies around it, a partially crushed-in skull, and what looked to be rotting flesh. The creature was carrying a tiny crude club with some sort of gem on it. When the hobbling gnoll started walking past the chanting ones, they stopped and looks of disgust on their face showed they were put off by its odor. The fly-covered creature pressed on, uninhibited by the others. Surprisingly, when one of the elite gnolls tried to stop it from approaching the altar, it gained a quick burst of speed. The creature swiftly approached the altar, swung its club, then BOOM!

"Yes!" Grim shouted. His plan had worked!

When Lukav had mentioned the opal, Grim realized they could use it to take out many of the group at once, as they had done with the undead. First, he decided to resurrect the ogre and two of the dead gnolls to use as kamikaze soldiers. Then, he set the opal on one of the undead gnoll's clubs and told it to go swing at the altar. Fortunately, Lukav gave him the foresight to also make the caveat that if anyone tried to stop it, to run straight at the altar as quickly as possible.

"Charge!" Grim yelled as he and his troops sprinted toward the injured gnolls.

It was time for the second part of his plan. Kill the motherfuckers while they were down! The ogre, being the largest, easily charged to the head of the group. Multiple thrum sounds rang through the air. Grim looked up to see that multiple arrows had pierced the undead behemoth.

"Ogre, take out the tower on the left! Manny, you and two of the gnolls kill archers on the right!" Grim commanded.

Quickly, his troops veered off in compliance.

In less than a minute, Grim and his five followers attacked the hurt and recovering gnolls. Smoke and dust in the air accompanied a few small fires. The gnolls' disorientation and damage served to the attackers' advantage as a few of them were swiftly killed in the first volley. The enchanted weapons also helped damaging and slowing them. Borril was busy keeping his brother preoccupied in combat. Grim fought with his greatsword in one hand and the greataxe in the other. His living rune was already proving its worth as he easily cut down his opponents. His newfound strength and reduction in his movement penalty when wearing heavy armor was very evident as well.

The sound of wood crashing rang out. Grim turned his head to see the undead ogre clotheslining the wooden beams of the archer tower, causing it to fall. He then received a mental projection from Manny that they had killed the archers in the right tower and were now shooting at the other gnolls. Borril had also killed Torril with the aid of the archers. By his count, there were ten on his side and twelve enemies left.

Grim smiled and thought, *This is going great!*

His optimism was then crushed. From the smoke, a beam of ice shot out at the watchtower Manny was in. The blast froze, then shattered the tower. Debris fell, quickly impaling Borril and one of the enemy gnolls below. A surge of concern for his familiar ran through Grim. Before he could call out for Manny, he felt a large hand squeeze down with crushing force on his shoulder. He heard the crunch of metal breaking, followed quickly by a sharp pain that shot through his body. Grim looked over his shoulder at a glowing, floating, sickly yellow-colored clawed hand pressing down on him. The sharp fingertips had broken through the metal of his armor and pierced his flesh. He felt a distinct warmth from the wounds as blood ran down the front and back of his shoulder. Ironically enough, a notification appeared that informed him:

Status Debuff Gained: Bleeding

You are being mauled by a magical claw. You should probably do something about that! It's fair to say that you are a bloody mess!

-3 Health per second while the claw is dug into you

-5 Health per second for 5 seconds after the claw unlatches

249

Grim dismissed the unhelpful and ill-timed notification and promptly fell to his knees. He looked at the smoke in front of him to see both Potor and the gnoll queen only twenty yards away. The assholes had survived the explosion with only minor injuries! The queen was cackling, her palm glowing the same sickly yellow as the floating hand. Grim gritted his teeth in pain. Not only was the spell damaging, it seemed to affect his psyche. Doubt and dread seemed to infect his very being. His resolve was dissolving by the second!

Luckily for the Progenitor, before any more damage could be done, the ogre returned to the fight. The undead behemoth jumped and swung its massive club at the queen and Potor. The queen had to stop concentrating on her offensive spell and cast a translucent shield of spikes to defend herself and the shaman. Grim sighed in relief, though his health had been drained in half. Then a soothing feeling overcame him and a notification appeared.

Xumi casts Heal Allies +15HP

Grim dismissed the notification as Xumi and Lukav came up beside him. Both were covered in dirt and wounds. The two orcs showed obvious concern at the resurgence of Potor and the queen. Grim did not share their feeling. He felt rage. These motherfuckers had hurt his friends and his familiar, and they were gonna pay!

"We've killed most of them, but how are we going to beat those two?" Lukav asked while gesturing to the two spellcasters.

Grim pursed his lips and looked at the ogre barely putting up a fight against the two spellcasters. The queen kept up a defensive shield as Potor slung spell after spell at it. The rotting creature was literally on its last limb as Potor used some sort of spell to chop its leg off.

If only we had more undead! Then another idea clicked. "Necro compeli!" Grim said, casting Summon Undead on one of the gnolls Lukav had killed. Then he cast Dominate on one that was fighting. As long as there were available dead bodies and enemies, Grim was a walking one-man army! "Xumi and Lukav, go keep Potor busy. I have an idea."

"But—"

"You don't have to beat them," Grim replied, resolve and anger distinct in his voice. "Just help the ogre and keep them distracted." To his new gnoll allies, he said, "You two, come with me."

Lukav and Xumi aided the ogre in fighting Potor and the queen, with Xumi casting Heal Allies and Lukav attacking the shield. They quickly broke down the magic shield of the gnoll. Unfortunately, when the queen's manna was almost out, Potor stopped attacking and cast his own magic shield of ice. The shaman was becoming desperate.

"Finish the ritual!" Potor yelled, looking back at the queen.

"But we do not have a sacrifice!" the queen barked with her shrill voice.

"Do it! When the time comes, I will get us one!" the shaman yelled, straining his voice.

Lukav began attacking the shield with renewed vigor. He did not want the ritual to finish!

The queen began chanting and cast some sort of spell on the ground below her.

"Grim, I do not know what you have planned, but hurry up!" Lukav yelled while still attacking.

Xumi did her best to heal both Lukav and the ogre, but

251

while her new spell was nice, it was not extremely powerful. She managed to get Lukav almost up to full health and the undead ogre around half. She was about to cast her spell again when the ground began to rumble beneath her. The ground underneath Potor and the queen glowed red with some sort of pentagram pattern. Brownish-yellow lightning began to emerge from the ground, lashing out erratically and striking Lukav, Xumi, and the undead ogre. The orcs were thrown backward and severely hurt by the infernal magic. The giant creature, however, was fatally wounded and broke down to black sludge. Lukav and Xumi were surprised to find Grim helping them up and that he was completely healed. They looked over at their enemies.

Both of the spellcasters smiled maliciously.

"And now for the sacrifice," Potor said.

The shaman unsheathed his handaxes and cleaved the gnoll queen in the head. Blood and brain matter shot out from the wound. The queen had a look of shock in her eyes at the instant of betrayal. Her knees hit the ground and the lightning stopped, then a flash occurred. All fighting stopped. Both the queen and Potor disappeared, replaced by a hulking figure eight feet tall with bright-blue skin over massive muscles. The only clothing it wore was a loincloth, which looked eerily similar to the gnoll queen's skin. Two large horns protruded from its head, along with massive upper and lower canines at least a foot long. The creature also had three bright red eyes with the third one in the middle of its forehead.

One look at the two handaxes it wielded made it obvious who it was. He used Analyze.

Potor (LVL 24)

Race: Demon

Type: Oni

Vocation: Shaman

Health: 500

Manna: 350

Stamina: 535

Resistances: Cold 15%, Soul Magic 50%

Onis are the result of a pact between a humanoid and a demonic beast. They are given a sacrifice and in repayment, are given the power of a demon and the one sacrificed.

Ohhhh, shit, Grim thought.

Potor examined his hands and then bellowed a maniacal laugh. His voice had changed to a demonic tone that sent a chill up Grim's spine. "Bwahahahaha! You weaklings have lost! I am unstoppable. I will kill all of you and bathe the entire Ashen Plane in your blood!"

Grim smirked. "You and what army?"

Potor scoffed. "My gnolls, of course." He gestured to his right and left. The smug look of satisfaction quickly faded as he found no troops around him or even at a distance. The demon growled in anger. "What have you done to my army, human!" Potor pointed an axe at the man.

Grim snapped his fingers as dozens of gnolls emerged from behind debris and buildings. Some had focused pupils while others had eyes of milky white, differentiating the dominated and the undead. "Oh, you mean this army? You see, we've been doing some talking, and we all agree that there needs to be a change in leadership. Time to *eat*!" he yelled.

At that familiar command, the creatures charged wildly at the demon and quickly swarmed him.

"Lukav, you and Xumi go free the prisoners," Grim said.

"What? No. We will not leave you!" Lukav retorted.

"This is no time to argue! There still might be guards watching over the others, and I don't want either one of you to get overwhelmed. Go get the prisoners and get them out!" Grim commanded.

Lukav sucked in his lips and nodded in acceptance. He then took off with Xumi toward the prisoners.

Grim looked back to the fighting and swallowed the last of his healing herbs.

Potor swung his axes with abandon at the gnolls, somehow keeping the horde at bay. Grim could see streaks of ice surrounding the wounds his axes caused. Since they could not hurt him in an up-close fight, Grim started hurtling magic while Potor was distracted by the gnolls. The demon oni was overwhelmed by the combination of magic and physical attacks. As soon as he would try to attack or block, he would be buffeted by a Death or Soul Orb reducing his health and stamina. Though they were able to inflict large wounds on the demon, his sheer tenacity kept him going.

Then Potor yelled, "Enough!" and instantly, a spiked shield of infernal magic surrounded him, impaling a gnoll in midair that had been about to claw him.

"Crap!" Grim muttered.

From his position on the uneven surface of the destroyed altar, Potor was able to swing through his shield without anything else getting through. He was cutting down Grim's minions with every swing of his axes, making the attack force rapidly dwindle. Some of the undead gnolls, immune to pain, kept attacking Potor in spite of the large, grievous wounds they received.

254

How do I break through the shield? Grim thought. This reminded him of his last fight in *Kingdoms & Valor*, which gave him an idea. The Progenitor ran toward the fighting.

"Move!" Grim yelled to his minions, looking like a berserker with a sword and axe in hand.

The four remaining gnolls parted out of the way but continued bombarding the shield.

Potor saw Grim coming and a malicious smile spread over his face. "Ahhh! Come to die with your slaves, human? Very well, come!"

As Grim approached, the demon oni focused solely on him. At the last minute, Potor swung both axes down. Grim rolled to the side, narrowly dodging the axes as they crashed down with a loud thud. Dust and dirt launched in the air. Before Potor could get in another swing, Grim cast a spell he had never used before—Decay. Rapidly, the wood, bones, and dirt on the ground turned black and fragile, extending past the cover of the shield. Large cracks spread across the wooden platform.

As Potor reared back for backhanded slash, the debris underneath his feet gave way to decay. The demon stumbled backward and fell, dropping his axes, and the lack of concentration caused his shield to dissipate.

Grim didn't hesitate. He grabbed one of the demon's handaxes and rushed in for a quick decapitation. Before he could begin his swing, Potor, still on the ground, stuck out his arm and the axe flew out of Grim's hands, into the demon's.

Grim just had time to think, *Oh, crap!* before the demon oni swung the axe at the side of his left leg, sinking it deep into his flesh. Grim fell to one knee. At first, he felt the warmth of blood running from the wound, but that was quickly replaced with a cold, sharp pain as ice crystals surrounded the cut from

255

the enchanted weapon. Fortunately, his heavy armor bonus helped prevent his leg from being immediately amputated.

Potor pulled out the axe and quickly rose up. The four gnolls recklessly attacked the demon who had struck their master. Potor quickly conjured another infernal spell in his free hand and released a rushing stream of tiny magic needles from his palm, quickly dispatching his attackers.

That was enough distraction for Grim to notice that Potor was seriously hurt, despite his new body. He used Analyze and found that he was at only a 125 HP. Even though Grim had a serious wound, he was healing quickly, which he attributed it to his Ogre Skin. The feat caused an increase to wound healing and a resistance to certain types of damage that made the Progenitor sturdier and more durable than your average man. That still did not mean he was invincible. Grim still had a large injury, and even though his body was slowly mending itself, he needed more HP.

Before Potor could attack him again, Grim touched the demon's leg and cast Absorb. A purple aura surrounded Grim's hand and the part of Potor he was touching. Grim could feel the life force leaving the demon oni and going into him. Only seconds passed, but Grim felt better. In fact, his health had gone back up into the triple digits. Before any more health could be absorbed, the demon oni kicked Grim back and pinned him underfoot. Grim looked up as Potor began conjuring a circle of infernal energy in the air.

Potor smiled down at Grim as a large skull of demonic hellfire shot out from the circle, straight at the Progenitor's chest. Grim let out a bloodcurdling scream as the flames started burning his skin. The demon smiled, enjoying the torture Grim was experiencing. The flames suddenly died out from a pulse of magic as Grim's Death Ward took effect. Grim let out a gasp of relief. Frustrated, Potor raised his enchanted ice axe to once more try to kill Grim.

Grim looked up at the demon and a pulse of panic surged through him as he was reminded of Gulag. He closed his eyes and winced in anticipation of the oncoming blow. Instead, he heard a feral cry and a muffled yell. He felt the demon's foot let off his chest and looked up to see Manny attacking Potor's face.

"That's my boy!" Grim shouted.

A huge surge of joy and relief ran through him as he realized his manticore was okay. In the short time Grim had known Manny, he had grown attached to the bloodthirsty familiar. When he thought Manny was hurt and possibly dead, he had hurt too. The pain was like that of losing a beloved family pet. With Manny now confirmed to be alive, Grim realized he never wanted to lose his familiar again. The demon had to die.

The small manticore didn't appear any the worse for wear and was doing a good job keeping Potor's attention, flying around and dodging attacks. Grim threw the last of the healing herbs in his mouth, then slowly and deliberately stood up. Being this close to death, Grim felt every bit of the aching muscles and sore joints, dirt and dried blood on his face, cold wind on his exposed skin, minty taste of his healing herbs, and pulsing of his ring more distinctly.

Wait. Why is my ring pulsing? Grim looked down to see it was his new Ring of Retribution and smiled in satisfaction. He knew how he was going to win.

"Manny, move!" he projected.

The familiar obeyed and flew away.

"You will not escape me, pest!" Potor yelled as he started to cast a spell at the manticore. He did not get to finish.

257

Grim covered the short distance and punched the demon in his side, activating his enchanted ring. A huge surge of pure force erupted from the ring, sending the demon airborne a few feet and knocking him prone. Grim's right arm launched back from the sudden recoil, sending pain tingling throughout the appendage. It felt like a bullet had been shot from his fist! He did not stop, though.

"Manny, attack while he's vulnerable!" Grim projected.

The manticore flew down to attack Potor. First hovering above Potor and flapping his wings quickly, the Slime-Manticore then began scratching, clawing, and biting like Potor was an all-you-can-eat buffet. The demon lay prone on his stomach, coughing up blood, and could barely put a hand up to swat away his tiny green attacker. Learning his lesson from last time, Grim picked up his own Greataxe of Leeching instead of Potor's handaxe and sprinted toward the demon. He was able to make it back to the fight just as Potor made it up on one knee. The demon oni turned his head in time to see Grim, but it was too late. The last thing he saw was Grim swinging an axe down at his neck, bringing the story of Potor to an abrupt end.

CHAPTER 23

RECOVERY

THE DEMON'S HEAD PLOPPED TO the ground, quickly followed by his body. Black blood oozed from the remaining stump of a neck.

"And that's why we had to chop you," Grim said. He stood panting but proud after his excellent punny one-liner. He did not have much HP left, and his skin was burnt and covered in blood. With the death of his enemy, exhaustion hit him hard, and he fell to his knees. There was a flashing notification icon, but he ignored it.

Manny flew down to him. *"Master? Master, are you alright?"*

Grim smiled up at his familiar. "Yeah. I'm just glad you're okay, Manny." He scratched the manticore behind his ears and petted the supple fur of his fluffy mane.

Manny closed his eyes and purred, then hopped on his master's shoulder as Grim carefully stood back up, using his axe for support.

Assessing his surroundings, Grim was surprised to see the surviving orcs about 150 feet away, looking at him in awe as they approached. Thrain leaned against Lukav for support, part of his right arm missing. It looked to have been cut off right at the elbow joint. When they reached the destroyed altar, the old orc broke the awkward pause first. He looked at Grim and raised his left fist up in the air, then looked at his clan members. Lukav and Xumi quickly followed his lead. With the same steely resolve as Thrain, the rest of the orcs held their fists up to acknowledge their hero.

Grim's eyes grew wide. He couldn't believe they were submitting themselves to him as their leader just like they had for Thrain after he beat Potor in the challenge. He was about to refute the offer, but then he saw his friends. They needed him, and he needed them. He had grown to care for the orcs, and if they wished to follow him, so be it.

In Orcish, Grim spoke the words he'd heard Thrain say. "Who is the chief?"

The clan pumped their fists in the air and chanted, "You! You! You!"

"Who do you follow!?"

"You! You! You!"

A notification appeared that Grim could not ignore.

Congratulations!

You have earned a new title: Chief of the Blood-Shield Clan. As the new chief, you have inherited and claimed your first village (Blood-Shield Village). You now have the ability to access Village Interface. More power will be available to you as you increase the tier of your village. You are now responsible for the lives of those other than yourself. Take care to help them thrive, and they will do the same for you.

"With great power comes great responsibility."

Your relationship status with all of the clan has increased to Loyal.

Grim was thrown by how this world could know a quote he'd heard from Peter Parker's Uncle Ben, but there were more pressing matters. He had a village! He had a people, and he had power! The high from his excitement instantly overrode any exhaustion he felt.

Grim walked over to Thrain, Lukav, and Xumi. "Is everyone alright?"

"We are okay," Lukav replied. "This is...all that's left."

Grim looked at the semicircle of orcs in front of him with a stern expression. Including Lukav and Xumi, there were only thirteen orcs remaining. He scanned the surrounding village and made a mental note of the four undead gnolls behind him, each in various states of decay and damage. "Where are the bodies?" he asked the group of orcs.

"What wasn't eaten by them gnolls was used for that altar. Their remains have been tainted somehow. I can smell 'em with my cook's nose from here," Riga replied.

Her brother Grogmar asked, "And what's that small lion on your shoulder?"

Grim was glad to see Riga and Grogmar had both survived. Gazing across the group of orcs, he said loud enough for everyone to hear, "This is my familiar. His name is Manny, and he is a manticore. He is our ally! He will not harm you, so do not harm him." Turning to Riga, he said, "Tainted? How so?"

"Figurin' it has something to do with that ritual thing Potor was doin'."

"We need to salt and burn the altar," Thrain interjected while still leaning on Lukav through difficult breaths. "After... fighting them enough, you learn some things."

> Quest unlocked! Ritual Cleansing
>
> Thrain has advised that you need to salt and burn the

261

remains of the demonic altar the gnolls constructed to properly cleanse it.

Requirements: Fire, 7 pounds of salt

Reward:

250 EXP

+500 Reputation with Blood-Shield Clan

Penalty for Failure: Eternal torture for the souls of the departed whose bodies were used for the altar

Do you accept?

Yes or No

Not seeing a reason to deny the quest, Grim mentally accepted the prompt. Thinking about where to get the salt, he quickly realized who might be able help with that.

"Riga, are you able to get enough salt and wood to cleanse the altar?" he asked.

The cook contemplated for a moment, then replied, "Yes, Chief. I've been collecting them hanzos since before we met. I have a secret supply hidden here in the village that I been usin' for tryin' new recipes."

Grogmar chuckled at his sister. "More like for personal snacks," the barber said while twirling his mustache.

Riga gave her brother an angry glare before continuing. "Point is, they should supply enough salt for the ritual."

Grim paused for a moment, truly taking in the chief thing and processing that Riga was a hoarder of hanzos. She was practically the equivalent of a squirrel in this world! Then he said with the confident tone of a leader, "I leave it to you, then. Take your brother with you to help. Once you're done, try to see if you can find some food and water for everyone. " He then addressed the rest of the clan. "The rest of you, I know it's been hard and so much has happened, but those of us who died deserve a proper send-off. Please, if you can, gather any remains of our clan and place them here," he said, pointing to the spot in front of him. "After that, see if we can gather any remaining bodies of our enemies. Make sure we loot them too. Anything you find just leave in a pile beside the bodies."

Covered in dirt and visibly beyond exhaustion, the orcs' resolve was not hampered. "Yes, Chief!" they all replied and then quickly dispersed.

Impressed by his newly adopted tribe, Grim then addressed his friends. "Did we find Vumira too?"

Xumi shook her head and somberly said, "No, we have not. Besides, Father is seriously hurt."

"Do not concern yourself with me, Xumi. Please, take Lukav and go find your mother. I saw her last when Potor had her taken to my cave."

Xumi, Lukav, and Grim all agreed that checking there was the logical first step.

"Go on. I'll stay here with Thrain," Grim said.

They helped Thrain sit down on a broken piece of wood as a makeshift bench, and the two orcs left him in their new chief's care. Besides having his right arm missing, the large orc did not look good. He was warm but also covered in a cold sweat, a duller green color than usual, and was breathing heavily.

"What is going on, Thrain? You look terrible," Grim said bluntly.

The usually stone-faced monk looked uncomfortable for a moment, but then relented to his new successor. "The queen cast some sort of curse on me. After she performed the spell, I received a notification that my fate was tied to that of Potor."

263

Grim's eyes widened in understanding at what that meant. "But Potor's dead! How come you aren't?"

Thrain gave a knowing nod. "Ever since you killed him, my health has been deteriorating. With my channeling skill, I have been able to slow its progress, but I cannot keep that up forever. Snow-Skin, I am dying." There was no regret in Thrain's voice, just his familiar stoic resolve.

Grim's heart sank low. "Is there anything I can do? Maybe my Death Ward can stop it," he said hopefully.

The orc shook his head no. "My fate is sealed, Snow-Skin. I have one recommendation, and one request. First, find someone with the administration skill to help you manage our people. The quicker you find that person, the better. Second, Xumi told me that you found our ancient burial site. I wish to join my ancestors once I die.

Quest unlocked! Burial Rite

Thrain has requested that you place his body in the Catacombs of Eternal Servitude once he leaves this mortal plane.

Reward:

250 EXP

+500 Reputation with Thrain, Vumira, and Xumi

Do you accept?

Yes or No

Grim's face conveyed a multitude of feelings as he processed what was going on. When he'd finally wrapped his head around the situation, he accepted the request and said, "Consider it done."

The old orc nodded his head and said "thanks" right before his and Grim's attention were drawn by Vumira and Xumi running toward their patriarch.

Grim left to give the family some privacy and walked over to Lukav, who had followed the female orcs back at a slower pace. The shocked look on his vassal's face worrying him, Grim asked, "Are you alright?"

"We found Vumira in Thrain's cave, tied up. I can only describe what I saw as a nightmare," the kind-hearted orc answered.

Grim looked back at the head hunter, now sitting by her husband and daughter on the broken piece of wood, holding hands. Tears were welling in both the females' eyes, they were so happy to be reunited. Vumira was covered in cuts and bruises, and her clothes were torn almost to shreds. He could imagine what had happened and decided not to press his friend further. He clapped Lukav on the back of his shoulder and flashed him an understanding grimace.

"Hey, we did it, man. We freed them! We freed your people and ended the war!" Grim said, trying to cheer his friend up.

Lukav gave a weak smile. He was about to reply when Xumi yelled for him to join them. Lukav was obviously torn, evidenced by a conflicted expression on his face, but Grim dis missed him to go join his love and her family.

Grim then turned around and walked off to a destroyed log cabin to go find a piece of rubble to rest on after his intense battle. After about thirty seconds, he heard a familiar voice in his head.

"Master?"

Grim looked over to his awesome familiar still perched on his shoulder. *"Yeah, Manny?"*

Manny cocked his head to the side and said, *"If we are not going to kill anything else, can I go to sleep?"*

Grim smiled at the odd request from the bloodthirsty creature. *"Yeah, sure. Where do you take naps?"* he asked while scratching his familiar behind the left ear.

Manny didn't answer immediately but just closed his eyes, leaned into Grim's hand, and purred affectionately. After ten seconds, to answer his question, Manny shifted into his dagger form and fell right into the sheath.

"You know what, Manny? I think taking some time to rest and process things is a good idea," Grim said out loud as he sat down on a pile of debris to take a break and review his notifications.

Quest Complete! War Games

You have successfully aided Blood-Shield Clan defeat the gnolls of the Cracked-Tooth Tribe, effectively ending the six-year war they have been in.

Reward:

500,000 EXP

Friendly Relationship with Blood-Shield Clan
New Quests
Automatic Disdain Relationships with all Gnolls

Level Up X 6!
You have acquired enough EXP to reach LVL 7-12!
30 Stat Points +6 Level Points +60 Health, Manna, or

Stamina are available to distribute

Do you wish to distribute them now?
Yes or No

Congratulations! Death Magic reached LVL 13!
+13% Damage
-1.3% Manna Cost

Skill gained! Dual Wielding LVL 1

Whoever said two is not better than one never was skewered with two swords at the same time!

+1% Speed of Weapons
+1% Chance of Critical Hit

Skill gained! Battle Leader LVL 1

You are able to strategize and lead others from the front. Current maximum number in party outside yourself: 5

+1% to Morale
+5% Damage done by you and all your party members

Skill gained! Administration LVL 1

By becoming the chief of a clan, you have gained the administration skill! It takes skill to lead oneself through adversity. It takes even more to manage and lead others.

+1% Amicability between others managed
+1% Efficiency

267

Congratulations! Traps reached LVL 7!

+7% Trap Effectiveness

-7% Chance of Trap Being Detected

+7% Chance of Detecting Traps

Congratulations! Death Magic skill reached
Initiate Rank!

Improvement to all known spells
in this branch of magic.

+1 Intelligence

As a reward for your ability to not only plan a coordinated attack but also be a frontline fighter bearing the brunt of attacks, you have received:

+5 Vitality and +2 Intelligence

Wow! This is awesome! Grim thought. His initiate rank in Death Magic allowed for interesting new possibilities. Quickly checking his Summon Undead spell, he found that it now lasted twenty-four hours. That was much improved from the original one hour. Two of his other skills could be upgraded to the initiate rank, so he decided to allocate his skill points next.

Congratulations! Great Weapon Wielding
skill reached Initiate Rank!

+25% Damage
+25% Attack Speed

Congratulations! Traps skill reached Initiate Rank!
+25% Trap Effectiveness

+25% Chance of Detecting Traps

Satisfied, Grim closed his interface. Before anything else could happen, his vision turned black. He tensed in the complete and utter darkness, truly confused as to what was going on until Zordell suddenly appeared before him. Even with Grim's newly improved physique, the Arch Necroid towered over him. Grim realized this was another mental connection and he was still sitting in the middle of the orc village, but that didn't make him feel any more at ease in the his patron's presence.

Zordell grabbed the shackle on his right wrist with his bony left hand and ripped it away, breaking several links that clanged and clattered as they fell away. He gave a terrifying smile and let out a satisfied growl like a predator that had finally cornered its prey.

"Wait! How did you do that?! I haven't destroyed any seals yet!" Grim blurted out.

Zordell smiled. "It seems that there is another way of breaking my seals. It is your strength, my progenitor. I have discovered that every ten levels you gain gives me the strength to break one of my seals!"

"Awesome!" Grim put a hand over his heart, immediately feeling a huge rush of relief. He hadn't completely realized it until that moment, but he had been holding a lot of tension about his lack of progress with the seals. He'd known Zordell's patience while he worked to grow stronger could run out at any moment, leading to drastic and violent measures.

Zordell chuckled in his haunting voice. "It is as you say, *awesome.* I am glad that you have shown continued dedication to our cause. While I'll admit your original plan to grow stronger in isolation was...frustrating," the Arch Necroid said through gritted teeth, then continued in a more pleasant tone, for a skeletal being of pure death, "your results are not disappointing."

Zordell admired his newly unchained wrist for a moment, then turned back to the human. "Grim, I will admit that in the beginning, our relationship was strained."

"Strained?" Grim said. "You stabbed me! Twice!"

"Would you like there to be a third time?" Zordell retorted.

Grim gulped and his eyes bulged in immediate regret of his outburst.

Unexpectedly, Zordell shook his head and apologized, "No, no, no. I am sorry. Centuries of isolation have degraded by ability to socialize with my subjects. As you know, I was desperate when I found you, and there was a phrase I had learned from your world. Ah! 'Desperate times call for desperate measures.' You see, I do not wish you to live in fear of me nor do I ever wish to treat you like I did again."

While eagerly listening, Grim was still understandably cautious of his patron. "Uh huh," he said warily.

"I wish for us to have a good working relationship. You have helped me, so I will help you." Zordell waved his newly freed hand as glowing white orbs appeared floating in front of him.

A notification came up in Grim's vision.

Quest Update! Death Comes for Us All

You have discovered an alternate way to free Zordell. For every 10 levels you gain, your patron will become strong enough to break one of his seals. This has pleased the Arch Necroid greatly, so you have been rewarded.

Current progress: 1/7 seals destroyed

> Reward:
>
> Trusted Relationship with Zordell
> One of three gifts from Zordell

Knowing what to do, he went up to each glowing orb and touched them. An information window appeared for each of them as to the item inside.

> Scorpio Chain
> Damage: N/A
> Durability: 20/20
> Rarity: Epic
> Quality: Great
> Weight: ½ kg
>
> Properties: 15-feet-long, extremely light, almost soundless chain that attaches to the handle of a small weapon. The wielder can use it to quickly recall the weapon or even pull their opponents into close range.

> Genmoira Seed
> Durability: 5/5
> Rarity: Fabled
> Quality: Average
> Weight: 0.1 kg
>
> Properties: Seed to the extremely rare and highly adaptable Genmoira. When eaten, it will provide a +1 boost to Strength and Stamina for 5 hours. The plants are carnivorous and sustained by living matter instead of water and sunlight.

Mask of the Masses
Durability: 10/10
Rarity: Exceptional
Quality: Fine
Weight: 0.5 kg

Properties: Enchanted to allow the wearer to look like any humanoid they've ever seen for a period of 30 minutes. Can be used up to three times every 24 hours.

Note: Mask must be taken off, then put back on for enchantment to restart.

"Thanks," Grim said cautiously as he stared at the three orbs and began pondering which one to choose. *Archers, ranged fighters, and mages can be a pain. The chain could help me close the gap as I have favored close combat. The mask could help conceal my identity, too, when I finally decide to go to other villages. I don't know if anyone knows who I am or is actively seeking me out to stop me from freeing Zordell yet. It could probably help with negotiations as I bet certain races have predispositions to treat others more favorably. There's something about that seed, though.* "Tell me about the Genmoira. Can it be used as a steady food source?" he asked.

"Genmoiras are magical plants. They and their seeds are favored for their sturdiness and ability to survive harsh conditions, though are notoriously bland. Twice a year they drop thousands of seeds. So yes, they can be used as a steady food source. But if you are not careful, you can be its food source!" Zordell cackled.

"What do you mean?" Grim asked, annoyed at the vagueness.

"You saw that they are carnivorous plants. If you do not

272

have the appropriate skillset, they will try to eat you instead of yielding fruit for you," the Arch Necroid replied.

Grim remembered that Lukav had said the area was very harsh. He reasoned that as the new leader of the tribe in this area, he would need to find a consistent food source outside of hunting. He might only need meat and blood but assumed the rest of his people needed more of a balanced diet.

"I'll take the seed," Grim said.

"A wise choice for a leader," Zordell said while nodding his head.

The two other glowing orbs disappeared while the one holding the seed floated toward Grim. When he touched it, the orb flashed. Grim's vision turned bright white, and he closed his eyes reflexively. When he opened his eyes and blinked to clear his vision, he saw that he was back in the remains of the village. Shaking off his disorientation, he noticed his right hand was clinched and felt something soft in his palm. He opened his hand, finding the bright-red plump seed Zordell had awarded him, and quickly put the seed in his pouch of holding.

Looking around the village, Grim noticed that no time seemed to have passed during his impromptu mental communication with Zordell. Lukav and Vumira and Xumi were all basically in the same positions around Thrain as when he'd last seen them.

A male orc with a bright red Mohawk and a tribal-style tattoo that went from one cheek to the other and across the bridge of his nose approached Grim. The orc held up his fist in the tribe's version of a salute and said in a deep voice, "Chief Snow-Skin."

Grim analyzed him, learning the orc was a tanner named Geld.

"Yes, Geld," Grim said.

The orc appeared a little uncomfortable as he replied, "We were collecting the remains of the gnolls when we noticed the other prisoner that was tied up with Thrain is alive."

"Alive? Well, did you untie them? Are they okay?" Grim asked.

"No, Chief. We wanted to wait on what you wanted to do with him," Geld replied.

"Why?" Grim asked.

"He is an ogre."

CHAPTER 24
EYE OF THE TIGER

GRIM WALKED OVER CAUTIOUSLY. AFTER following Geld to the other side of the destroyed village, he was just fifteen feet away from the hulking ogre. It looked similar to the one they'd encountered on their way to liberate the village. Unlike the previous time though, this one was very much alive. It had light brown skin and wore only a loincloth. Its hands were shackled and chained to a large wooden pole on each side, and its ankles and knees were shackled together. It had some sunburnt skin and was imprisoned on the open field where the training grounds used to be. What was interesting about the brute was that it wore a large feline skull as some sort of adorned helmet with the lower jawbone as a chinstrap. There were many thick scars on its skin that appeared to be in some sort of pattern and multiple wounds with various spears sticking out of its body. The odors of blood, infection, and body odor permeated the air. In obvious pain and exhaustion, its head rested on its chest as it breathed heavily.

Grim analyzed the creature.

Crunch (LVL 22)

Race: Ogre

Vocation: Chieftain

Health: 200/1278

Manna: 40

Stamina: 50/558

Resistances: Slashing Damage 25%, Blunt Damage 25%

Ogres are giant brutes who live by the saying, "Might Makes Right." Many live solitary lifestyles unless forced into submission by a bigger, stronger ogre that they accept as their leader.

Level 22! Grim thought. Besides Vumira and Potor, this thing was the highest level creature he had ever analyzed. He kept a stern expression so as not to show weakness to the hulking behemoth.

"You are Crunch, the ogre chief?" Grim asked.

The ogre wearily lifted his head up to look at Grim. "Me Crunch. Who you?" he asked in broken Common.

"I am Grim. I am also a chief. Chief of the Blood-Shield Clan."

The ogre seemed both confused and angry at Grim's statement.

"You chief? But you puny human. Me could crush you! Me true chief!" Crunch said defiantly, pulling against his chains with newfound energy. Fortunately, he didn't break his bindings.

Grim took a breath, grateful he'd kept his distance, and quickly regained his composure. "Hmm. You maybe could in a different situation, *but* it looks like currently, you can't. *I,*

276

on the other hand, could kill you on the spot." Grim drew his greataxe and placed its blade against Crunch's exposed neck.

The ogre's eyes widened in surprise, but he kept a serious look focused on Grim.

"Or," Grim said as he pulled away his blade. "I could free you."

The ogre growled, "Err, free Crunch!"

"Why? One of my tribe members, Geld, told me that ogres have always tried to kill my clan on sight. Though I don't want to see someone die a cruel death, what's in it for me? What can you provide my people?" Grim asked.

The ogre looked down, contemplating Grim's question. "Me used to have sharp club, but gone now," Crunch said.

"Okay, so you have nothing to give. What can you do?" Grim asked.

"Crunch strong. Crunch strongest in mountains. Why me chief!" the ogre said proudly.

"Well, I can tell you're strong. What skills do you have exactly?" Grim asked.

The ogre stared directly at Grim for a moment, then his complete information appeared in the Progenitor's vision.

Crunch (LVL 22)

Race: Ogre

Vocation: None

Strength: 124

Agility: 25

Vitality: 426

Intelligence: 9

Mind: 9

277

Endurance: 111

Charisma: 11

Health: 200/1278

Manna: 40

Stamina: 50/558

Feats: Ogre Skin, Big-Boned

Skills: Great Weapon Wielding LVL 58, Tracking LVL 25, Blunt Weapons LVL 58, Unarmed Combat LVL 20, Battle Leader LV 19, Administration LVL 11

Resistances: Slashing Damage 25%, Blunt Damage 25%, Death Damage 10%

Languages: Common

Titles: Bone Breaker

Ogres are giant brutes who live by the saying, "Might Makes Right." Many live solitary lifestyles unless forced into submission by a bigger, stronger ogre that they accept as their leader. Owing to their thick hide, scars they receive make them tougher and increase their Vitality. This one has risen to become a leader by being much tougher and slightly smarter than the others.

Grim noticed that the ogre had the feat Ogre Skin, which seemed pretty obvious. What really stuck out to him was the administration skill. He remembered Thrain saying he needed to find someone to help him manage the village with that skill. Grim had mixed feelings about having Crunch utilize that skill for the clan because having a low intelligence ogre organize orcs who were his recent former enemies might not go well. He was in an isolated area, though, and beggars can't be choosers. Plus, having an ogre as an ally sounded awesome!

If he could convince Crunch to pledge loyalty to him,

maybe the ogre could become a Greater Vassal. Grim's ability to make a Greater Vassal had dramatically changed Lukav's body. Maybe it could affect the ogre's intelligence. The ogre needed a Death Magic affinity of 50% for the metamorphosis to a Greater Vassal to even occur. And Grim's Analyze skill wasn't high enough yet to show Affinities, but seeing as Crunch had a Death damage resistance of 10%, he was hopeful that there could be a correlation with that and magical affinity. He decided to approach the ogre for more information.

"Thank you, Crunch. You do have some useful skills. So, how did you end up here?"

The ogre looked annoyed at Grim asking the question, then answered, "Tiny smelly things attack Crunch and ogres. Crunch squash many of them, but ice guy cheat with magic."

That made sense to Grim. He assumed the gnolls were the "tiny smelly things." To the ogre, they were tiny. The "ice guy" was obviously Potor. Apparently when the shaman joined the gnolls, the Blood-Shield Clan had not been his only target.

"Did any other ogres survive?" Grim asked.

At that, the ogre pursed his lips, obviously upset. "Crunch strongest in tribe. Crunch...only lived," the ogre said sadly.

Satisfied with the information, Grim decided to make the ogre realize that joining him would logically be the best choice. First, he decided to lay it on thick. "Ogre Chief Crunch, you certainly are strong. What if I could make you stronger?"

The ogre raised an eyebrow in surprise at Grim's question. "You make Crunch stronger? You not stronger than me."

"Actually, big guy, I was able to beat ice guy, and he cheated with magic again," Grim replied.

Crunch's eyes widened. "You beat ice guy?"

Grim nodded and said, "And if you pledge your loyalty

to me, I will help you become the strongest ogre in all of the Spine of Zulnixia."

The ogre looked down, thinking and contemplating what the man had said. After a bit, the brute looked back to Grim. "I pledge to follow puny human if you free me and make strongest ogre in mountains."

"In life and death now and always?" Grim asked with a wide grin.

The ogre just grunted in agreement.

Quest unlocked! King of the Hill

Crunch has agreed to become your vassal if you will free him from his bondage and help him become the strongest ogre throughout the entire Spine of Zulnixia.

Reward:

Ogre Chieftain Crunch as your new Vassal

Do you accept?

Yes or No

Grim selected yes, then Geld handed him a key and the new chief unlocked the ogre.

The brute gave an ecstatic sigh of relief, then quickly and brutally ripped out all of the spears and weapons still impaled in his body. Then the ogre looked down and locked eyes with Grim, and a thread of purple magic extended from Grim and to the top of the ogre's chest, turning him into Grim's vassal.

"Now make Crunch stronger!" the ogre demanded beating his chest.

"Whoa, whoa, big guy!" Grim said with his hands out, placating the ogre. "Making you the strongest ogre will take time, but if you take a knee, I might be able to help make you better than you are now."

The ogre grunted in frustration but complied.

Grim stuck out his arm and touched the brute's chest. He focused and tried to keep his face composed despite how bad the ogre reeked with festering wounds and body odor. Fortunately, something appeared to distract Grim's thoughts from what he smelled.

> Devotion I
>
> Current follower status (3/50)
>
> Would you like to make this follower a Greater Vassal?
>
> Yes or No
>
> Note: Your follower must undergo an awakening of Death Magic in order to become a Greater Vassal.

He was about to select yes when he saw one of the poles Crunch was shackled to fall toward the ogre. Before Grim could say anything, the ogre caught it quicker than Grim thought possible. Surprised by the ogre's speed, it gave him an idea for the ritual words he wanted to say.

"Crunch, the ogre Administrator with cat-like reflexes, become more."

A thread of Death Magic extended through Grim's palm, into the brute, like he had done with Lukav and Xumi. He quickly found a spark! When he disconnected from the ogre, Crunch started to glow purple and examined himself. Then he groaned as if in pain as he started to change. Wounds started to heal, his body grew bigger, and fingers and toes grew longer with sharp black nails extending off them. The most dramatic changes were to his head and skin. The giant cat skull he had adorned as a helmet began to fuse with his head! Muscles, tendons, and skin grew over it. Orange, black, and white fur grew to encompass his entire body.

Soon enough, the change was complete, and Grim was rewarded with a new greater vassal. He looked up at the new Crunch, now a giant tiger/ogre/humanoid hybrid.

Crunch looked at Grim with obvious intelligence in his eyes, then stood up straight in a formal gesture with his hands behind his back. He pulled out a pair of small, thin circular glasses and set them on his nose before returning his arms to their previous position.

Where did he pull those from? Grim thought.

"Purrfect. Thank you, Chief," Crunch said. His voice and speech had changed from broken sentences with little intelligence to a silky smooth, deep, sophisticated tone like that of an experienced aristocrat. Well, outside of the purring.

Grim analyzed him again.

Crunch (LVL 25)

Race: Ogre

Type: Togre

Vocation: Administrator

Strength: 140

Agility: 45

Vitality: 500

Intelligence: 30

Mind: 20

Endurance: 135

Charisma: 20

Health: 2000/2000

Manna: 100

Stamina: 675/675

Feats: Ogre Skin, Big-Boned

Skills: Great Weapon Wielding LVL 58, Tracking LVL 25, Blunt Weapons LVL 58, Unarmed Combat LVL 20, Battle Leader LV 19, Administration LVL 20

Death Magic LVL 1

Death Orb

Resistances: Slashing Damage 25%, Blunt Damage 25%, Death Damage 15%

Languages: Common

Titles: Bone Breaker

Ogres are giant brutes who live by the saying, "Might Makes Right." Many live solitary lifestyles unless forced into submission by a bigger, stronger ogre that they accept as their leader. Togres are ogres with the hide and head of a tiger. They are typically more savage and smarter than their brethren and are considered a step up in the evolutionary chain. This one, in particular, has the ability to use magic and has extremely high intelligence for an ogre.

"Whoa!" Grim said, surprised to learn there was more than one kind of ogre in the world.

"Yes, sire. My change was, er, hm, dramatic. I thank you for my growth and humbly submit to your wisdom," the togre said as he bowed his head toward Grim.

Grim looked at the giant figure, then the orcs surrounding them. Once again, the orcs of his tribe were all looking at him in amazement.

How did they all know to look over here right at this moment? he thought. Grim realized he could use this moment to his advantage. "Let it be known that if you wish to pledge fealty to me, not just follow the tribe, there are benefits." Turning back

283

to Crunch, he said loud enough for everyone to hear, "I hereby welcome you as a new member of the Blood-Shield Clan and appoint you as Village Administrator!"

> You have gained +500 Relationship Points with Crunch.
>
> Current Relationship with Crunch: Loyal
>
> Congratulations! You have appointed Crunch to fill an open job for your village: Administrator
>
> "You know appointing a smart ogre sounds like an oxymoron right?"
>
> To look at other available jobs, check your village interface.
>
> Your display of power has helped you gain +500 Relationship Points with the orcs of your clan.
>
> Current Relationship with orcs of the Blood-Shield Clan: Allied

The togre's eyes became unfocused as Grim assumed he was reading a message on his interface. Grim remembered at that moment that he should have gained something too. When he made Lukav a greater vassal, he had learned orcish. He opened his character screen to find out, hoping for some awesome, unique ogre trait.

> Skill Gained: Blunt Weapons LVL 1
>
> "When others see a stick, you see a way to bash their faces in."
>
> +1% damage when using blunt weapons
>
> +5% chance to damage armor

While Grim wasn't overly excited about gaining this skill compared to something more rare, he figured beggars can't be choosers. He dismissed the notification and looked up at Crunch.

"This is wwwonderful!" the togre said while chuffing like a tiger as he rose up from his knees. "I will get to work on our efficiency once we organize our resources."

"Good," Grim replied.

Before he could say anything else, all the villagers approached and formed a circle around him. Crunch took a step back, casting a respectful gaze at his leader and their people. All the orcs then took a knee and bowed their heads to Grim. They uniformly pledged their eternal loyalty to him.

Their saying the same words together was a bit creepy, but having an entire people trust you enough to submit themselves was one of the most confidence-building moments in Grim's life. It made him realize how some rulers could become so egotistical and obsessed with power, and that's not the kind of leader he wanted to be.

Forcing himself to take a calming breath, he said, "I accept your pledges."

Tendrils of purple magic extended out of his body and touched all of the orcs, making them all glow purple for a moment.

After Grim dismissed the notification telling him he now had fourteen out of fifty followers for his Devotion I quest, he saw that all of the orcs had stood up and were looking at their chief with gratitude and firm resolve.

"Chief," Geld said. "We have gathered all the bodies of our enemies and taken all of the valuables from them." Then shifting uneasily from one foot to the other, he said, "We have also gathered the remains of our tribe."

Grim could tell this was difficult not only for Geld but all of the orcs. Thrain was sitting down on a fallen log surrounded by his family and Lukav. He was slightly pale but still had an aura of strength coming from him.

"Take me to them," Grim said firmly to Geld.

Grim was brought to the bodily remains of the members of his tribe. Seeing them truly sent a chill down his spine. They were bones, just bones, and not many of them. There weren't even enough to make one entire skeleton. Many had small indentations that were obvious chew marks. What finally broke the man was when he saw the small skull of an orc child. Tears flowed down his cheeks as pangs of guilt racked him. He had accepted the quest to defeat the gnolls and decided to wait the night before attacking. Maybe if he hadn't, this child would have still been alive. Grim turned his head and saw the orcs behind him crying as well.

"I'm sorry. I'm so sorry," Grim said through his tears.

Geld stuck out his arm and grabbed Grim's shoulder. "My sister and niece were among the victims. They died a death they did not deserve. Their deaths were not your fault, and it brings me comfort to know they received retribution. I know their spirits will be comforted too. You made that happen. Hold your head up high, Chief. You deserve it."

Grim smiled and wiped away his tears. "Thank you, Geld. I needed that."

The orc nodded in response.

After Grim informed the whole tribe that their ancient burial ground had been rediscovered, it was decided to take the remains there, to hopefully bring their spirits some peace. The bones were carefully tied up in a hide sack and given to Geld to carry in honor for his kindness. Once that was decided upon, Grim had the orcs go help Riga and Grogmar with getting ready to cleanse the altar. He left to go check the bodies and items of the dead gnolls. He planned on raising them and at least using the undead as pack mules for the group. Grim also brought Xumi along because of her identify spell. They found the bodies and items neatly arranged and organized with Crunch there, patiently waiting.

"Chief, I have organized these bodies and items of our enemies for your examination. I assume you shall use your magic to reincarnate the remains, so I have taken the liberty of sorting the bodies that were intact enough to provide the best functioning servants. I have also organized the items they had by category. They are assorted into weapons, armor, rings, and necklaces."

"Wow! That's really thoughtful. Thanks, Crunch!" Grim said, already grateful to have his new administrator but wondering how the togre didn't have a spot of blood on him.

Grim then thought about sorting through the remains, but quickly changed his mind. Dying had led to certain orifices of the gnolls releasing their contents. Fortunately, the ones Crunch had sorted out weren't in as bad a shape. There were ten gnolls corpses Grim could use. He would address them later. First, he wanted to see the loot.

You have found Minor Ring of Health!

Durability: 4/5

Weight: 0.1 kg

Rarity: Common

Quality: Average

Properties: Gives +2 HP

You have found Crude Copper Dagger!

Damage: +3-5

Durability: 10/15

Rarity: Common

Quality: Below Average

Weight: .3 kg

You have found Steel Mace!

Damage: +18-20

Durability: 22/25

Rarity: Uncommon

Quality: Above Average

Weight: 5.8 kg

You have found Leather Shoulder Guard!

Durability: 6/12

Weight: 1 kg

Rarity: Common

Quality: Below Average

Type: Light Armor

Properties: +9 Armor

You have found Slaver's Whip!

Damage: +20-25

Durability: 24/25

Rarity: Common

Quality: Average

Weight: 2.3kg

Properties: +10% chance to cause bleeding

You have found Manna Storage Ring!

Durability: 12/12

Weight: 0.1 kg

Rarity: Uncommon

Quality: Average

Properties: Will regenerate +18 Manna over 2 seconds up to twice a day on owner's mental command.

You have found Runic Ice Handaxe of Recall X 2!

Damage: +10-12

Weight: 3 kg

Durability: 28/30

Rarity: Fabled

Quality: Excellent

Properties: +5 Ice Damage, Soulbound

This axe can be summoned directly to the owner's hand from up to 100 feet away.

You have found Necklace of Pain!

Durability: 8/9

Weight: 0.1 kg

Rarity: Exceptional

Quality: Average

Properties: A necklace formed from the exoskeleton of a dead Mana-Centipede. It sinks into the flesh of the wearer, providing a consistent source of pain. Every spell cast by the wearer results in a burning sensation to their body but results in their spells causing 5% more damage.

You have found Ring of Hunger!

Durability: 10/10

Weight: 0.1 kg

Rarity: Uncommon

Quality: Average

Properties: Causes the wearer to experience unrelenting, extreme hunger, but in return, they will never have to eat anything to keep nourished.

You have found Gold Ring of Strength X 2!

Durability: 5/5

Weight: 0.1 kg

Rarity: Uncommon

Quality: Good

Properties: Provides +3 Strength

You have found Bronze Earring of Comprehension!

Durability: 3/3

Weight: 0.1 kg

Rarity: Fabled

Quality: Superb

Properties: Once pierced on one's ear, it allows that target to be able to hear and understand any language. The target will not be able to speak the language. Does not apply to written forms, including codes.

You have found Magika Core!
Durability: 995/1000

Weight: 17 kg
Rarity: Mythic
Quality: Excellent

Properties: Once attuned, this large crystal can provide an extra 5,550 manna to a target once every 24 hours.

Nice!!! Grim inwardly celebrated over the list of choice loot. The runic handaxes and earring were great, but the magika core was the definition of amazing. 5,550 manna a day! He could rain down some serious terror on his enemies with that much ammo. Plus, he could finally try out his Fusion Spell, though he did not know on who yet. He planned on calling dibs later, once they got the village more settled. There were also a number of shoddy spears that he was used to seeing the gnolls carry.

Grim learned from Crunch that the villagers could at most have six rings equipped, so he would have to carefully choose which ones he would wear, which ones to give to whom, and which others to possibly sell. Crunch also showed him a chest of coins that weighed about ten pounds and a pile of coins from the bodies that added up to 54 copper, 34 silver, and 1 gold piece. Cha-ching! He left the contents in the chest and poured the pile of coins into his pouch of holding. Fortunately, each coin only took up one slot. He then equipped himself with the manna storage ring and the two rings of strength since they were easy to carry. He was not a sadist and definitely did not plan on wearing the ring of hunger or necklace of pain anytime soon! He left the rest of the items with Crunch as his bag of holding had a limited number of spaces.

Next, Grim examined the bodies. The ten gnolls Crunch had sorted out were in pretty good condition, most of their bodies still intact. Realizing how morbid it was looking at dead bodies and their condition, he was surprised by how well he was

291

processing all this information without being overwhelmed. He figured Zordell had been right about him. He was able to be a Death Mage. Before he started to use his raise undead spell, Grim inquired as to what happened to Potor's body. He learned that for some reason, the body actually self-combusted and burned away. Grim figured it was the demonic version of decay. What was interesting was that the head had remained intact. On Crunch's recommendation, Grim put it inside his pouch of holding as there might be some sort of use for it later.

Grim then cast Summon Undead on the ten gnoll corpses. Once the zombies stood, he gave command of them to Crunch and instructed the togre to direct the cleanup of the debris and organize any materials that could be of use for the village, which included the rest of the items. Once finished giving orders, Grim headed back toward the altar. It was time to cleanse the altar.

The ritual was very straightforward. They simply poured enough hanzos to meet the seven pounds of salt requirement on the altar and ignited a dry piece of wood. Not long after, the entire structure went ablaze. Everyone there quickly believed that it really was tainted because of the creepy screams and wails coming from the altar. Black smoke sometimes shifted into the appearance of suffering orcs and gnolls. Grim and company quickly equipped themselves with their weapons in case something unexpected happened. After a couple of minutes, the screaming died down as the dark smoke dissipated.

Everyone's tension eased except Grim's. He had not received a notification that he had completed his quest. His concern was validated as another large spew of black smoke violently surged out of the pyre. It did not dissipate like regular smoke but coalesced and floated about ten feet up in the air. Claws, eyes, then ears quickly formed out of the black smoke, followed by a maniacal cackle.

It was a gnoll laugh, but the smoke figure was not just any gnoll. Grim could tell it was the queen! Somehow she had survived being sacrificed by Potor and was now some kind of spirit creature. She pointed a finger at Grim and started spouting something in a tongue he could not understand.

"Uh...Thrain? Is this supposed to happen?" Grim asked in a panic.

"No," the orc said matter-of-factly.

Grim groaned at the unhelpful statement. Not wanting to waste time, he charged and yelled, "Attack!"

After he took a few steps, the queen slapped the ground hard with her smoky hand, causing the entire village to quake for a couple of seconds.

Losing his balance, Grim fell face-first. He looked up to see the queen looming over his head. Smiling down at him maliciously, she breathed some sort of green gas in his face. It entered Grim's mouth and nostrils, stinging his airways and causing him to cough reflexively. The man quickly stood up and moved back, coughing and swatting away at whatever fumes were assaulting him. After five seconds, they went away and Grim could see the queen looking directly at him. She cackled once more, waved goodbye, then disappeared.

Quest Complete! Ritual Cleansing

You have successfully cleansed the altar in your village and freed the tortured souls attached to it.

Reward:

+250 EXP

+500 Reputation with Blood-Shield Clan

There were more notifications, but before Grim could read them, the ground underfoot shook. The sounds of breaking rock echoed throughout the village. Cracks spread over the ground and underneath the burnt altar. The remains of the altar then plummeted down a ten-by-ten-foot hole that suddenly appeared. Then the shaking stopped, and everyone looked at each other in shock.

"What was that?" Grim exclaimed.

Before anyone could answer, the ground around the hole started to develop more cracks. Chips could be seen breaking off, increasing the hole's size.

Grim knew there wasn't much time. "Everyone grab as many supplies as you can and get out of the village!"

Agreeing with Grim's plan, the obedient orcs bolted away as fast as they could while trying to pick up anything important along the way. Lukav carried Thrain on his back, his face showing the strain of carrying the large orc at a good speed. They reminded Grim of people after a natural disaster, running into and quickly looting anything from any store possible. Crunch had apparently heard the message because even Grim's undead were already getting out of Dodge with items in their hands.

Grim quickly grabbed some shoddy-looking tools and a couple of dirty blankets by him and took off for the village exit. The flashing icon of a notification was still in his vision, but he ignored it. He had to focus on his environment. He spared a glance behind him and saw that the hole was about thirty feet out and growing larger by the second.

"Crap, crap, crap, crap!" he yelled as he dodged a collapsing wooden cabin to his right. Running toward the only exit, he could see the stone walls developing cracks and fragments starting to fall off.

A large piece of rubble broke off and crushed an undead gnoll, forcing it to drop its loot as coagulated blood and squished organs shot out from the impact. Despite wanting to stop and vomit on the spot, Grim was intently focused on not plummeting to his death. As fast as he could, he made it past the stone wall edge of the village by some large trees where the rest of his followers were gathered. About fifteen seconds later, the entire stone wall surrounding the village collapsed and the shaking stopped.

After Grim confirmed that only two undead gnolls were lost, they approached the village boundary cautiously. They were surprised to see that the entire village had turned into one giant hole! There was no ground, no stream running through the middle, and no stone wall. The mountain where Thrain's cave had been was still there, but there was nothing else. Grim was grateful he'd made it out! He moved and leaned his head above the hole. It was massive and pitch black. Grim could see no bottom to it! He kicked a rock nearby into it trying to gauge its depth. He strained his ear to hear it land, but it never came. The hole was so deep that Grim could not hear the rock land. Pretty sure that a fall would lead to anyone's certain doom, he had his clan move off to a patch of rocks and trees to rest, recover, and allow Crunch to reorganize what items and resources they had left. Fortunately, no one appeared seriously injured.

Not long after, the togre came by and informed Grim that they were able to save most of the loot but did lose the slavers whip, the earring of comprehension, and the magika core. He tried to not let his Administrator know it, but his frustration at the loss of the amazing items was too obvious. That magika core was going to be a gamechanger! He would have been able to cast high level and high cost spells despite being only level 12.

"Errr!" Grim groaned out loud while massaging his temples.

"I am sorry, Chief," Thrain said as he limped over to join the conversation between Grim and the feline humanoid.

"Yeah, no shit, Thrain! What exactly was that?!" Grim yelled at the injured orc. If Thrain had known anything like that could happen, the clan could have been better prepared and moved all valuables outside of the village with time to spare.

At his outburst, all of the clan became silent and looked at him.

Thrain kept his stoic visage. "I have only ever had to cleanse an altar the gnolls made once. While there was the moaning smoke, I never saw an entity like that which came out of the one you cleansed," he replied. Then his look became contemplative. "The one I cleansed years ago was a lot smaller, though, and we destroyed it before the gnolls could ever use it. It could be that a successful ritual was performed on it, making it stronger."

Grim noticed the layer of sweat on the old orc's body, evidence of his curse taking effect. Though frustrated, he was satisfied with the response. "Thank you, Thrain. That makes sense. Fortunately, everyone made it out alive, and that's what counts. Go rest. We all need to recover."

The sick orc gave Grim one of his rare smiles and hobbled off to be with his family.

That helped make Grim's mood less sour. Getting Thrain to smile was like winning a badge of honor! He then turned to Crunch, who was waiting patiently. "You rest too, big guy. We have a lot to do if we're going to rebuild."

The togre nodded his head and went to go rest against a large tree.

Well, I don't think it can get any worse, Grim thought. Upon checking his flashing notification, he really wished he hadn't tempted fate.

You have been cursed with an unknown spell by Gnoll Queen Revenant!

Penalties:

-1 to Personal Level

-1 to all Stats

-1 to all Skills (if skill is at level 1 there will be no penalty)

-3 to total Stat Points gained per Level

-5 to total Health, Manna, or Stamina Points gained per Level

Loss of half of unallocated points

Note: Until curse is remedied, your penalties will remain.

Great Weapon Wielding and Traps have fallen back to Novice rank, stripping all benefits from having them in the Associate rank.

Penalties:

-25% Damage with Great Weapons

-25% Attack Speed with Great Weapons

-25% Trap Effectiveness

-25% Chance of Detecting Traps

Quest unlocked! Break the Curse

You have been cursed by a spell from the Gnoll Queen Revenant and received serious penalties to your ability to grow.

"Let this be a lesson when dealing with crazy women to always use protection."

Goals:

Discover what exactly is your curse

Break your curse

Reward:

Removal of Penalties

Unknown

Do you accept?

Yes or No

"Fuuuuccccckkkkk." Grim quietly groaned. He accepted his quest and immediately went to allocating his points before something else happened. With the fifteen points he had left, he put one in all seven statistics to make up for the loss from the curse. Then he allocated the rest into the only stat he hadn't directly invested in yet—Charisma. Grim reasoned now that he was a leader and his interactions with others could directly mean the success or failure of his clan, the increased points in that stat would become useful. He then put his thirty other unused points into Stamina to balance himself better as it was a lot lower than both Health and Intelligence. Not long after he was done, Lukav approached him.

"How are you, Chief?" Lukav asked.

"Well, I just learned that I have somehow been cursed by some revenant gnoll, but I'm making the most of it. You? Also, with you, I'm just Grim, okay? None of that Chief stuff, please."

"Wow. That sounds awful. Is it anything that can be spread?" Lukav asked, taking a step back.

Grim chuckled. "Not that I'm aware of, man. Come on. Have a seat. What's on your mind?"

"You know I'm an orc, right? It is a little strange being called 'man,'" Lukav said chuckling. "Well, I was wondering, have you thought of what we're going to do now that the village is gone?"

"Honestly, dude, I haven't fully thought of what we should do. Maybe we should just rebuild right here. We have wood to build, and I bet there is a water source nearby. The clan can clearly hunt for food. It doesn't sound like a bad option, now that I think of it. First though, we need to get Thrain to the catacombs. I promised him that I would bury him with his ancestors, and I would like to bring all of the remains we gathered to be buried there as well."

"Well, if I can offer a suggestion, why don't we just rebuild by the catacombs? There is a large amount of land and water with ample resources there. Plus, it is defendable!"

Grim thought about it for a moment, soon realizing it was an excellent suggestion. He then stood up and addressed everyone. "My people, it is clear we cannot stay here. We are exposed and don't know who else knows where the village was. Fear not, though. A clan is not a place. A clan is its people. Blow after punishing blow we've been given, but we did not give in. I promise that we will rise again, not only by standing on the bodies of our enemies but by protecting and helping each other to grow stronger as well. We have lost our home, but we have not lost our will. We will rebuild!"

At that, multiple cheers rang out from the orcs.

Grim then continued, "Xumi, Lukav, and I have found where the Catacombs of Eternal Servitude are. It is a day's journey from here, at a very defensible location with ample resources. I have decided we shall go there. Are there any objections?"

Grim looked around, concentrating hard to keep from looking surprised or nervous. He'd never been any good at giving speeches, but the one he'd just given was awesome. Increased Charisma for the win!

When no one responded, he said, "Good. Xumi, you and Vumira are both skilled hunters and have been to the area where the tomb is. I want both of you to scout out the area ahead of us, in case there are any enemies or wild beasts, but first I think there are many hungry mouths here. Would you please go search for some food? I know Riga probably brought some, but we're gonna need more."

"It will be our honor, Chief," Vumira said with true respect in her voice.

It was definitely nice to hear the usually grumpy hunter in such a good tone despite the circumstances. *It's good to be Chief,* he thought.

> Congratulations! Administration reached LVL 2!

After the clan ate some charred woohig, they were ready to depart. Crunch was very effective in organizing the clan to make for effective travel. On his recommendation, Grim allowed the undead he controlled to be pack mules for the supplies and items the clan had while having two of them carry

Thrain against the old orc's objections. They had almost made it to the site when Xumi and her mother rushed through the brush and appeared before the group, both looking very disturbed and in a cold sweat.

"What is it? What's going on?" Grim asked.

Xumi looked at her chief and said one word, "Slavers."

TO BE CONTINUED

EPILOGUE

THE COUNCIL LOOKED AT EACH other uneasily. They knew why they had been brought there. Zordell's soul had somehow been set free. What they did not understand, though, was how. How could they feel his presence on the Ashen Plane, but he was still locked up in the chamber? Their interrogation of the Arch Necroid came up fruitless. He had withstood their methods for centuries, and this time was no different.

While they could not agree as to how or why Zordell's soul was set upon the plane, they did agree on one thing. It had to be stopped…

GRIM'S STATS AT THE END OF BOOK 1

Grim Snow-Skin (LVL 11) (stat points to allocate 0)
Race: Human (Living-Dead)
Strength: 32 (+6)
Agility: 15
Vitality: 22
Intelligence: 16
Mind: 22
Endurance: 16
Charisma: 20
Health: 195
Manna: 170
Stamina: 165

Feats:

Ogre Skin
Shrewd
Sapper
+50% Affinity for Slimes
+10% Chance to Intimidate
Kahn Living Rune

Skills: (Points to allocate 0)
Culinary LVL 1
Great Weapon Wielding LVL 9
Analyze LVL 1
Commerce LVL 2
Heavy Armor LVL 10
Shields LVL 2 →Shield Bash Augment

Short Blades LVL 2
Stealth LVL 2
Herbalism LVL 2
Tracking LVL 1
Traps LVL 9
Manna Manipulation LVL 2
Runesmithing LVL 1
Dual Wielding LVL 1
Battle Leader LVL 1
Administration LVL 2
Blunt Weapons LVL 1

Death Magic LVL 12

Death Ward
Death Orb
Commune with Dead
Decay
Summon Undead
Death Spear
Absorb
Dominate

Soul Magic LVL 1

Soul Spear
Fusion
Soul Orb
Resistances: Death Magic 99%, Cold 25%, Slashing
Damage 25%, Soul Magic 50%, Fire -25%

Languages: Common, Orcish

Titles: Progenitor of Death, Death Mage (Novice), Soul
Mage (Novice)

Familiar: Slime Manticore (Manny)

Items Equipped:
Black Clothing Set x1 (Shirt, Pants, Shoes)
Iron Armor Set x1 (Body, Helmet, Bracers, Boots) (+50 Armor)
Ring of Death's Protection
Ring of Certain Scry
Ring of Retribution

Gold Ring of Strength x2
Ring of Manna Storage
Wolf Fur Cape
Daria's Dagger (Manny)
Iron Greatsword of Slowing
Blood-Shield Greataxe of Leeching

Active quests:

Burial Rites
King of the Hill
Death Comes for Us All
Devotion I
Riga's Recipes
Wisdom of a Lost Leader II
Break the Curse

Thank you so much for reading this book! This novel has been a labor of love, and I truly hope you enjoyed it! If you did, please be sure to leave a positive review on Amazon. It really does help out. Keep an eye out for the next book in this series as well as an Audiobook version in the future!

Best,
Maxwell Farmer

ABOUT THE AUTHOR

Hi there! I'm Maxwell Farmer. I'm an avid nerd, gamer, and veterinarian who fell in love with LitRPG back in college. I was inspired to write the Ashen Plane Series from the multitude of LitRPG I consumed as well as the games I've played that made an impact on me. They opened up worlds of wonder and possibility and brought much joy to me. I hope my books will do the same for you.

Feel free to reach out to me on my Facebook page and/or through my website. I'd love to hear your thoughts on the book and would love to talk about nerd stuff in general. Keep living your best life!

Website: maxfarmer3.wixsite.com/ashenplane
Facebook: https://www.facebook.com/authormaxwellfarmer/

Made in the USA
Monee, IL
22 March 2020

23732764R00174